GEODE Copyright © 2025 by John A. McColley

For more information, please contact:

www.ascendentmedia.org

ISBN: 978-1-963970-20-3

Table of Contents

PART I: THE SHELL

Chapter One

"Haral," someone said his name, but the syllables slipped through his awareness, dissolving into the darkness behind his eyelids. The world was filled with a warm, steady, pressure of rising along the sunlit side of the spar, one of millions of angular crystal points which were at once parallels to Old World sky scrapers and city blocks making up the Central Equatorial Band, where almost everyone lived. This warmth gave way, to the cooler relief of sliding down into shadows. His head lolled from one shoulder to the other.

"Haral," the same voice—he was pretty sure, being closer to the surface of wakefulness—called again, buzzing with annoyance. He groaned a response but couldn't seem to manage opening his eyes. It was so comfortable here, and he had gotten so little sleep…

"Haral!" The voice came again, not as a phantom haunting the edge of his dream, but as a full, forceful burst of sound from the speakers of the train car's announcement system. Haral started, sitting up as he sniffed and blinked. He ran a light brown hand through brown hair just long enough to show its curl, dislodging his billed cap. It fell into his lap and tumbled to the floor before the discordant signals from his brain could pull together to snatch it up.

A number of other people seemed as disconcerted as he. Some were standard humani, like Haral, but there were also some heavily-modified humani with insectoid eyes and bristles along their scalp in lieu of hair, a pair of ribbon-like Flexxe, and a Rulab. The latter had been so startled by the sudden, stern, voice coming from above that their standard appearance of a blue-green scoop of ice cream had more of the appearance of a black and purple hedgehog trying to cram itself under the nearest seat.

"Yes, Gann, I'm here," Haral said aloud, groggily.

"Fallen asleep on the train again?"

"Mm… no. Just… studying," he mumbled. This drew laughs from a number of other riders.

"Right, that's why you're a millie off from Swanton Spar and still moving at three hundred mikes an hour."

"I'm not a millidegree from-," Haral sat up properly and peered outside. Millidegrees and Microdegrees, "Millies and Mikes," had become the standard measures of distance centuries before, living on the inner surface of a giant sphere, they served as degrees longitude and latitude once had, but Geode was a much larger sphere than Old Earth. Whole degrees were too large to be of use.

His Overlay—a heads-up display within his visual cortex—popped up names of local spars. These were massive blocks of crystal built up into farms, dorms, businesses, or labs that covered most of the Central Equatorial Band, the civilized part of the interior of Geode. Unfamiliar spar names scrolled through his Overlay as links to more information about each:

Geroo Spar
Hendrick Spar
Menalee Spar
LiFang Spar

Corp! he swore mentally.

"Uhh, yeah, Gann, I'll get the next transfer and be back as soon as I can." At least he was far enough from home he didn't recognize anyone… He was so embarrassed, for falling asleep, and getting caught lying about it…

"Hop an express. I'll pick up the ticket," the steely voice said, now only in his head. Haral's eyes widened at this. Gann Surai was not known to spend more Pull than was strictly necessary. It must be serious.

"What's up?" Haral asked over the NeuroNet connection.

"Getting some weird readings. Need you to investigate." Cryptic.

Haral's interest was piqued. Most days, his job as a maintenance engineer meant picking up debris that Geode had pulled from the great void or scrubbing the thrusters that kept the world spinning, giving a goodly portion of the inner surface gravity, of a sort. He knew better than to ask for more details. While his job wasn't secret per se, there was an understanding from the top that people should be made to think about what was outside Geode's skin as little as possible. There was plenty of room within the great egg of civilization, with four species of folk that had come together to build the megastructure, capturing all of Sol's radiation, represented by nearly a trillion individuals. Why should anyone want to leave?

And yet…

Haral always stopped to look up when he went out on the surface, the darkness unlike anything one saw inside Geode, set with uncountable gems of other, unharnessed stars. How many other worlds spun there?

"Haral?"

"Sorry, yes, express in… two minutes and a half, according to my Overlay. Booking now." And he did, sending the charge through to Gann while he watched unfamiliar monoliths coated in solar-converting film slide by, flashing gold from one angle, deep purple from another.

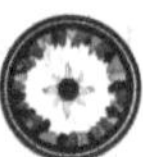

The ride back was tedious, with tension creeping into Haral's neck and shoulders. Not for the first time, he wished he had enough Pull for physical amenities apps like Autorelax. In school, he had pursued programming for a while, hoping to generate Pull by making bioapps people would rave about, but he just hadn't had the knack for it. The gleaming landscape rolled by, majesty now tainted by anxiety.

Work was work, but he wasn't often relieved or particularly glad to be there, except when his repair jobs took him outside the Shell or into the Warehouse. *Is there something wrong at the repository of space junk? Is Chopper all right?* Haral's blood pressure crept up as he hurried past the yellow and black striped doorway into the observatory.

"Gann?" He called out, eager to get answers to relieve his worry. The expression on the other man's tall, silvered, face did not give him that relief. "What's going on?"

"Finally! Come with me." Gann spun on his heel and waved Haral forward with both right arms. Folding his four powder-blue arms across his chest, Gann just nodded at a bank of screens. Many were simple video. Others normally showed alternate spectra, like IR and UV or more specialized data. Now, though, every screen was in its fail mode, for some that was bars of bold color, for others, a prickly pattern Gann called "snow," —whatever that was. The guy was always pulling ancient words out like they proved he was smarter than everyone else. Haral was pretty sure he just made them up sometimes.

"Do we have recordings from just before this happened?" Haral asked.

"Why didn't I think of that?" Gann asked, acid on his tongue.

"I'm sorry I was late. I haven't been sleeping well, and you know they pipe lulling sensations into trains to keep us pacified as we ride."

"Not the time for Chopper's conspiracy theories. We need to find the source of the problem and fix it. Could have been done by now. Could have been back in the game if our best mechanic knew how to plan his rest periods."

"I wasn't out, not even watching streams. I just couldn't sleep."

"Again, later. Now, watch this."

The screens all reset to their normal outputs, relaying information from scanners and telescopes keeping tabs on Gann's little corner of Geode's outer shell. The snow cleared up to stable points of light. Other displays showed wavy auras in different shades, a lance of energy from some distant pulsar. One by one, the images flicked over to the way they had been a moment before, disconnected from their feeds and in total disarray.

"You said 'weird readings.' This is *no* readings. It's like the wires were all cut."

"Then that's the first thing you should check."

"Where should I start?" Haral wondered aloud.

"That's *your* job."

"No, I mean… Can you play the record again?"

Gann sighed and dragged a finger along a series of parallel lines at the bottom of his specialized control console. The man had four arms, after all. He could type more than twice as fast as Haral, when typing was necessary, for low-level coding and such. Coding and crunching numbers were Gann's strength, where finding trouble —hopefully in a failing system or device—and fixing it, were Haral's.

The normal screens appeared again.

"Can you slow down the playback?" Haral asked, studying the screens carefully.

"What did you see?"

"It's more of a hunch, something I saw without realizing what I saw, or that I saw anything."

"Ah, sweet clarity," Gann condescended.

"There's something… Can I see it again?"

"Are you sure you're not just procrastinating?"

"Please, I'll know it when I see it." Gann sighed again and ran the feed back. The screens popped back to normal in the same order as with the first swipe.

"Gann."

"Yes, Haral?" Gann responded his tone hovering between annoyance and boredom.

"How are these oriented?"

"Pardon?"

"The feeds. How are they ordered?"

"By importance, of course," Gann said, like it was the most obvious thing in the world. "The ones along the bottom rarely show anything, and largely cover gray zones, between our sector and the next. The next row up have hits monthly —or better—but don't include thrusters, just basic surface plates. The top ones are the thrusters and spectra feeds focused on stars I'm certain there are planets around."

"OK, great. Can we re-align them to their relative geography?"

"You mean like east to west, north to south?"

"Yes."

"It will take a few minutes."

"Great, I'll get some breakfast… Oh!" he said, looking at the time in his Overlay. "Maybe lunch… no wonder I'm so hungry. Be right back." Gann didn't respond, already typing and swiping, deep into realigning the feeds.

The nearest mess station was a floor above and a few dozen steps away. Banks of food weavers hummed and hissed out fats and proteins and carbohydrate chains into a panoply of edibles, tweaked and tuned by chefs for a bustling luncheon crowd. The air itself simmered with spice profiles thousands of years old, from around old Earth, and the handful of planets and moons from which the non-humani species originated.

"Haral!" Everyone was yelling his name today. He felt as though his Pull must be halfway to the sun. Sadly, he knew his ranking hadn't budged in months and he would have to forgo chef-made cuisine for recipes-as-written codes that were nearly as old as Geode itself. That food was fine, just as long as no one *saw* him eating it. He'd lose even more Pull if they did. The poor got poorer.

"Hey Haral!" The voice came again, much closer, and accompanied by a waft of meat patties with sear. "Great timing! I just wove this for you not three minutes ago." The burger, replete with condiments and tubular fries, hovered before him on a yellow plate gripped between two brown tentacles. The owner of the tentacles was largely hidden from Haral's view by the offering.

"Nez! I didn't know you were back!" Haral lifted the plate from the offering limbs and took in his long-absent friend. The other was a head shorter than him, and a Xochat, four great lobes of nose arranged radially, with membranes for intercepting sound stretched between them on a low, plump, body capable of climbing most any surface with its pliable foot. This one was displaying red and orange coloration despite its people not having light receptors of any kind. "How was the culinary academy?"

"Amazing! I'm sorry I didn't call you more often," Nez hummed, "They had us running spice level and flavor discrimination drills and fine-tuning tests for like twenty-eight hours a day!"

"Sounds grueling."

"Oh, it was. About fifteen percent of students generally drop out. It was eighteen percent this year. Tell me what you think." The Xochat stood silently billowing its tympanic membranes like the Old Earth jellyfish Gann had shown him once after meeting Nez.

"Yeah, let's find a table." Haral found an empty high-top table with two chairs. The table popped up a small hologram warning him it had been reserved beginning in twelve minutes. He would be long gone by then. He waved to dismiss the alert and sat. Nez stood by, impatiently awaiting the verdict on his meal. Haral gave the burger a good long sniff, as was Xochat custom, and lifted it to his mouth.

"Haral!" Gann popped up in his Overlay. "Where are you?"

"I told you, getting breakfast." Haral took a bite before Gann could tell him to leave it and come running. The vegetables were crisp, the meat was juicy, hot, and had a good texture and firmness to it. The spices Nez had chosen danced and sang on his tongue, and down his chin, as he chewed. He lifted one hand, cupped, palm up, as a sign of appreciation.

"At 11:50? Ridiculous! Anyway, the displays are realigned." The burger began to slide apart and Haral brought his other hand back to it just as someone bumped him from behind.

"This is *my* table," the words hit nearly as hard as the appendage which had shoved Haral. High-powered vocal cords, or an amplifier of some sort. Haral lurched forward, trying to catch the remainder of his sandwich, when the speaker grabbed him by the shoulder. Spinning around, he saw a face familiar to a good portion of Geode: Merit Lang, influencer from a dynasty of influencers going back to before any formalized system of Pull. For a fraction of a second, the angular, golden jaw and piercing blue eyes were eclipsed by a curled-up hand adorned with gleaming gems set along the fingers. Then that fist knocked Haral backward over the table.

Nez screeched, tentacles scraping the inside of his tympana.

Geode rolled above Haral before the mess station came back around and slammed into him.

"Are you on your way?" demanded Gann.

"I'm…" Haral spit, blood and meat mingling before splattering on the textured flooring tiles. "Working on it."

"Aww… 'work,' that sounds so… boring. Who could stand it?" Merit sneered. Tiny recording drones orbited him like electrons around an atomic nucleus. No doubt millions of people were watching Haral being attacked. But if he fought back, he'd be the one punished with down votes and possibly legal entanglements Merit would never have to deal with. How could he possibly turn it around?

Tentacles appeared from beneath Nez's tympana, wrapping around Haral's arm and helping him to his feet. Haral's mind swirled, seeking the most scathing retort, since he couldn't match Merit physically.

"Who are *you?*" Haral spat. Merit, who had been posing for his viewers, reveling in the glory of his sneak attack and abuse of personal power turned. Eyes wide, face slack, he looked like someone in one of Gann's old movies who had been 'shot,' which was some kind of attack that had led to a long and complicated discussion of injury, death, and other words Haral wasn't certain had ever existed. Merit fell back a step.

Nez pushed Haral toward the periphery of the clot of fans Merit's appearance had begun to accrete. He stumbled forward. The crowd, mostly humani, but all races represented, backed away from him like he had a force field around him. Many held up hands, as though trying to stop him, but none actually barred his exit from the mess.

Chapter Two

"This is as close an approximation of relative position as we're going to get without dismantling my desk," Gann said, squinting at Haral. "No." He played the collapse of the sensor array again. The outage moved from east to west across the displays.

"You see that? I think that will give us a direction to look, but there's… something else." Haral studied the images intently, searching for whatever had tickled his subconscious brain the first time. He made a looping gesture with one finger.

Gann swiped the controls.

Again.

Now Haral squinted. His Overlay signaled a new message, but he was busy and snoozed it.

Again.

"There! Oh boy…"

"What?" Gann squinted at the screens.

"There's a wobble."

"Okay…?" Gann said, trying to draw more from Haral. The younger man stepped up to the wall of displays, pointing to a spray of stars. "Amina Globulae, so?"

"Watch those stars over the preceding five seconds," Haral said as Gann swiped a short distance back and played them again.

"A wobble… but there's nothing there."

"Or is there? I think we need real eyes on that section of sky."

"It's more important to get the sensor array working again. What if something happens and we can't see it?" Gann challenged.

"What if something *is* happening and we can't see it?" Haral threw back. "What if that ripple was an energy wave that knocked out the whole array… It's unlikely that it would be just our sector… unless it's sabotage…"

"More conspiracy theories. You spend too much time with Chopper."

"Or maybe… not enough." Haral's Overlay pinged again and he snoozed the alert, turning off all except dire emergency notifications and government announcements. He needed to concentrate on the problem at hand. It was probably just Nez checking up on him. Only a few other people ever messaged him.

"Are you just going to flip everything I say around and try to make it sound revelatory? Or are you going to do your job?" Gann demanded.

"As much fun as the former sounds, I am actually doing the latter. I can't fix anything if I don't know what's broken."

"Check the wires; then, if there are no breaks, check the equipment."

"But what would cause all of it to fail at the same time? East to west?" Haral continued, ignoring Gann's instructions. "Not cut wires unless someone was very particular about their snipping. There's something extraordinary happening here, and that's no conspiracy."

"Wires!" Gann said, pointing toward the repair bay where Haral kept his tools. Several other bays stood empty. This job took a special set of interests, skills, and lack of Pull to get a better one that culminated in a sad summation of Haral Adjani.

Haral popped open a small conduit at the back of Gann's desk and clamped a small metallic ring around the bunched wires. It would send periodic signals he could trace with a scanner to see where the break was, if there was one. He had doubts. Something about that wobble in Amina Globulae set off alarms somewhere at the back of his mind.

As Haral trudged along waiting for a tone from the scanner, he hummed to himself and wondered what Nez was up to.

"Ah crap. He's probably left me a dozen messages by now." The Xochat had few other friends, and no family, beyond a cousin, or something like one, a few spars over from Swanton. He had adopted Haral as his brother over a decade before.

Haral turned notifications back on and was flooded with more pings than he could track, individual tones blending into a vibrating note that drew his attention completely. There was no way Nez had sent *that* many messages. He looked at the subject lines of the last dozen or so. They were all a standard system message that he, admittedly, didn't see very often.

He scrolled back for half a minute, holding the button, then moving to the "jump back a page" button for almost as long before reaching the start of his unread messages. What was happening?

***Nez - Hey Haral, just chec...**
***PullSys - You have a new follower!**
***PullSys - You have a new follower!**
***PullSys - You have a new follower!**
***PullSys - You're going viral!**
***PullSys - You have a new follower!**
***PullSys - You have a new follower!**
***PullSys - Congrats! Your PullTier...**
***PullSys - You have a new follower!**
***PullSys - You have a new follower!**
***Nez - Haral, have you seen...**
***PullSys - You have a new follower!**

***PullSys - You have a new follower!**
***PullSys - You have a new follower!**
***MeritLang1 - You really stepped i...**
***PullSys - You have a new follower!**

He clicked into Nez's message with a focused thought on the button at the side of his Overlay:

Hey Haral, just checking in to make sure you're all right after the kerfuffle with Merit. Not quite as good as getting a selfie, eh?

The words hung in a yellow-orange light in his vision. He hit "**Reply**."

Hey Nez, thanks for checking in. I'm fine. I'll feel it for a bit, but no worries. Sorry I didn't get to eat the whole burger, but what I got was great. Thanks for making it for me. Glad you're back! I'll see you later. Gann's got me chasing down a wire break.

Curious, he clicked on the next message.

Haral_Adjani1773! You have a new follower! Record a message for:
1. **Your New Fan, Mysray119418**
2. **All Fans**

He closed out of the message and saw that most of the new alerts had the same subject line. Was there a member rush on? He didn't really keep track of such things but knew that nobodies sometimes got caught in the wild currents of rushes, having their followings, and Pull, temporarily boosted. He had no interest in whatever Merit Lang had messaged him, and was tempted to just delete the note... but it might be worth something later. Anything with a celebrity name on it seemed worth Pull these days.

He shrugged to himself and continued the scan, tracking the wires along the bulkhead and down a number of levels to the last access point before they went through Geode's outer wall and met up to their respective sensors and detectors. He opened a NeuroNet chat.

Hey Gann, I'm at the Shell, nothing but bulkheads and conduits spaceward. No luck on the wire. Activating a drone.

He sent the message and scrolled through his Overlay to get to drone controls. He had to pass a number of security pages; Gann had gotten even more paranoid about someone stealing one or joyriding and crashing one of the small machines into a sensor array or something after a few of them had unexplained battery drain.

>> Welcome to drone X-471554.

Hey Alissa, please bring full sensor array and one extra battery pack to accommodate the weight. We're hunting shadows.

>> Sure thing, Haral_Adjani1773.

The drone acknowledged the directions with a quick trill, but was not equipped to understand his last comment. It wasn't truly AI, and had only accepted "Alissa" as a name after he messed around in the system, adding the label to its code. Whole-scale apps may have been beyond him, but a bit of tinkering and hacking was something else. Another trill alerted him to the text message appearing in his Overlay.

>> *X-471554 equipped and awaiting flight path.*

Alissa, begin Manual Pilot Mode. I'll take her out. I'm not sure where she needs to go, but I'll know the target when I see it.

>> *X-471554 Manual Pilot Mode engaged.*

Haral sent the drone straight up from the surface of Geode, commonly called The Shell by those who actually thought about things outside the world. The stars were magnificent, as always, but there was something… off about the view. It took him a moment to realize what it was.

Geode, being a shell wrapped all the way around its sun, didn't really have an orbit like moons and planets of old. It relied on spin for artificial gravity. It gained that spin mainly from shunting solar winds through thrusters on the Shell. All this meant that the particles of solar wind shot out away from Geode. Usually, this took the form of plumes visible only in their collisions with the thin veil of gases, mostly the cooled remnants of earlier plumes, that caused a secondary light show. It was similar to pictures Gann had shown him of "auroras" from Old Earth.

Now, these plumes were colliding with something else. It took Haral a moment for his brain to accept what his virtual eyes saw through Alissa: four thrusters before him fired off energized particles in streams angled up away from the Shell. Each tore jagged holes in sky through which were visible glowing patches of some kind of rippled material like the tread of a shoe. The streams caused the material to incandesce, brightly toward the middle of the hole, and fainter along the edges, which shifted with a chaotic ripple of their own. Curious.

"Gann, I've found something," Haral sent via NeuroNet.

"Great, kid, what is it?"

"Um, well, I don't know. It's some kind of… I mean, the thrusters…"

"No problem with the thrusters yet. Should I anticipate one? Which thrusters are affected?" Gann shot in quick succession.

"I can see four. If… It seems like… Oh wow!"

Haral said in realization that all of the "holes" were at the same height, and seemed to be behaving exactly the same… It was one object, hidden by a projected image of the stars behind it, but the illusion was broken by the thrusters.

"What? Don't hold out on me now. Patching into the drone's feed. You know, they used to call this 'piggybacking.'"

"Whaty-whating?"

"A piggy was a kind of-" Gann fell silent, but Haral didn't need to ask why. The stars shifted, a ripple reaching out toward the drone. The ripple split into four fingers which lost their illusion, revealed as dark claws reflecting purple red in Alissa's small external navigation lights. A second later, the feed cut out entirely, sending a feedback wave along the connection which slammed into Haral's brain and knocked him from consciousness.

"Haral!" Once again, he woke to Gann yelling his name. The tone was different this time, but it was still a rude awakening. He tried to sit up and found himself bound to a stretcher. "There you are. You took so long waking up I summoned aid," his superior said.

"Great. Can you let me go?"

"We must ensure your complete health before releasing you, Mr. Adjani," one of the two mechanical med techs told him. The speaker was a teardrop-shaped bulb atop a stalk which rode back and forth along the length of the stretcher, scanning his body. Haral assumed that the stretcher itself was probably the med tech, with the sensor bulb being the closest thing it had to a head. Its partner glided away, a tall, narrow pyramid of yellow plastic with a thick, white plus sign on each angled face and a spinning yellow light within its transparent apex.

"'Mr. Adjani?'" Gann laughed despite the situation. "When did you become a 'Mister?'"

"Beats me." Haral gave a chuckle that throbbed through his brain, forcing him to lie back with a small groan.

"How long before I can get my repair tech back?" Gann asked the med techs as the gurney mechanical followed its partner.

"We will assess Mr. Adjani for twelve hours. After that time, we will know whether he is in need of further treatment," The gurney med tech responded.

"Where are we going?" Haral asked.

"To Swanton Spar Hospital, of course," the med tech replied.

"What? There's got to be some mistake," Haral protested. He didn't have that kind of Pull to spend.

"When did you become king?" Gann asked at almost the same time.

"There is none. Sleep," the med tech said. A slight dizzy feeling slid over Haral. He lost consciousness again.

Haral reawoke in a room full of gentle pastels, swirls of orange and pink shifting and overlapping through a field of blue while he watched. As his mind cleared, he was able to pull his attention away from the ceiling and look around the room. Two figures entered his awareness. One, a golden-skinned humani, sat on one of the rounded chairs of the same colors as the wall. The other was a Xochat whose orange and red coloring from earlier was washed out and gray with worry. They almost matched the decor.

"Nez! Thank you for coming to see me. They said twelve hours… it hasn't really been that long, has it?"

"No, Haral," the humani broke in, "That's just the standard holding time after head trauma. They wouldn't tell me exactly what happened, or maybe they did and I didn't understand, but it sounds like you took a pretty good hit to the ol' thinkin' muscle. I can't help but assume that was my fault," Merit said, barely looking up at him.

"No, no, Merit… Mr. Lang-"

"No, you can definitely call me Merit. Not only did I do something stupid to send me spiraling into an eventual redemption arc — I can say that, because they didn't let me bring my paparazzi drones in here, but we can do a re-creation later. I think this scene would play huge… Where was I?"

"Stupid," Nez said in a low, flat tone.

"Right, yeah. I guess I owe you both an apology. It's just easy to get caught up in doing anything that gets more eyes on your feed. I was a real jerk. At least it worked out for both us… I mean, aside from possible brain damage… Sorry.”

“Ah… Ok?” Haral said, “Wait, *how* am I here? I don’t know if I even *know* anyone who’s been in the hospital before. You have to have Pull to rate real doctors looking at you.”

“You got it, man. I mean, we’re not peers, or anything, but you’re a rising star. That’s why I’m here, you know, besides the apology thing. I want to team up. If we play this rivalry thing right, we could both see a bump of millions of followers, maybe tens of millions. A solid wave could keep us trending for a week, maybe more, and the long tail… once you’re someone, you’ll always have ups and downs, but you won’t hit bottom like you were at unless you like… kill someone…” Merit said matter-of-factly.

Of course, no one had actually committed murder in centuries. Standard nano-arrays were resilient and capable of maintaining life after quite a bit of damage. This was one of the reasons hospitals had become boutique experiences. If one broke a bone, one usually let the nanos do their work, either toughing out the pain for a few days or getting a temporary subscription to an anesthesia app.

“Millions?” Haral said aloud while searching his Overlay for his Pull chart. He had hidden it off the main interface ages ago as irrelevant to daily life and frankly depressing. He did spot that there were more alerts waiting. The oval which usually displayed the number of new notifications instead had the stylized plus sign beside a slightly higher plus sign that meant the number wouldn’t display properly. He was tempted to open his messages but stayed on task.

Accessing the graph of recent activity, he saw a jagged landscape of the "Views" line jump up from seemingly, or perhaps literally, zero into the hundreds of thousands. Another line in a lighter orange showed his followers. It had also jumped into the tens of thousands, far more than he'd ever had, or dreamed of having, since giving up on get rich quick schemes in his later teens.

"Thirty-two thousand? I have thirty-two *thousand* followers?"

"Aw man, I'm sorry, I thought this would work out for both of us. We can just forget it if it's going to tank your ratings," Merit said, standing from the chair.

"Tanking? No… definitely not the word, but… Yesterday," Haral said, not quite believing the numbers. Merit turned back to Haral as he spoke. "I literally would have jumped off a spar for ten thousand followers. I was no one, no importance, replaceable at my job…"

"Haral…" Nez said, moping. His colors, which had brightened a few shades on hearing the news about Haral's follower count, faded again, dipping darker than they had been when Haral first woke.

"No, no, I know. You don't approve. You kept me from doing all kinds of things that would have gotten me views and follows when I was a stupid kid, and a bunch of broken bones and all that, maybe even dead." Haral said to Nez before looking back to Merit. "Look, I don't know how we got here, but I just can't right now. There's something going on… outside."

"Yeah, my fans tend to follow me around. I-"

"No, outside Geode," Haral interrupted.

"I don't know what you're talking about."

"You know how Geode is a big shell, right? A massive bubble around the sun that our collective ancestors built centuries ago?"

"I can't say I paid that much attention in school…" Merit said, shrugging.

"I did," Nez said, sliding closer to the bed. "What's out there?"

"We don't even know yet, but it's projecting a view of the stars behind it."

"Invisibility? Or at least active camouflage? That's pretty cool. I have a few friends with good camouflage gear." Nez didn't have many friends but the ones they did have always had some special skill or related trait tied to the topic at hand.

"But this is like the size of a spar, maybe bigger," Haral insisted. Merit moved to the window and looked up.

"It's down."

"Huh?" Merit grunted.

"The Shell, the outside, is down. We're used to looking up to see out, the stars and such, after millennia, tens of millennia, on Earth," Haral said, "At least that's what Gann tells me. I didn't pay that much attention in school, either, but 'out' is down now, beneath our feet."

Chapter Three

"Sorry, Gann, I've tried, trust me," Haral said aloud. NeuroNet had weird interference on it and had dropped their chat, so now they were speaking, like savages. "I've had enough of this place. I'd rather be figuring out how to see past that projection, but it's all thought experiments from here." Haral paced as he spoke.

"Elevated heart rate detected," one of the med techs said from the doorway, "Cease labor. You need your rest."

"Look, Gann," he continued, ignoring the med tech, "I'll be out of here in two more hours. I'll see you then."

"Blood sugar and other reports indicate you need food. Choose from this menu," the med tech said. A beautifully rendered image of food stuffs arranged in a garden tableau—benches, trees, and a pond with reeds at one side, hemmed in by blocks of color representing flowers—scrolled into Haral's Overlay. Below lay a text list of options. When focused in, each expanded to show slowly rotating images of top-tier foodstuffs, from steaks to vegetables that were actually distinguishable as the plants they once came from, such as carrots and celery, rather than pastes and blocks as the lowly food weavers he could afford generally offered.

The first dish he looked at made his mouth water, which was something he'd heard of but not really experienced before. Food that looked so good it made you hungry? It was almost inconceivable. Just in case, he clicked into the next one to see how it looked. A fish steak that actually looked like it was cut from an Old World, pre-Geode, water creature… Some people might find the concept of food that came from other living things repugnant, but it had always fascinated Haral. The next was less obviously this, a battered and breaded mass surrounded by more vegetables, but then he'd never had anything so fancily prepared… Except that burger Nez had made, and he was only allowed a single bite…

No, he stopped himself. If he kept looking, he would just make himself dizzy with choices. On the other hand, this might be his only chance to eat this well. Nez's burger had been pretty amazing, but it would have no doubt cost him days worth of Pull rations were he to actually buy it from a weaver. It was a celebration of crossing a finish line. This was like he was living someone else's life. The Pull bubble that his interaction with Merit had caused would pop soon and he'd be back to unembellished protein blocks and vitamin paste, at least unless and until Nez got his own food weaver stand…

All of this steered him back around to Merit's proposal, working together to get more Pull. Mysterious strangers hovering above the Shell notwithstanding, what could it hurt to improve his life? Even if it was just for a few days or a week? He ordered almost without looking, certain that anything on the menu would be mind-blowing and turned back to the golden celebrity.

"So, how would this work? If we were to play this game?" A smile crept onto Merit's lips from one side of his mouth in response.

"I knew you were smart. OK, I've been playing this 'game,' as you say, all my life. You'd think it would be complicated, twists and turns like some movie. And it can be, if we want to really go for the long ride, but I don't want to get into anything too binding just yet. Let's call it three days. We'll do a scene before dinner, someplace public where we run into one another 'by accident.' Lots

of yelling, chest-thumping," Merit said, mimicking Old
World apes he had seen video of in school. Then one of us
will storm out. You did it last time, so it's probably my
turn. Then we clash a couple of times tomorrow and three,
maay-be four times the next day. Don't want to make it
too obvious, but we can't lose momentum, either. Gotta
keep it rampin' up, keep 'em interested in our feud."

"I've never had a feud with anyone before," Haral
said. "And that will get us both a bunch of followers?"

"Guaranteed. I've done this a bunch of times.
When I'm not feuding with Ynna Sram-"

"Oh! I love the Harbingers! They're my favorite
sportsball team!" Nez said, brightening visibly.

"… Ahcor Lommaru… Sadre Theim… I mean
really anyone within plus or minus five million Pull is fair
game, probably a bit narrower for you, you know. I'm an
exception, because we kind of stumbled into this.
Stretching this far outside of my normal territory is risky
for me. People may not care, but it seems like we're
getting some traction. Oh, yeah, and as you're getting to
be somebody now, you should do some livestreams to let
people know who you are, what music, sports teams,
meals or chefs you're into. Maybe plug your buddy here,"
he gestured to Nez,"that kind of stuff. And when I say
'you,' I of course mean… your character, the 'you' you'll
be playing when we do our public interactions."

Haral blinked. "Wow, that's… a lot to think about."

"We can discuss what kind of stuff should happen,
maybe script the first one if you're nervous, but you did
fine earlier. I would have milked it a bit more before
running off…"

"I was called to work."

"Mmm hmm. You said."

"I was."

"I believe you. I don't really know about work and all that. I hear it sucks."

Haral nodded. "It can. I've had good days and-"

"Meal time," a med tech chimed in, rolling on triangular treads through the door which slid shut behind them. They set a covered tray upon a table which swung around in front of Haral. He nearly passed out when the narrow-fingered hand lifted the cover away and the scent of the new life Merit promised him wafted out, filling his senses as they had never been affected before.

The only thing that ruined the succulent meat and tender vegetables as he worked his way through his plate was the thought that he could lose it, that he *would* lose it again if he didn't go along with Merit's plan. Would it be better to never have had the meal than to live with the ghost of it while choking down relatively tasteless, texture homogenized, common food?

No, like seeing a great work of art one could hold in one's mind's eye for the rest of one's life; to witness the beauty of a towering forest or majesty of a whale, it would hang as a jewel on the chain of life's events. Another concern wriggled at the back of his mind, but did not make itself known yet.

As the med tech took the plate away, Merit stepped back in. "So, what do you think? Pretty good, huh?"

"No… I've programmed some recipes before and managed 'pretty good' a few times. That was… I'm no poet. I don't have the words," Haral admitted.

"But you want more, right?"

"No, I'm full. That was very satisfying."

Merit looked over his shoulder at Nez. "I thought you said he was smart."

"Maybe the drugs are dulling his mind, or the daydreams of being famous. We should just call all this off. You have more important things to do, Haral," Nez buzzed.

"No, no, no, no, no," Merit said, holding a hand, palm out, toward each of them. "Let's not backpedal here. I'm pretty sure Haral wants what I'm offering. Who wouldn't? Better food? Better digs? Lady friends? Or boyfriends. You know what I'm saying. More Pull means *more*. Of everything. All the good stuff. You wouldn't have to work anymore; broken wires or pumps or whatever wouldn't be your problem. I've talked to a few people with normal jobs. None of them seem happy. There's always someone, a boss, customers, co-workers, who screws things up for them. They're always bored or stressed." Haral couldn't argue with anything Merit was saying. He would probably miss Gann if he didn't see him every day, but the man wasn't easy to deal with, very demanding, critical.

"You would never see the stars again," Nez said.

"Stars? I'd dazzle you with stars. You could get gems, light shows, whatever it is you'd want."

"They are amazing," Haral admitted. Before he could continue, the room shivered ever so slightly; the pattern on the wall skipped. Machinery inside the bed rattled. "What was that?"

"What? I didn't see anything," Merit said, gold a bit paler than it had been a moment before. Clearly, he was lying. Haral leveled a stare at him. "I dunno, a tremor. They used to have them on Earth all the time, right?"

"But Geode doesn't have tremors, not unless something is very wrong." Haral frowned.

"And *you're* going to fix it?" Merit asked incredulously.

"Who else?" Haral asked, pulling back the blankets from over his legs and shifting his body so he could stand up from the bed. Merit watched him for a moment, hands raising from his sides slightly, then falling back. He stepped toward the door.

"I'll send you a time and place for our meet up. Be there, for both of our sakes, Haral."

"I'll see what I can do. My priorities are bigger than me and you right now, no matter how good the food is." Merit stood, stunned, while Haral and Nez shuffled out of the room.

"Sir, you have one hour and twenty minutes until you are cleared to leave," a med tech called down the hallway.

"I'm fine. I have work to do," Haral said. A waiver popped up in his Overlay. "Yes, sure, thank you for your help, and the meal, but I'm needed." He ticked the acknowledgments and signed the waiver as they walked toward the elevator.

We're on our way, Gann. Haral messaged as they walked through a section of Swanton Spar dominated by clusters of trees and raised gardens of flowers and bushes. People sat around here and there, chatting, making videos for their followers amid the greenery, and generally enjoying themselves.

"Hey!" A young woman's voice called out, trying to get someone's attention. The pair kept walking.

"Hey! Adjani!" she yelled, followed by rapid footsteps. Before Haral could turn all the way around, the humani was upon them—brilliant purple hair in tall spikes along one side of her scalp, pink curls occupying the other. Her eyes, a mix of light brown and green, bored into him. "I called to you."

"I didn't think you were talking to me until you said my name. I… That doesn't happen to me very often," Haral said.

"I followed you hours ago, sent you like half a dozen messages, and another just now when I saw you," she persisted.

"Sorry, I started getting a lot of alerts earlier today and turned off my notifications." Haral held a hand up in a placating gesture while he navigated his Overlay.

"Well, that's rude."

"They were very distracting. Apparently, my run-in with Merit Lang put me on people's feeds."

"Ah yeah, I was wondering why I hadn't seen you before. Laeua." The girl stuck her hand out in a way he had seen in Gann's videos. When he didn't react immediately, she advanced half a step and jammed her palm against his, grabbed hold and pumped up and down a few times before letting go.

"Haral."

"I know, silly, didn't I just call your name to get you to turn around?"

"Ah, yeah. This is all just a little strange… OK, *a lot* strange. My friend is Nez."

"Hey, Nez," the girl said, wiggling her fingers at the Xochat. "No, wait, I know this…" She held both hands out before her and rubbed the fingers and thumb of each hand separately in a manner Haral knew was the humani equivalent of Xochat speech.

"Pleased to meet you, as well," Nez rasped back via sliding tentacles along the inside of his tympana. Haral wasn't fluent, but he caught that much of the conversation. He wondered if she had known some Xochat before today, or learned that greeting after seeing them in Merit's video. Then he shook his head. This whole other stratum of life was already messing with his mind. What a thing to think about someone he had just met.

"I-" Haral sighed, "I'm sorry about the alerts and all. Let's start again. Hi, I'm Haral Adjani, nice to meet you," he began again, holding his hand out. For a fraction of a second, he thought Laeua was going to laugh him off, but then she took his hand and gave it the same firm pumps she had the first time.

"Laeua Kio, nice to meet you, too. I see you're a history buff. Any chance you're a reenactor?"

"Not me, but my friend… my boss, really, at my job, though he's ok, is always showing me old videos and renderings of artifacts and spewing factoids and quotes. He's the expert."

"Nice, you wanna head to the mess station?"

"I would like to, but the previously mentioned boss needs me back at work. We have something of a crisis going on, and not one I can just blow off to hang out with a pretty girl-" Haral realized his boldness a moment too late. What would Merit do? He had no idea. The guy was famous, tons of followers, but Haral wasn't one of them. There were just so many people out there. He guessed he'd better follow him now, though.

"Look, I'll follow you," Haral said, opening his notifications and suffering a torrent of alerts of new followers. He concentrated past it for a moment and selectively silenced them, while allowing messages from people he knew, and opening the follow function. He held his hand, palm up, to Laeua. She returned the gesture, sliding her hand against his even though contact wasn't necessary for the function. "So I can message you when I know what times I have open."

"You'd better. We've just touched three times in a couple of minutes. In some spars, we'd be married already." Laeua laughed. Haral smiled awkwardly. "I'm kidding! Man, you just turned the brightest shade of cerise, on your way to crimson!" She rubbed fingers at Nez, who responded in kind.

"She seems nice," Nez said, then in a sing-song, reedy voice, "Haral has a girlfriend. Haral has a girlfriend."

"Very mature. She's not my girlfriend."

"Oh! I forgot, she's your wife! Haral has a wiiife, Haral has a wiiife."

"I can walk faster than you, you know." Haral scowled.

"Only for a little while. I'd catch up with you eventually."

"Can we just go, please?"

"Nobody's stopping you," Nez said, then, quietly, "Haral's got a groupy! Haral's got a groupy!"

Haral picked up his pace.

Chapter Four

"What took you so long?" Gann said, tapping and twisting and sliding his way across his console.

"I uh, had to stay at the hospital until they cleared me."

"Actually," Nez piped up, coming in on Haral's heels, "We snuck him out early, but then there was a girl."

"Seriously? You just had to run all the way back here alone and you're already back on that?"

"Was she cute?" Gann asked, one bare, silver eyebrow raised.

"Yes," Nez answered before Haral could formulate an answer that didn't make him sound too eager or as though he was already taking advantage of his new fame, however minor.

"Can. We. Work. Please?" Haral said through clenched teeth.

"I thought you'd never ask," Gann said. "So, I've been poking around the Inter-Sector-Messaging System, and it looks like we're not the only ones experiencing… whatever is happening out there. No one's coming out and saying what they've seen, but you're not the only drone operator who got backlash. Half a dozen mechanics in this hemisphere are in the infirmary and two have… died."

"Wow, that's just… Who was it?" Haral asked.

"Not really the point right now, but I don't think you knew them. It does point to the seriousness of the situation, though. If that's an alien force, they've just committed, even if accidentally, the first murder we've had in centuries. This could be war."

"We're not equipped for war. Most people don't even know what it is, except from old movies and videos, ancient texts decrying the atrocities… If we have to fight… how?” Haral asked.

"Let's not get ahead of ourselves," Gann warned. "There are also plenty of surviving movies about people making bad assumptions and leaping to action causing the kind of conflict they're trying to avoid. If they had just communicated, things could have been resolved."

"So what do we do?" Nez asked.

"This is really Sector business, Nez. Don't you have a job?" Gann asked.

"I completed my culinary course and am awaiting food weaver assignment. It could be days before I'm placed," Nez replied.

"Lovely. Fine, do your people have any knowledge about distant races that use active camouflage on their ships?"

Nez contemplated before replying, "We have few stories of races beyond those who came to Geode. Visitors from beyond our local neighborhood were quite rare. Nothing comes to mind, though I can check in with my own historian friends."

"Please do that, when you get the chance," Gann said, turning back to Haral, "OK, so, we know they have relatively sophisticated travel tech, faster than light or some kind of wormhole tech, maybe."

"Or they have the luxury of drifting through space for extended periods," Haral pointed out. "We live basically forever now, even though our ancestors were ephemeral. They might too."

"Or they could have generation ships that have soared through the black for millennia," Nez said wistfully.

"What do you know about black?" Gann asked.

"I am familiar with the concept. It's the easiest of your colors to understand."

Gann conceded, "Fair enough."

Nez recalled a distant memory. "…Though someone once tried to equate color and tone in music, which made some sense to me."

"Got it, we need to move on," Gann said, "So basically, we know nothing about their technology except that they can project images of what's behind them, but solar ions disrupt the illusion without, presumably, destroying the ship itself. That… is not a lot."

"What if… no, let me back up… Why would something sit in the path of the streams? Does it need to be close to the Shell and just happened to intersect the streams? Or is it possible it's using the jets for something? Charging batteries or filling fuel tanks?" Haral wondered.

"I see what you're getting at, but we just… don't know enough to even make that conjecture," Gann said, "Or any conjecture. We need more data."

"You want me to go out there, when we *know* this phenomenon has *killed* people?" Haral asked.

Gann nodded. "I don't see another option. It's possible the camouflage only works against our sensors and cameras."

"They figured out their camouflage was breached by the streams and instead of backing away, they knocked out the sensors that could reveal them," Haral pointed out. "I'm not going out there in a standard suit." Haral turned toward the door.

"So you're just going to walk away?" Gann challenged. "Go be a streaming star while these quakes, or whatever is causing them, tear Geode apart?"

Haral paused with his hand on the door frame. "I'm *going* to see Chopper." Nez slid past him and he followed. The door whirred shut behind them.

URS ⊓ B17 the Overlay called it. UnRecyclable Storage Bay 17 was more spacious than most spars, and occupied by only one sapient being.

"Chopper! Chopper! You hear me?" Haral called long and clear from the grid balcony just inside the entrance. His mechanical friend was not connected to PullSys, and Haral needed a hardwired workstation to use the ISMS. Nez pulled in the middle of his stalk like a man sucking in his gut, angling his noses down and giving his tympana slack so Haral's yelling wouldn't harm his sensitive hearing.

Great, foot-thick doors slid shut to Haral's left, a long hum ending with a thump, revealing "URS ⊓ B17" written in a variety of scripts, the common scrawl being most prominent in letters as high as his leg in case you might forget where you were.

Below and away into the dwindling distance ran rows of stanchions holding thousands, perhaps millions, of shelves, each as long as a sportsball pitch. All that space, but still they overflowed with centuries of detritus— potentially contaminated, toxic, or otherwise dangerous items and materials gathered from the surface of Geode. These were measured, cataloged, labeled, and cared for by an ageless overseer.

"I'm here, boy, no need to yell. I do get alerts when the doors open, even though I gave you the code. You can

never be too careful," a flat, ancient, robotic voice warned
him. A dinged and scratched metal chevron once painted
warning yellow hovered up to meet him, the cozy
binocular eyes spinning this way and that to optimize
focus. His head, a silver and black chevron, rose on a
black conduit the width of Haral's arm to look him over.
"Something's different about you… both of you. Nez."
Chopper nodded in greeting. "Welcome back."

"Thank you! I had a great visit and learned a lot
last time, but we're not here for a social call," Nez said,
handing the conversation back to Haral.

"Yeah, um, I'm not sure how to say what I need to
say here…" Haral said, knowing the wrong groupings of
words could send Chopper over the edge into a diatribe
about "external intelligences." "We're… having some
difficulties with the sensor arrays and I need to go out
there to check things out."

"I've been tracking the chatter. It's *them!*" Chopper
said excitedly. Haral sighed.

"Which them?" Haral asked in what he hoped was
a calming but serious tone. If Chopper had anything real to
offer besides the decommissioned exosuit prototype, he
might get some insight into how to proceed.

"C'mon, I'll *show* you," the mechanical caretaker
promised.

"Uh oh…" Nez said by rubbing his limbs against
his tympani in his native language, something he knew
Haral would understand, but Chopper had never been
programmed to. Nevertheless, they descended, Nez sliding
along the wall, Haral taking the stairs which were far
better suited to humani than Xochat. They reconvened at a
clear area of decking surrounded by screens and crates of
uncatalogued items still being studied. Many of these,
Haral had brought in himself.

Chopper stood on black, spindly legs—the same style and size as his neck—facing a large crate. As the others came to stand beside him, the near face of the gray box became transparent, showing a swarm of metallic shards hovering and bouncing off the walls in unison like a school of fish.

"These were collected about a hundred and twenty years ago, not far from the southern border of the sector. I inspected them thoroughly at the time, searching every square millimeter for energy signatures, inscriptions, language of any kind, and nothing. Now this." Chopper turned toward Haral.

"'These?'" Nez whispered to Haral in Xochat.

Before he could respond, Chopper pressed for an answer, "So, what have *you* seen? What do you know about our visitors?"

"You seem very... calm." Haral regarded Chopper. To Nez he rubbed his fingers, "What?"

"Calm?" Chopper let out a warbling, mechanical laugh. "I suppose I've considered so many possibilities over the years, hashed and rehashed every angle that I'm just out of guesses. Until you give me some real information."

Haral considered this for a moment. "Only if you can keep your head on. We need your help. People have... died."

"We're pretty sure it was an accident," Nez chimed in. "I mean, from what Haral said about his experience..."

"You've already interacted with them?" Chopper asked, sounding hurt.

"Not on purpose," Haral said, turning away from the mechanical, angling his head to one side and shooting Nez a glare he knew the mechanical couldn't see as he was watching the odd shapes in the crate. "But yes, they… let me start at the start." And he did.

"Well, now…" Chopper said, speaking slowly as he did while he was thinking fast. This was usually a prelude to an explosive hour-long discourse on the circumstances around a particular artifact's usage and the purposes of its individual features. "You've reset my probability matrices quite nicely with that tale, m'boy! It seems to me that the visitors are here looking for their probe, to retrieve the data it might have captured before crashing and being hauled inside. Alternatively, it learned what it needed to from the probe which transmitted data back to their people before being destroyed.

"Presumably, this gives us a range of distances to their homeworld, or at least outpost, if they have such, or are multiplanetary… Assuming the signal moving at the speed of light, one hundred twenty years, a round trip… Traveling at or close to the speed of light… somewhere less than 60 lightyears away, which, checking our most recent data, looking for anomalies in the general directions of those places… maybe we saw them coming and didn't know it…"

"And he was off…" Nez stridulated.

"Yeah…" Haral rubbed his fingers in response. But he didn't, strictly speaking, *need* Chopper to walk him through signing out the exosuit. He was official, on the job. He walked over to one of the display walls and pulled a drawer from a low-slung filing cabinet. He quickly found the keyboard that Chopper never used, as he could communicate directly with the monitors, security sensors, etc, even if all those feeds were too much for him to internalize all at once. Haral plugged in the device. He waited a few seconds for the system to recognize it, then began typing, logging himself into the system and calling the exosuit closet.

The rumble and squeal of the chamber trundling along the floor tracks echoed to them, announcing the device's imminent arrival.

The exosuit was in the vague form of a rotund man with thick limbs and the slightest bubble of a separate clear dome for a head. In a pinch, he *might* be able to adjust his body and move the limbs manually, but the suit was really meant for him to hang in a harness at the center of the main sphere and access controls and sensor readouts more like a pilot than someone in a snorkeling get up.

Merit's message came just as Haral was buttoning up the armored EVA suit, making sure the seals pressurized. He read quickly, hoping he could placate the other rather than running to his side like some pet.

***PullSys - Follow reports autom...**
***Laeua_Kio1792 - How about dinner? I ...**
***MeritLang1 - 5pm <u>Meet</u> at <u>Discotec...</u>**

Haral groaned to himself. Yesterday, he was no one, with just one responsibility. Now, things were collecting on his proverbial plate faster than he could process them.

"Hold on, I've got to answer these messages before I get outside and lose signal," he told Nez.

"Girlfriend troubles already?" Nez prodded.

"Ha… ha… Though one of these *is* from Laeua…"

"OoOOooooH!" Nez exclaimed excitedly. Haral could feel his cheeks growing pink again. He was glad Nez couldn't see it. Even his tentacles' thermal sense—

which might have given him a clue—was blocked by the thick armor.

He clicked on the PullSys alert just to get it out of his sight. Apparently, he was getting so many follows now that they were sending hourly digests instead of individual notifications. It was a step up, and a nice feature, not having to deal with each one individually. He wondered briefly how many he had gotten, but didn't want the number to go to his head and clicked over to Laeua's message.

How about dinner? I know you're a busy guy now, but you gotta eat, right? I'd like to hang out and get to know you better over some home-cooked food, but maybe we can just hit a restaurant if you're more comfortable with that? I usually shoot for 6pm. LMK. Laeua

Hey Laeua!
Haral deleted the exclamation point as too excited, but then put it back. He was already going to have to give her less attention than she deserved, at least until this crisis was over. He wanted to signal his interest to make sure she knew.

...I'm working right now, about to... be unavailable for messages for a bit, but I would love dinner, at a restaurant or wherever you like. I'll do my best to be back by 6, but if we could we make it tomorrow, I feel like I'd have a better chance. I don't want to have to cancel if I'm all grungy from work. -Haral

Hi Merit. I've had something come up at work. I can't guarantee I'll be back for 5pm, and I may have just gotten a date for 6. Maybe sometime later in the evening? Or earlier tomorrow? I know you had

this big time line set up, but life doesn't always bow to our plotting. I still want to do this, but I need to see to things here, too. -Haral

Messaging taken care of, Haral walked slowly, heavily, into the innermost airlock. There were a series of them because a breech to the outside would be catastrophic. At least the suit had rockets to make the five kilometer trek go by faster. It had been referred to as a "suit" by those who had worked closely with it on the daily, but it was officially classed as a "single person vehicle." So he was in command of his own spaceship.

That was fun.

He almost wished he had some of the drones that followed Merit around for this part. It seemed worthy of one of Gann's old videos: the intrepid stellanaut Haral Adjani, passing through corridors of stone and metal into the deep void—one that only a few thousand humani had seen with their own eyes in the centuries since Geode was completed.

At the outermost lock, he took a moment to energize the magnetic clamps in the feet of the suit before beginning the cycle. Not that there was much air at this point. He had been self-contained since entering the first lock, and it was better not to let oxygen eat away at the components.

"Heading out," he told Nez and Chopper waiting below.

"Be careful out there, Haral," Nez said back through some speakers above and to either side of his head. Another strange sensation.

"Thanks."

The last door opened, and he immediately saw the difference between the projected stars to his right and the real things on his left. There was no sign of Alissa, the drone he'd lost, nor of any of the sensor embankments what had dotted this area of the sector. He was familiar with all of them due to his repair work and rare actual visits to the surface. It was odd to think of it as the surface when in his perspective he had just traveled downward for nearly ten minutes like an ancient miner headed to work.

There might not be any data to extract from the sensors themselves, but he made for where the nearest sensor had been located yesterday and found a fused layer of shining metal, not yet corroded by the thin cloud of gasses that swirled around his suit's feet. He looked up now, searching for the spots where the solar winds had been routed. Shifting the spectrum of the cameras, he could see on some face-sized screens what his eyes refused to show him: the wash of ions shooting from the thrusters, roiling and launching into the gap between Geode and… something that was trying to make itself invisible.

From here, he could see material that looked vaguely like the shards Chopper had in the crate being heated by the energetic particles to a vague nimbus of light that shifted with the chaos of the jet. Most Geode-made ships would have melted in minutes, if not seconds, under such onslaught.

Perhaps this had all been a terrible mistake.

That rogue thought was reinforced by others in a quick stream of words, mostly Old World curses, as something unseen knocked him backward.

Chapter Five

Gasping, Haral rolled to one side to try to get onto his belly and push himself up. He remembered the hand-thing grasping the drone just before he had lost contact...then consciousness. There would be no med techs out here to drag him to the hospital. Just as he regained his feet, something grabbed one of them and pulled.

"Fuah!" He exclaimed involuntarily as he was jerked backward, his arms flailing forward but finding nothing to grab onto. A small, but insistently bright red display popped up in his Overlay:

WARNING!

You are experiencing a health emergency!
Your heart rate and blood pressure are well above healthy levels.
Find a place to quiet your mind.
Think of quiet waves upon a sandy beach, or small animals frolicking.
Would you like to contact Emergency Services?

WARNING!

Before Haral could respond to the pop-up dialog, sparks exploded and smoke rose from the suit's right leg. An alarm from the suit itself bored into his brain via his ears. He silenced it, swatting away all the open windows crowding his consciousness.

He tried to run, but the limb didn't respond, except with a whine and series of angry clicks from the hip servos. The status readout down and to his right showed the entire leg flashing red. Not a good sign.

*No, no, NO! If I can't run, or even walk, away…
No!* Haral denied the alerts and alarms, but they beat against his mind.

The suit pitched forward as the shiny patch of burned-away metal pulled away from him, first straight ahead, then down. The whole suit swung upside down. He spotted a familiar wedge of yellow paint followed immediately by bright flashes of blue and gold light. Twisting, he saw bursts of weapon fire for a moment before everything vanished behind a rippling field of stars. Purely from instinct, his arms fanned out to the sides, seeking any kind of handhold.

His Overlay popped back to life.

WARNING!

You are experiencing a health emer-

Haral swiped the alert away. He needed many things right now, from a vacation to a stiff drink, but loud, insistent reminders he was about to die were not on the list.

The sky settled below him, giving him a moment to breathe. He realized that he was looking at the inside of the projected illusion, which meant he was inside the ship! Or soon would be… He hit the booster rockets, usually a dangerous tactic on the surface. One wrong thrust and one might never be seen again, but he felt there was a strong chance of that, anyway. The suit rumbled with the force exerted, but the thrusters didn't affect his trajectory.

The suit had no weapons, but Haral deployed a handful of sensor drones, hoping to get more information about his attackers. He waited impatiently for additional readouts to blossom across the panel beneath the helmet.

Each showed a view from the camera, battery life, direction and distance from the suit in 3D space. A secondary display showed this latter information numerically in millies and mikes. He was a round, smoking planet. The four drones were moons orbiting at different angles and distances.

Information about the object above him began pouring in. He tapped through a menu to relay the feed back to Chopper's station. Who knew if he'd be back to carry it himself? Wow, it was large, if the scans were correct. Somehow, this realization filled his stomach with butterflies. It wasn't just fear anymore, but awe. It might be tiny compared to Geode, perhaps, but larger than any ship the humani had ever built for travel. There were all kinds of polymerized molecules, as one might expect, but many seemed very similar to ones he had studied when learning to program… Organic, or meant to interface with organics.

One of the drones bounced off something it couldn't see, whirling out of control, but still recording. Thus, it caught on video two things: a tangle of gray tentacles emerging from the surface of the massive form, and the other drones all being speared in one sudden flash of movement as the tentacles straightened as one into spears.

One of these thrust through the clear canopy, inches thick super-hard polymer. Alarms blared that a handful of other spots on the side of the suit closest to the invader—it was hard to think of them as visitors in the middle of a misunderstanding at this point—fell victim to the spear-tentacles. Conduits and wires were severed. The hull was compromised. Jets of atmosphere venting caused the whole suit to rattle.

Before Haral could react beyond widened eyes and dropped jaw, he was pulled back and down into a tiny ball just big enough for him to fit with his knees to his chest and arms tucked around them. A message flashed in his Overlay.

***EMERGENCY*EMERGENCY*EMERGENCY**
LIFEBOAT protocol engaged.
Hull compromised
Atmosphere venting
Multiple systems damaged
Repair time unknown
Rescue beacon initiated.
EMERGENCY*EMERGENCY*EMERGENCY

Folded into the "lifeboat," with his knees pressed into the front of his shoulders, Haral poked around at the limited interface, thankful he didn't actually have to move to do so. He tried to get communications, or even a single view of what was going on outside, but the lifeboat protocol was bare bones to say the least.

The sphere slammed to the left, bumping his head against the cushioned bulkhead. Something pinged against the metal hull. He hung in the center of the cramped space, his inner ear and stomach arguing over whether he was plummeting back toward Geode or hurtling out into the void and whether his lunch should follow suit.

Either way, he was fairly sure he'd be missing both his first date with Laeua and his Pull-boosting appointment with Merit. What a strange name, "Merit," as though his parents had been so uncertain of his future worth that they had to start him off with some additional unearned Pull. Or perhaps it was a name he had taken later, like a stage name or a pen name from Old Earth.

Where were these thoughts coming from? Surely the latest blow to the head couldn't have caused any harm, even given the punch to the face earlier. Perhaps he was running out of oxygen. It was rather tight in here, after all. How much air could there be? Maybe he couldn't get enough because he was all folded up like one of Gann's reproduction street maps. And what was with Gann, anyway? You'd think, with all the junk he collected, he'd get along famously with Chopper, but he acted like the old mechanoid had a different screw loose than him. They were two… two… peeps in a pack… no… peeps in a pond.

The Overlay faded and Haral drifted, wondering where his limbs had gone, where Nez had gone, and hadn't he just seen Chopper?

Sudden light woke Haral. He flinched in his harness, but had nowhere to go. He could barely turn his head away. The light faded in brightness by degrees over a span of seconds until it was a faint gray that seemed to slide over everything, limning the dissected console before him, the edges of the wall of the tiny capsule, the straps holding him in place, and finally his jumpsuit and hands. It was cool to the touch, like a glass of water that had been left partly drunk.

Beyond a ragged hole in the emergency pod hull was a room. The floor had the same striated, segmented, pattern as the shards of metal floating in Chopper's crate, confirming what Haral had thought he'd seen earlier. That material stretched beyond the gray light's curved edge, showing nothing else occupying the space.

There's no way I'm alone. Someone has to be watching, at least. He tried to speak, but the pod, the chamber beyond, even what he could see of his knees wavered and washed away.

Colors swirled, unrecognizable blobs growing, then fading away. Green came to dominate the field, resolving into a massive wall of vegetation, flat as any spar, but clearly made up of twisting branches and thousands, millions of tiny leaves. At the center of the wall stood a tall arch of carefully guided trees, one on either side, their limbs entwining at the apex of the entry.

Ventren Gardens, Haral remembered. At the upper reaches of Swanton Spar, one of the only places plants grew and birds flew in the CEB. There were many spars, many gardens and ponds, but true wilderness only existed toward the poles.

Mrs. Humphries brought us here in fourth grade, he reached back to that day. She explained the purpose of the wilderness zones, how important species diversity was, and how much had been lost during early humani civilization. Much had been rebuilt, complex webs of plants, animals, producers and consumers. The gardens he was used to were tiny reflections of these, with suitably small, more or less controllable, species held in proximity to people for their entertaining and soothing effect on the oldest parts of humani brains.

Likewise, this was a calm memory, peaceful.

Colors blurred and blended, fading from green to grays and white before resolving. The classroom. Mrs. Humphries lectured them about the structure of Geode. The outer layers of rocky material were threaded with metallics that could intercept and convert cosmic rays into

energy in a similar way to how the films coating the spars
and other habitation zone structures turned the spectrum of
energies from the sun into usable power. This made the
trains run, regulated temperature within the habitation
spars, and pumped water in the rivers around the equator.
The rivers aided in generating spin for artificial gravity.
This same energy helped create the magnetic fields that
directed the solar winds through the tunnels in the Shell to
the thrusters to create spin and adjust Geode's trajectory as
needed. The whole lesson was conveyed in images,
moving and still, but not a single word from the generally
talkative woman. Was that how it had happened?

"Why am I…?" Haral struggled to get out. The
words were suddenly heavy, clunky, unmanageable,
foreign objects. It was like trying to communicate by
rolling boulders down a hill. His harness snapped open,
the silvery light sinking into the seams and releasing him
to fall forward, tumbling from the life pod onto the foreign
floor as the whole orb rolled forward, releasing him, then
fell back.

The floor was less rigid than he expected, and even
sank a little under his weight. It was like sitting on a bed.

"You're in my head!" He said finally, pulling his
attention back from the gray material. The only response
he got was the capsule spreading apart along the crack like
a jagged, metallic flower. The light played over every
inch, separating components and holding them, hovering,
spinning in pseudopods of liquid gray light away from the
rest as if inspecting them individually before dropping
them onto the floor as unceremoniously as he had been
ejected.

"If you want to know something just ask!"

Mrs. Humphries came back to his mind, standing
before his whole class, pointing to the holo-projection of

Geode. She said something, her words blurred as when an object vibrates violently. They felt like an Old World building of earthen slabs... bricks, cracking apart along one side and leaning over in one of Gann's movies. Words a mystery, annoyance was plain in her tone.

The projection, a cross-section of the great sphere encapsulating the sun, expanded, growing closer to him, focus shifting to the open edge. Small gray lines pointed to the various strata of the Shell, and features embedded in it. The outer crust and inner spars filled in quickly, conduits for the solar winds and carrying water, the pumps for creating the flow of the river and spin were identified next. He recognized one location as a warehouse, like the one Chopper oversaw.

He resisted, trying to think of something else, anything else. Laeua came swimming by, but the spikes and curls of her hair failed to solidify, blown away like mist on the wind. He tried Merit, to much the same result, his golden features a metallic blur before fading, his mind drawn back to a crate in Chopper's workspace.

The nearest wall of the container went transparent, revealing the shards which writhed through the air like a cohesive being, not just a school or swarm as he had thought before. But it wasn't all there. Pieces had been left behind, or taken by other collectors. Chopper had said they had been found near the south border of the sector... The floor vibrated, and he felt a sensation like he was being pulled apart. He felt like vomiting, or crying, but only wrapped his arms around himself in a tight hug as though in vain attempt to hold his pieces together.

Another push on his mind. They were searching his more recent memories. His new acquaintances slid through his vision again, the hospital, the mess station, Nez, Gann, then it all ran back the other way, forward, he realized, past Gann again down to Chopper and then the tunnel to the outer Shell. The last lock opened. He rolled to one side, involuntarily lying down. The ridged floor curled up around him, cradling him as he slid toward the direction of his feet, hugging him close and preventing him from sliding further. Shards of the lifeboat rained down from above his head. A memory of water slides washed over him, the sun shining, people shrieking in delighted fear.

Giggling.

Splashing.

Joy.

Coinciding with a final splash into a sun-drenched pool atop Fendil Spar, Haral felt his body come to a sudden, but still-cradled, halt. The memory of his visit to the outer lock swept over him. The controls loomed close. He saw his hand reach out, tapping a certain pattern. The doors opened, allowing him to see farther into Geode.

Zip.

Splash.

The second lock blocked his way. He was standing… standing? Or hovering? He wondered groggily, peering at the controls. He tried to think of other things—Laeua, Nez—but felt himself reaching out as though plying the buttons again, a video clip on repeat.

Splash.

Thrashing, at least within his mind, resisting, but then movement again, lost in the cyclical moment of slipping down the water slide, only to pause and take off again. Every thought he had, every attempt to deflect and delay was swept aside, the summoner of memories either becoming adept at opening the locks, or at playing him like an instrument. Neither idea held any comfort.

In a final, disconcerting flash, all sensation of infinite water slides was gone. Haral sat on the rubberized grate floor of Chopper's workstation, Chopper lying to one side, and a completely washed-out Nez quaking a few feet away. A shape Gann would later liken to a giant leech hovered in the air, tapered more sharply at the front and more gradually toward the back of the flattened tube. In a flutter of movement, it swooped past the crate, slicing it open with a means Haral couldn't fathom, then swung back around to float overhead.

The shards swam up through the air to meet it. A vertical seam opened toward the front end of the larger form, allowing the smaller to enter. The seam sealed and the thing rolled in the air, starting for the lock.

Haral found his voice again. "Wait! We didn't hurt anybody! That… They, maybe? Crashed before I was even born. I don't know what happened. I don't know that anyone does."

A memory surfaced of a wildlife encounter field trip where the students got to interact with small mammals, reptiles, and birds. He remembered one bird huddled in his hand, tiny heart beating a thousand degrees a minute. He cooed to it, stroked its tiny feathers, tried to feed it the little tan crumbs the staff said were its food.

The creature, or ship, or both? Shot into the lock. The doors closed, leaving him with a story no one would believe. He crawled over to his mech friend.

"Chopper? Can you hear me?" Haral reached out to touch the yellow frame, but the air around it was shockingly cold. If he made contact, he would suffer frostbite immediately. "Chopper, come on, man!"

"Is he okay?" Nez asked as he picked his way across the rough flooring.

"I don't know. I can't see any movement. He came up after me," Haral said, realizing why the mech was so cold. It was the only explanation. "We should have found some other way. This is my fault…"

"Any other drone would suffer the same fate," Nez pointed out. "The wave that sent you to the hospital killed others. You were brave to go. There wasn't anything else we could have done but go up and look." Haral nodded vaguely, searching desperately for any sign of flickering lights or movement of lenses on Chopper's face. "I'm sending an alert to nearby sectors for a repair mech. We won't be able to fix him on our own," Nez said.

"Right, good idea." Instinctively, Haral reached out a comforting hand again. He felt the cold boring into his flesh and yanked it back just before making contact. Alerts flashed in his Overlay now that he was back inside Geode.

PullSys - New features, perks,…
MeritLang1 - Urgent: Hey man, don…
Senrach221 - HighPull visibility override message: Hey, Haral!
Themis42 - HighPull visibility override message: Welcome to the club!…
Laeua1792 - I understand if you'…
YnnaSram010 - HighPull visibility override message: Re: Merit's Feud
PullSys - MeritLang1 mentioned you in a stream!

Haral's eyes widened at some of the names on the messages. These were legitimately famous people, writing to *him*. But there was only one that warranted addressing in this moment, even when his friend was unresponsive on the floor. He couldn't not.

I understand if you're too important for me now. I haven't been stalking your numbers, but you've kind of been on the news, between your thing with Merit Lang and being in the hospital and all. Even some thing about technical stuff with your job? I don't know, but I don't expect a HighPuller to be interested in some nobody artist... Laeua

Haral composed a reply immediately.

Laeua! I am absolutely not blowing you off. I am back from my trip, but dealing with a medical emergency with a friend. Why is life so exciting now? I will do my best to be at dinner. Just let me know where and when. HighPuller? Crazy huh? And that's not even the wildest thing I have to talk with you about. LMK re: dinner. -Haral

"Haral! There you are. Messaging your girlfriend again?" Nez needled.

"…She's not my girlfriend."

"That's not a 'no," Nez retorted.

"Just shut up. Do we have someone on the way for Chopper?"

"It looks like everyone within a few sectors south and west is in the middle of some kind of emergency, but the northern sectors are diverting a team here from their aid mission to the south. They were already in transit and should be here soon," Nez said.

Haral checked the time with a flick of his attention, considered responding to some of the other messages, but honestly, they could wait. Of all the paths before him, some fake feud with Merit Lang to get more people watching his every move seemed like a fairly low priority one.

Nez stared at Haral, considering. "Need to go get ready for your date? I can wait here with Chopper. He's my friend, too. Just… what happened up there? I can guess it was exciting by the way you suddenly appeared, but… where's your exosuit?"

"*That* is a long story in itself…"

Chapter Six

Nez had reassured Haral that he would stay by Chopper until help arrived, and had shoved his indecision off a cliff with the words, "They'll probably want to look you over, too." The Xochat had been absolutely right. Sneaking out of a hospital where you had voluntarily checked yourself in was one thing, being strapped to a table and have hundreds of tests run on you because you'd been on a previously unknown alien race's ship… out of your environment suit…

Haral had run, not walked, to the stairs and up a service ladder, avoiding the normal elevator approach to the warehouse. Now he was on his way back to his apartment when he realized they would look for him there first. As soon as Chopper came around, they would most likely realize Haral had been there, and send someone to lock him down, or just turn his apartment into a prison. No, he had to find some acceptable clothes, get cleaned up in as anonymous place as possible, and get to wherever place Laeua had chosen for dinner.

Head on a swivel for anyone tracking his movements, he ducked into a side-hall between storefronts to check his messages. In addition to the previous messages he had left in place were:

PullSys - Create a message for...
EscamillasAuthentic - Confirming reservation
Laeua_Kio1792 - reservation at Escamilla's
MeritLang1 - Discotech! Be there...

I went ahead and made a reservation for six tonight at Escamilla's. I know you might not be able to make it, but I figure I'd better get in before you

Scrolling back up, he noted Merit's stream notification and played the recording:

"Hey fam! So this Haral has been ducking me since our first run in, but I'm tracking him down. If you see him, take a still or a video and tag him, me, and his location! We're gonna have this out, bro!" Merit said, bouncing around and flailing his arms as though throwing punches.

Did he think he was a boxer now? Did he expect Haral to fight? Anyway, setting even more eyes than the government could muster to look for Haral didn't bode well for sneaking his way through the next hour. There was no real choice but to flip in the completely opposite direction. Or directions.

In his paranoid teens, Haral had downloaded an illegal app that allowed him to spoof his location marker. Later, he learned that one could also take a recording of oneself and remove or replace the background so it looked like you were wherever you wanted people to think you were… Your apartment, studying… at the library… He wouldn't say he'd used it wisely before, but now… The blank section of wall behind him in the narrow alley was perfect for replacing.

One of Gann's movies was a collection of ancient —even for Old Earth—folk tales acted out by handmade puppets while a narrator read the stories. In one, a hunter captured a faerie of some kind and demanded its treasure. The hunter marked the location of the treasure with a red ribbon tied to the tree, making the faerie swear not to remove the ribbon or turn it invisible. When he returned to the forest with a shovel and wagon to take the hoard of coins away, he found every tree in the first with a red ribbon, making it impossible to find the treasure. This was the seed of Haral's idea. He hoped it didn't obligate him to not complain about Gann's movie choices in the future.

"Hey everyone!" Haral said into the camera in his manual ID, holding the palm-sized card up with two fingers while he waved with his other hand and smiled. "Welcome to my first stream. I've seen so many of these, but have never… well, you don't care about that. The game today is, 'Where's Haral?' Can you find me and get Merit's reward? I'll be around Swanton Spar at various shops and sports arenas for the next few hours. Follow me and Merit Lang for continuing updates!"

After ending the short stream, he took a handful of short vids of him waving, or pointing at things in the distance and ran them through the spoofer, sending himself virtually all over the spar, in different outfits, his own red ribbons, spread liberally around, from gardens to climbing walls to sportsball arenas and the water park which he'd remembered during his return from the surface of Geode. It wasn't technically on Swanton Spar, but it was close enough that adventurous citizens like Merit could buy a short-term app to grow a variety of wings or go truly stone age and use a hang glider to fly to Fendil Spar in a matter of minutes. Even less adventurous or LowPullers could ride the train over in less than an hour.

He hoped these false positives would fool not only Merit's fanbase, but also whatever authorities might be on his trail.

One might not be able to erase one's digital footprint, but one could make false trails to maintain confusion, as long as he didn't trigger any direct locators. Haral slid the ID into a metal mesh envelope to prevent automatic reading and tracking by sensors all around and headed for the nearest gym. After a trip into actual space and back in an alien device, or was it a being? He owed Laeua a shower, at the very least. In the locker room, he got cleaned up. Standing in a towel, staring at his grubby work clothes, he looked around for another solution. He pulled a second ID, provided on the silent by Chopper some years ago, and bought a pair of pants and relatively fashionable shirt from a kiosk. Three minutes later, he slipped back out into foot traffic.

Having second thoughts about the brazen approach as there were just so many people around, Haral ducked into a shop and bought a billed hat with the anonymous card tied to an account he kept aside for emergencies. Maybe Chopper's stories *had* sunk too deep into his brain. But for now, he was grateful. He would be able to go undetected longer.

"He's at the water park!" Someone yelled and a clot of schoolagers rushed by, headed for the train to Fendil. This could be working. His Overlay pinged with a new message. Since he had set the filters, he knew it had to be one of only a few people.

MeritLang1 - Nice. This'll be fun...

Five, right. Haral scrolled back up to Merit's earlier message about where to meet him. Could they take care of this business and leave Haral time to get back to Escamilla's for Laeua? It seemed reasonable they could. *All right, Merit, you're on.*

Haral looked around. There was a lull in traffic. He pulled out his ID and shot another quick segment.

"Hey, Merit! I know it's not your fault you're a spoiled jerk," Haral jumped into making a new video without thinking very much about what he'd say, but stumbled through it. "Almost breaking my nose over a mess station table is pretty gradeschool, but that doesn't mean everything is forgiven. We're going to have a showdown someday, and you'll regret your foolishness!" Haral made certain to get the screen over the train he was standing near in the shot and then boarded before cutting off the recording. He got right back off and scheduled the clip to release five minutes later. By then, he'd be safely on another train headed in a different direction. Maybe Gann's old spy movies had some use, too.

He boarded the train that would take him closest to the Discotech—a dance club slash roller skating rink and more—at the west edge of the spar. Finding a seat, he leaned back with his long-brimmed powder blue hat pulled down.

"Hey," a very young voice intruded quietly on his moment of rest. "You're the one Merit punched, aren't ya?" Haral was tempted to pretend to be fully asleep or deny it, but it seemed a poor start to a life of Pull to lie about being the recognizable person.

"Don't tell anybody, OK? I'm trying to lie low for right now," Haral said just above a whisper.

"'Lie low?'" the child asked.

"It's an expression from Old Earth. It means like 'try not to be seen' or 'go around unnoticed.'"

"Huh… why would you want that?"

"I'm trying to sneak up on someone without them knowing I'm coming," Haral said, voice still quiet.

"Ahhh," the child said knowingly. Their chin, the only part of their face he could see under the edge of his hat, bobbed. Suddenly, the hat flew off his face, waving around in the air over the kid's head as he ran away. The kid yelled, "Hashtag MeritLang1! Hashtag TeamMerit!" laughing the whole time. He jumped up on the seats near the end of the train car and danced around, then pointed at Haral. "Hashtag Haralsucks! Hashtag Haralisnobody!" He waved the hat at him, and he tried to grab it, but the kid snatched it back too fast and jumped off the seat, running one way as though trying to get past Haral, then turning and running out the door. If he ever went into sportsball, he'd probably go far. He had moves. A second later, Haral heard a frightened scream and the flash of powder blue as his hat shot past the window.

"Ah crap!" Haral said, charging for the door.

"Leave the kid alone!" A burly man jumped up from the side of the train the hat had flown by. The man planted his feet, crossing his thick arms before his chest.

"Are you kidding me right now?" Haral demanded. "He fell. He could be hurt."

"*You* could be hurt. Sit down." The large man cracked the knuckles of one fist in the palm of his other hand.

"You didn't see, didn't hear?" Haral asked.

"You're not fooling anyone, and you're not getting past." The other's frown deepened. He thought he was protecting the kid.

"You can't hear him screaming?"

"That's just the wind. The door didn't get closed all the way. Happens all the time." The man stood resolute. Haral glanced past him and saw the door, perfectly sealed as it had been before the kid rushed through.

"Help!" The child screeched, barely audible through the wall, and invisible from this vantage.

Haral's mind raced. How could he get past this guy? He thought he was doing right, but there wasn't time to prove him wrong, and he couldn't force his way past or even hope to injure the man to save the kid. A gray light came from the windows on the right, or perhaps the overhead light strips. Or maybe he was having a stroke, as the light crawled across the man like… like the light on the alien craft! He felt something push on his mind, trying to find a moment of imbalance, of losing his footing. Back they were at the water park again, a wave rolling up and lifting him from his feet, toppling him over.

The bulwark of a man before him cried out, flailing his limbs as he fell over in exactly the way Haral remembered doing. Not wasting any time, he rushed by, grabbed the door handle and slid it open. The kid hung, elbow wrapped around railing support while his body flapped in the hundreds of mikes an hour wind. Haral edged out toward the boy.

"Help me!"

"I'm trying!" Haral yelled against the wind.

"Try harder!" The boy demanded.

Haral shuffled closer and managed to get his hands under the other's armpits. He hauled backward, dragging the kid up. The train, tilted, taking a turn. The boy rose up in the air. The pull of the wind grew stronger, as though playing tug-o-war. "Aaah!" The kid screamed. Haral almost screamed back, but then turned and hauled, bringing the boy back on the safe side of the railing. Haral sank against the wall of the train car, letting the boy go, first with one hand, then the other, as he grabbed hold of the door handle.

"Th-thanks, Haral. Sorry I stole your hat." The boy said, regaining his breath.

"Don't worry about it. I'm just glad you're safe." Haral patted the kid on the shoulder.

"And lost it." The child said, head down.

"Yeah, I saw that. No worries."

"How will you lie low now?"

"Good question, but I think it's too late for that." Haral said, looking up at the windows of the next car. Faces, drones, and ID card recorders were pressed up against the glass.

"You'd better get back inside. I've got to figure out how to get off this train without being mobbed," Haral said, standing. The kid hadn't opened the door yet, so he tried it himself. It was locked, or someone was holding it shut. "Come on!" he yelled through the glass. "At least let the kid in!"

"You go over there! We saw what you did to the big guy!" said a lean man with four parallel blue lines angled across his cheek. It probably signified something, a group association or pronoun preference, but Haral didn't recognize it.

What *had* he done to the large man? Even he wasn't sure. Had he really done anything? How could someone else be affected by *his* memories? Nevertheless, he nodded and crossed the tiny platform, coming to the narrow gap between the rails of this car and the next. The door slid open. A hand reached out and grabbed the boy, dragging him back to safety. The door slammed shut and definitely locked this time. He could hear the clicking and grinding even over the wind shooting by. He thought to himself that it was good he didn't have drones like Merit's, or they'd all be gone like his hat.

His Overlay pinged a new alert, flashing it before his eyes without his having to acknowledge or open it.

SWANTON SPAR REGULATORY FORCE

AN INCIDENT HAS OCCURRED
IN YOUR AREA.
REMAIN IN PLACE UNTIL UNITS
HAVE RECEIVED RECORDS OF
THE INCIDENT FROM ALL
WITNESSES AND DEVICES.
FAILURE TO DO SO MAY RESULT
IN LEGAL ACTION, DETENTION,
AND OTHER PENALTIES.

SWANTON SPAR REGULATORY FORCE

At first, Haral thought it was a specific order to him, that the Regs blamed him as that one Reina had. He relaxed against the rail for a moment, breathing easier, but he knew he still had to try to get back inside to hide among the crowd, if not off the train, before the Regs showed up. There was no way to explain what had happened with the large man blocking his way, and if he tried, he'd be sent to psychiatric lockdown or, if they believed him, worse. He had already fled the scene of an incident today… Was that related? Had the alien intelligence done something to him? Given him… superpowers?

Haral's Overlay pinged again. This time, it was Merit.

Whoa, man, taking it a little far on the first day. We need to work up to getting the Regs involved. Great shot with the kid, though. He-Ro-Ic! Too bad that part's getting buried by the algorithm. You attacked someone? That's real news, but way above your pay grade. I got away with it because I've got like tens of millions of followers. My Pull puts me above most petty laws. You just broke 3 mill. Cool it. I'll see what I can do to get you cleared, but don't do anything else before we talk in person. -ML

Attack? They thought Haral had somehow shoved that man three times his size out of the way? Or knocked him out with a punch or something? He'd have had better odds crawling along the outside of the train like a spider to get to the kid… The whole thing was ridiculous. Would Merit be able to clear it up? Would he really try? How invested was this guy in their team-up? Haral couldn't chance it. He had to find a way off before the Regs got on. A message flashed across the windows as well as, unintelligibly, over the speakers. Luckily, the words ran in a chyron at the bottom of his Overlay as well.

"Destination Advisory
Danton Quarter Station: Ninety seconds!
<u>Discotech</u>

•

<u>Rebels' Bar and Grille</u>

•

<u>Harris Studios</u>

•

<u>Art House Multiplex</u>
Destination Advisory"

Discotech had a pool, right? A massive one. Could he launch himself from the train and land in it? It seemed possible for *someone* to do so, but him? He remembered the wave pool incident again and the whole train rocked discomfitingly.

Water sloshed high in the windows of the car before him, where they'd taken the boy in. The rising water was edged in an increasingly familiar silver-gray shimmer. Passengers tried in vain to hold onto hanging loops or vertical poles, but ended up slamming into the windows and supports, falling limp in the water. He glanced over his shoulder and the next car was in the same state, filling with cloudy water full of bubbles, dark shapes that were definitely people, mostly humani, being washed back and forth in the stiff artificial tide.

No, he thought, then louder, screaming inside his head. The water continued to rise. "No!" He finally yelled aloud. "Stop!" He grabbed the handle of the nearest door, but it held fast. He slammed on the window with his hand, sending shockwaves of pain up his arm, but doing nothing to the clear panel. Alarms went off overhead. Lights flashed. Another message forced its way into Haral's perception.

72

SWANTON SPAR REGULATORY FORCE

AN INCIDENT IN YOUR AREA HAS BEEN UPGRADED TO:

VERY DANGEROUS.

EVACUATE IF POSSIBLE.
SHELTER IN PLACE IF NOT.
AUTHORITIES AND RESCUE VEHICLES ARE ON THE WAY.

SWANTON SPAR REGULATORY FORCE

"I'd vote evacuate… if I could," Haral muttered to himself. The water in the cars was almost to the ceilings. Lights within flickered and went out, leaving only the vaguest of shadows hanging limp in the water. What was happening? How did he happen to be the only one to avoid the accident, however it was happening? A gray light hovered along the edge of the water, appearing now only where the surface dipped below the edge of the window. Maybe… maybe he could pull it back down? But where would the water go?

With a strange wobble, the panel in the door bulged, then started spewing water. The force of it knocked Haral from his feet. He grabbed for the railing, but it shot by faster than he could react and he found himself soaring, no… falling! He flailed his arms and legs as though he could suddenly learn to fly, but the water was all around him, surrounding him, almost cradling him.

Tumbling, he spotted the multiplex with its many domes, and the flashy, angular structure of the Discotech. He was too far away, surely. There was no way he would reach the pool from here.

Chapter Seven

Desperate, Haral tried thrusting his arms and legs out to create as much of a surface as he could, perhaps slowing himself. The wind howled. Water hung around him as if it were a twisting, rippling curtain he could catch himself on rather than a torrent that was pacing him to the ground. A floor of deep green rushed up toward him, then wheeled away as he lost stability and rolled. Something slapped him across the back, broad and leathery, edges whipping around and snapping at his arms and neck. Another, and still more attacked in a barrage until he slammed into a puddle.

No, it was moving. A stream. Someone gasped. Another screamed.

"Who is that?"

"Where did he come from?"

"I think he fell out of the trees."

"Hey!" But then the voices were gone in a roar of falling water. The shade of the stream let out into clouds of mist and an amazing panorama. All upside down, of course, as he slipped over the edge of a nature-embedded water slide facing the wrong way. He screamed, reaching behind him for the slide. His hand bounced off, carrying him out into thin air again, but a second later, the smooth trough slammed into his back.

Just as he began to scream again, roiling water engulfed him, and he was thrown sharply into a more horizontal trajectory. A handful of seconds later, he skidded to a stop and began to sink, stunned, into a pool. He paddled weakly, but water pressed in all around him. He tried to get a breath, thrusting his head up, but it wasn't enough, and he sucked in water. This activated a primal part of his brain and he thrashed without coordination, sputtering and choking, until hands drew him out of the water and laid him down on his side on warm, textured concrete.

"All right, bud?" An attendant in bright orange shorts and foam shoes asked. His deeply tanned face creased with wrinkles of concern as he leaned close over him. Haral continued to sputter for long seconds, but tried to nod in response to the question. The look of concern only deepened. "You're gonna be OK, just breathe." A quick pat on the shoulder, then the attendant sat back on his heels to keep an eye on Haral.

After a few moments, Haral recovered enough to sit up, but he didn't think he'd be running anywhere for a while. It was amazing that he hadn't been too seriously injured. Or was he? Would he even know? What if he was in shock and couldn't feel a broken bone or damaged nerves? Falling from that height might have landed him back in the hospital for days. There, he'd definitely be found by everyone looking for him.

His neck hurt. As he took stock, he became fairly certain he had broken a couple of ribs, and his vision was blurry, but this he could walk off… At least soon. For now, sitting was his speed. His Overlay flashed as more messages arrived.

WARNING!

You are experiencing a health emergency!
Your heart rate and blood pressure are well above healthy levels.
SelfMed app reports:
- **possible concussion,**
- **broken ribs,**
- **strained intercostal, neck, and back muscles,**

- **multiple contusions**
Remain where you are and do not exert yourself.
Doing so may aggravate your injuries
Find a place to quiet your mind.
Think of your favorite food or relaxing activity.
Would you like to contact Emergency Services?
WARNING!

Haral swiped the pop up away. The last thing he needed was even more people charging toward his location, or some app telling them where he was. The thought triggered a memory of Chopper on one of his rants about the surveillance state,"We're always being watched by people we don't even know are there." Or some such.

PullSys - Congrats on reaching 5 million followers!
MeritLang1 - I said, "take it eas...
Laeua_Kio1792 - Wanted?

As usual, Haral skipped the PullSys notifications. If he made it through the day, he could bask in the surreal climb his Pull had taken. He clicked into Merit's message first.

Hey, Haral. Look, man, you might be too extreme for me. What happened on the train? The authorities are looking for you. Again, you might be making gains here, but you're playing in big boy territory without the Pull to handle the consequences. Just come to the Discotech. I'm here now. We can do our little thing and then I can find you a place to hang while the heat dies down a bit. You've got a lot going for you now. Don't throw it away. I've been in this game a long time. I know what I'm talking about. Stay safe, -ML

Stay safe? Did someone record his fall from the train? If so, the authorities might know exactly where he was. He tried to stand. The world swam around him. Silver light edged the palm trees and the concrete, even the people.

"Hey, just take it slow. Give your nanos a chance to clear up your head, at least. I think you have a concussion," the attendant said. The other backed off and let him pass when he kept walking, though. As he went, he tried to read Laeua's message, but couldn't focus enough to get it open. Finally, he gave up and put everything he had into following the buff pathway that wound from the pool to the nearest building.

He collapsed onto the bench of a picnic table under a large, domed pavilion. Seeing as he had finally made it to the Discotech, if not exactly the front door, he figured he would message Merit and see where this confrontation was meant to take place.

Hhhee mmm....
Merr)(&*

Haral sighed. There was no way he was going to write a whole message. He couldn't even say "hi." Saying… that was it. He fumbled with his Overlay for a minute, traveling through menus to dead ends, clicking off and having to start over. Finally, he managed to activate voice dictation. The words swam before his eyes as he spoke, but they seemed right enough.

Hey, Mer-it, I don't... really know what... ~~I'm, no strike that~~ to say about my day. It's has been over the top, for sure certain. I'll tell you about it, if I survive this whole chain, train, down the drain... of... events. I'm at the Discotech, near one of the pools. There's a hard ten.. tent Where are you at? -Haral

Haral got an immediate response. Luckily, the voice to text app, "ReadToMe," worked both ways. From the interface he had it read Merit's message.

Haral! I just saw the capper to your train ride. The Regs reconstructed it from some traincams outside the cars and a couple of watersliders' drones. That must have been a five-hundred foot fall! And the landing? With all those trees? You're either a master of aerodynamics with some great head for math, or you're a total psycho. Anyway, great slide... head first! I've tried to go down that way a few times, but attendants always stop me. -ML

"Hey! Haral Adjani! Stay where you are. We need to speak with you!" Haral looked up at the mention of his name, expecting to see uniformed Regs bearing down on him, or having formed a perimeter, net launchers and stun guns at the ready. Instead, it was a quintet of business-suited figures and a squadron of broadcast drones. "Leonardo Sperra, COO of PullSys," said the man leading the chevron composed of a second humani; a Xochat; a ribbon-like Flexxe, twisted and bent into an approximation of a humani; and a Rulab, in what was basically a gray cummerbund and nothing else around their little hill of deep blue gel. Sperra clapped his hands together once, fingers pointed toward Haral in greeting.

"This is my team, Tyla," the humani woman waved with a half smile as her rainbow freckles slow-flashed and her auburn hair shifted, but not in the wind.

"Duran Doran, no relation," Sperra laughed, but Haral didn't get the joke, if there was one. The Flexxe extended two flat green-gray loops from the arms of their suit, imitating Sperra's gesture. "My advertising guy."

"Clieth, outreach," the Xochat wobbled at him and scratched out a Xochat greeting. Haral returned it with his own fingers rubbing together. A ripple of pale green delight cascaded across the umbrella-shaped membrane.

"And, of course, host of seventeen different shows over an illustrious career, and programming manager, you must know Zan-DAZ Kelmert!" Sperra said the Rulab's name as though introducing him to millions of audience members rather than a single befuddled humani.

"Nice to… uh… meet you all. But why?"

"'Why?'" Sperra repeated, looking dumbfounded and turning to his companions to show his wide-eyed expression again. "The 'why,' my dear boy is that you've hit your five millions viewer mark, and in just about record time, too. Obviously, many have become more popular by your age, but they all had, let's say… a head start. To be no one and in a *day* hit the 5 mill club… Well, the sky's the limit, as they used to say."

"So you came all this way to…congratulate me?"

"Do you live under a rock, son? There are celebrations to be had, *parties!* And this…" Sperra said, still facing Haral with his plastered smile, but waving his hand impatiently behind him until a package was placed in it. With a flourish of his other hand, Leonardo Sperra held forth the box, covered in a pale blue fuzzy material and the size of a small viewing tablet or one of those *books* Gann had standing all in a row on a shelf in his office…

Haral began to reach for it, but Sperra was faster, his free hand coming to the front of the case and lifting it open to reveal a rectangular slab of gleaming gold metal with the PullSys logo. His name was inscribed below. The whole thing, he saw as Sperra drew it forth, was on a blue ribbon the same shade as the box.

"May I?" Leonardo Sperra asked. He was clearly not someone used to asking for anything. He looked pained enough Haral almost asked him to repeat himself, but then thought better and nodded, lowering his head to allow the man to hang the award on him.

When Haral sat up again, he caught a different glimpse of gold as Merit stepped back into some bushes. The other shook his head from side to side, a warning hand held out before him. He didn't want them to see him for some reason.

"So, what are your plans now that you can live anywhere in Geode? Will you take a penthouse with your own pool here on Swanton Spar? Or do some traveling first and perhaps learn about our other spars? There is an awful lot of Geode to see," Duran Doran asked in their breezy Flexxe voice.

"That's a great question," Haral said, stalling as he had done in school when he didn't know the answer. "Travel does sound good. I hear the poles are amazing, all that nature still roaming free, soaring through the low gravity zones and all."

"That does sound exciting," Sperra agreed. "Well, we've got a few more of these to do today, so we're going to head out. If you have any technical questions, want to hire sidekicks or a 'girlfriend' to play off for better views, just contact us through the system. You have a whole new 'advanced help for advanced users' section. Zai jian!"

"Uh, yeah… Bye…" Haral was still unsteady from the concussion, and the whirlwind of whatever just happened probably wasn't helping him regain his center.

"Nice, five mill in a *day!* Up top!" Merit was suddenly beside him again, holding a hand up for him to strike. He did so.

"Uh, hi again. Yeah. Thanks. I… don't really know what's going on, but it's been a day, for sure. Are we going to do the rivalry thing?"

"Totally, but I can tell by the way you're swaying and crossing your eyes you're not really up for it. That dive was epic, though, like s-w-e-e-t, epic!"

"That's not how… Oh, right, ok, changed how the word was spelled, clever… I should sit down."

"You're already sitting, bro. Don't worry. We'll go again, in the morning. Eat good tonight, but light in the morning. We're going to do a killer squirrel flight to XinShu Spar. Obstacle course, get the teams-sides thing really going with live voting for who should win, who they think will win… It'll be boisterous."

"Yeah, boisterous," Haral said, still feeling lost.

"That's the spirit!" Merit clapped him on the back, jostling his tired body. "Go home. Rest up. Beat you tomorrow."

"Can't go home… Regs…"

Merit waved a hand dismissively. "Nah, that's already taken care of. I had 'em keep it off blast, but you're clear. Nobody got hurt. It was all just some kind of mass hallucination or something? I dunno. So they were good dropping it. But… because they're not announcing it, you might still get finger wavers and Reinas calling you in, which will only be great for your ratings. It's all good. 'Til the AMs!" Merit said, patting Haral on the shoulder—mercifully gentler this time—before stepping behind a pillar.

On the train home, Haral checked his messages again as his head cleared.

PullSys - Your hourly follow report
Laeua_Kio1792 - Dinner
Nez110119 - Chopper and... stuff...

Feeling badly that he had left Nez in the lurch with Chopper and the incoming sector teams, Haral opened the Xochat's message first.

Haral, just wanted to get in touch with you and let you know that Chopper is back up and running. He's compiling all the data from the original crash and what the warehouse sensors got when you both... reappeared like that. We've also gotten updates from the other sectors which held fragments like the ones in the crate and they've been raided, too. The quakes seem to have stopped. Hopefully whatever is happening is over? More when we're face to face. -Nez

Well, that was some good news, anyway, Chopper was OK and the sector folks hadn't given them too much trouble. Haral still felt bad about leaving them, but would have felt worse if he was strung up to all kinds of mind-reading sensors and being grilled about his experience. Of course, that day might still come…

I don't know exactly who I thought you were, but it definitely wasn't a train-sabotaging daredevil attention seeker. After all, you'd gone how long without making such a nuisance of yourself? Anyway, I don't think it's a good idea for us to see each other. -Laeua

What? Oh no… This was supposed to be it! Rising to the top! Gaining Pull like crazy, this award, my fake rivalry with Merit, and possibly a real connection, finding a girl who thought I was cool *for some reason. And* she *seems cool…* Fatigue and nausea washed over Haral. He felt himself slide off the seat onto the train floor and couldn't bring himself to resist. He lay, limbs at odd angles, staring up at the ceiling.

On one hand, it was a relief, being let off the hook of having to go out again tonight. He could just crash on his bed and deal with tomorrow when it came. No. For some reason he really liked Laeua after just the one meeting. She seemed great. And she liked him. There had to be *something* he could do. Flowers? But which did she like? What did she like in general? He had to get to know her better. He scrolled up to the previous message from her.

I see now you're wanted by the Regs? What is going on? I hope you'll explain it all at dinner.

Merit had said he'd cleared things up with the Regs, but had them keep it quiet so the buzz would stay up. If he could prove that to Laeua somehow, it should clear things up. He clicked the reply button in the message interface, but instead of a field to type into, he saw a banner.

This user has blocked you. You cannot message, follow, ping, or otherwise interact with them through any PullSys products.

Great. No way to find out about flowers or favorite color or food or anything now before dinner. Where had she said? Escamilla's? 6PM? So much for resting… But would she even be there? The reservations weren't easy to get for a regular person. Hadn't she said something about going with her family if he couldn't show? A plan began to bubble in his mind. First, though, home, and another shower. He smelled of wild places and pool water. His new clothes were ruined. What might have been a panic-inducing realization there before barely registered now. He had the Pull to get any clothes he wanted. He could *fill* his current apartment with clothing, wall to wall, floor to-.

Someone sat down beside him. At first, he was deep enough in thought that he didn't register them, but then they began speaking.

"So here we are, with one of the newest rising stars of Geode, managing the amazing feat of five mill Pull increase in a day. From nothing." Humani, female, at a guess, though that was always dangerous, and might change for some people by the week, or day…

"Are you talking to me?" Haral asked.

The humani spared him a glance. "To? Not exactly. I'm recording an interview. I was just introducing you, Haral Adjani, fugitive, but not fugitive. Again, quite the feat on your first day famous. Have some inside help? Are you a secret heir? Bastard son of Harper Sanchez, perhaps? I could see it, with your eyes, that chin… OR perhaps Alamondo? Certainly, your hair is the same, but that's easy enough to get changed. I'm sure millions of people have had their follicles tickled to resemble the leading man. Perhaps you're just a fan… Care to weigh in? Let my viewers know a bit about the *real* you? How did you manage your rocketing up the charts?"

"No, no relation to Alamondo or Sanchez, as far as I know. Um… Who are you?"

"Natalie Tattle-y, of course! Interviewer to the stars!" said the humani with pale skin, gold and blond hair, high, wide eyes that reminded Haral of an owl, and shimmering, color-shifting eyeshadow that was almost mesmerizing. A mic drone had attached itself to the window behind the humani, and a pair of video drones hovered at angles before them.

"Natalie! Of course!" Haral played at remembering, even though he couldn't recall hearing of her before. Was it just his concussion? Perhaps not. There were so many vloggers out there… One could hardly be expected to keep up with them all. "I've got a few minutes. What… what's on your mind?"

"Let me turn that around and ask what's on *your* mind," Natalie said. "Yesterday at this time, no one had ever heard of you. You had a hundred followers, and most of them were friends and family, standard story. What happened and how do you feel?"

"I guess the big thing is crossing paths with Merit Lang. I had met my friend Nez (Nez110119, hey man!) at the mess station. He just finished up a culinary certification and had been gone for a while. He wove me up this fantastic burger and I sat down at a table…" Natalie leaned in. Maybe he was good at this storytelling thing… "And just as I took the first bite, BAM! Someone hits me from behind, total sucker punch. It caught me completely unawares, you know? I'm just sitting there eating, catching up with my friend-"

"And that was Merit?"

"It turns out, yeah! So there I am, he pushes me down, I barely save the burger, and he comes at me again. Lunch is a bust. That thing was a work of art, something I'd have to spend days of Pull to buy just last week…

Anyway, Nez and I hightail it out of there. I'm not a fighter. Violence is not the answer."

Natalie nodded, lips pursed. "Mm hmm, mm hmm, for sure. And that was just this morning. A lot has happened since then."

"Yeah, no doubt. I can't really quantify it, but I've met some new friends, and possibly some new enemies. I've never been one to have enemies, but… it seems like there's always got to be conflict, right? I also went to work for a little while, but that went… unexpectedly. Sorry, this is my stop. Message me and maybe we can do a recap of day two sometime!" Haral said, standing, and thankful for not feeling woozy anymore. He still held the vertical rail by the door until the train stopped. Natalie did her sign off, but he couldn't really hear as others got between them, chatting about a shopping trip.

Chapter Eight

Haral stopped halfway through the lobby of his apartment building, wondering why it was so crowded. What had to be a hundred people were crammed in shoulder to shoulder. Someone said his name. He looked up to see everyone turning to stare at him. Some held signs like old picket signs. Others held more modern glowing banners on two sticks. Drones hovered near walls, playing light-borne text over pale blue paint. The messages ranged from #JailforHaral to #FreeHaralAdjani, and people seemed to be equally happy and aghast to see him, in their own measures. After a moment of stunned silence, roughly half of those gathered cheered, and the other half booed and hissed and began chanting hateful slogans.

Uncertain of how to handle this, he tried to smile and wave at friendly faces and ignore those screeching and roaring at him. He resolved not to stop for either group. He was on a schedule if he wanted to track Laeua down at Escamilla's.

Halfway to the elevators, someone shoved him. He lurched forward into a broad, olive green, Flexxe who immediately bumped him backward.

"Don't you touch him!" One woman yelled.

"He almost killed all those people!" A man bellowed.

"If the Regs hadn't arrived…"

"No! He *saved* that kid!" Words and limbs flew all around. Haral struggled to his feet and avoided a sweeping tentacle from a Xochat. Someone grabbed him around the waist.

"I've got you!" The other whispered and barreled through at least three humani and a Flexxe before being tackled from the side by a massive Rulab moving faster than Haral had ever seen one go. They all rolled across the floor in a sticky tangle while the melee continued. Team Free and Team Jail went at it like the freedom of the entire world was on the line.

Haral rolled off the humani and pulled away from the Rulab, an angry dark purple, something else he had never seen before, and got to his knees. Near the left wall, a decorative tree toppled. Somewhere else, a vase or bottle broke, shards of glass scattering on the polished stone floor. Someone shrieked and blood flew through the air. Someone behind the business counter finally hit an alarm and the lights flashed.

A piercing, rolling wail battered Haral and many others backward. A few reacted for a moment, then clearly turned their hearing off via apps and continued on as they were. The rest staggered for the door, hands over ears. Haral had access to such apps, now, but had none downloaded. His only choice was to get out of there as quickly as possible. He patted the fallen massive humani who had tried to help him on the shoulder and lurched to the silver doors nearby. The Rulab jiggled and rippled in the sonic attack, sliding away and letting the humani up.

At the elevators, he turned and raised his hand in a shoulder-rooted wave. "Hi folks, thank you all for coming out. I appreciate all the support from those so give it and am sorry for any misunderstanding with the rest. Have a good evening!" The doors opened behind him and he stepped backward. The single humani rider slipped past him, saw the crowd and turned back to see who had just entered the car. Their eyes widened satisfyingly as the doors slid shut.

On his floor, thankfully he spotted no one waiting to ambush him. He reached his door and entered with no

problem, quickly closing and locking it at the highest
security level, just in case, before slipping out of his shoes
and clothes and stepping into the shower. There wasn't
time for a nap, but he would darn-well show up clean.

Properly cleansed, Haral picked out a new set of
clothes and arranged his dark hair. Stomach growling at
him, he decided to risk a small meal in case he didn't find
Laeua—or she told him to go away before hearing him
out. He overshot the temp on the frozen veggie foldy,
burning his fingers on the folded tortilla, even as steam
escaped from the vegetables trapped within. He let it sit on
the plate for a moment while he looked up the location of
the restaurant. How long would it really take to get there?
It turned out to be on the east side of the spar, not terribly
far away, and with a train that had a stop nearby.

Overlay told Haral that it was 5:32PM now, and
the trip would normally take ten to twelve minutes. If he
didn't dawdle, he'd have time to stop for flowers. He
hoped there wasn't a wrong botanical answer, but was sure
that bringing nothing was the wrong answer.

Now, how to get past the lobby mob… He tapped
into the building security feed, available to residents.
Some folk had dispersed, but if anything, those remaining
were more dangerous, equipped with science knew what
apps. Would they stand against the Regs when they
showed up? It occurred to Haral that Merit might have
ideas… he tapped into the messaging system. Of course,
there were a number of messages waiting for him,
including three from Gann… Oops. He had not put his
boss on the whitelist when he set up his blocks… The man
was probably fuming. He tapped into the first.

Haral, how did the investigation go? Any idea when we'll be back up and running with the telescopes and all? -GS

Of course, he hadn't answered that unseen first message, so he expected a bit more heat with #2…

Mr. Adjani, even if you haven't managed to track down the source of the disturbance in our system, I expect you to report in regularly. Failing that, at the very least, when I request said report. -Your boss, Gann Surai

Yup, "Mr. Adjani" was a dead giveaway. Haral was going to have some explaining to do. He held his breath as he opened the last.

Haral, just heard from Chopper. He's still pretty scrambled, but hopefully working back toward wellness. Nez reports not having seen anything… you know what I mean. I'd like to get your report, but I understand from what little Chopper could relay that it was a traumatic trip to the Shell. The exosuit was destroyed? Take the rest of the day and I'll talk with you tomorrow. -Gann

Well, that certainly de-escalated quickly. He hadn't even had to say anything. Chopper still being affected wasn't a good sign, though. Perhaps that's why Gann took it easy on Haral. How much better shape could he be in? To be honest, not much. He would rather crash out until morning than go deal with whatever minefield lay around Laeua, but if he had any chance with her, it had to be today.

Gann, I am sorry I missed your earlier messages. I had a surge of incoming alerts and I must have set up the blocks wrong. I'm fixing it now. As for what happened at the warehouse... That should definitely be an in-person convo. Thanks for understanding. I hope Chopper is feeling better. See you tomorrow. -Haral

That taken care of, Haral saw that he no longer had time to consult Merit for a way to get through the lobby. Wait, Merit… He had been watching some of his vids to get more familiar with how he did things and his character… There was one where he sneaked out of a hotel by some back entrance that only HighPullers had access to… Was it possible that Haral had gotten that high on the social ladder? He queried his Overlay.

QUERY: Do I have access to a privacy elevator?

PullSys Affirmative, do you desire a route?

Yes, please. Get me out of here.

PullSys Route is ready. Please follow the purple line.

A bright purple streak of light appeared in his Overlay, leading to his bedroom… Curious, a bit disturbed by the thought that there was a back door in his bedroom all this time, he tracked the line through the open doorway as though trying to sneak up on something. A knock came at the apartment door. He typed mentally:

WhoIsThere: FrontDoor

He sent the command. A small window opened in his Overlay showing him the hallway. Half a dozen humani, nearly as many Flexxe, and a pair of Rulab crowded in the narrow space, all pushing for position closest to the door. One of the humani males knocked again.

"Haral! We know you're in there! We're making a citizen's arrest!"

Oh, hell no. Haral picked up his pace while trying to remain quiet. The carpeting in his bedroom aided in this, but the thumping of his heart did not. The humani slammed on the apartment door with a meaty fist. Every strike seemed harder, louder, making him jump in his skin. Coming around the bed, he saw the purple line run into the wall. When he stepped up to the space, the line slid into the base of the wall, and ran upward, outlining in purple a door with a single button the size of his palm. He struck it.

His front door crashed open, the plastic panel bouncing and making a warbling sound that would be comical in another context. The door before him opened a fraction of a second later. He stepped through without looking.

"Hey! Where do you think *you're* going?" the humani bellowed. Two of the Flexxe charged across the living room and were entering the bedroom before the humani took a step. Haral had forgotten they could be so fast, never really having seen it himself firsthand. Haral shuddered as the elevator doors slid shut before him. Heavy Flexxe bodies crashed into it a fraction of a second later. He looked at the keypad beside the door and hit the button labeled "Street."

The car began descending, but he could still hear the Flexxe battering against the outer door, then something struck the top of the small car. Did one… jump down?

Were they all so crazed? He listened, but didn't hear anything for a long moment. Maybe they have just thrown something down after him, or broken the door in.

WARZING!

**PullSys_Security@lert
Your apahhhhtment has
been b/reached by unknown
indiv!duals.
Would ewe like to contact Emergency Services?**

WARNING!

"Yeah, thanks, I got that…" Haral said to himself with a roll of his eyes. "On second thought, yes, send the Regs."

Thirty seconds later, the doors behind him slid open and a whiff of, if not *fresh* air, at least open air, rushed through the door, pulling at his shirt. He stepped out of the elevator and the doors slid shut, becoming all but invisible again. The street itself was actually the alley between his apartment building and the next one. The gray-blue towers held layers of graffiti—months, *years*, of stories and impressions from disgruntled artists and a few advertisers who thought they were clever, stealing advertising space by mimicking taggers' styles.

QUERY: How do I order drones to improve my followers' experience?

PullSys - What packa8e w*uld you lik@?

The Overlay came back within half a second. There was a string of product shots and specs along the bottom of his view.

Get me whatever MeritLang1 had when he had my number of followers.

PullSys - That mOde7 is oot of date and unaVailable for prinnnting. Would ewe like the latest motel in the same liÑe?

That sounds fine, sure, yeah.

PullSys – Hors derrrrveded.ed. They will be deLIVEred to your residunce within six hours.

AdjustOrder Please change delivery to my person. As previously noted, my residence has been... uh... breached.

PullSys - Swanton Spar Regulatory Force is onesies, onsides! ...onsite, intervieWing witnesses and suss-pex. Do you deseyere a replacement dUOr?

That sounds like a great idea, perhaps with more locks, and reinforcement.

PullSys – Acknowlendged.

QUERY: Find me a quick route to Escamilla's restaurant that keeps me off the main streets.

PullSys – Route is red, E. Please follow the pOrple liÑe.

QUERY: Addendum: find me a flower shop en route.

He didn't know what he was looking for, but hopefully when he saw it, and smelled it, he would recognize it. Given that, flowers were not something he felt he could just order via Overlay.

PullSys - Addendum appled. Rooot is red eyE. Please follow the perpule leeeen.

Again, a guide appeared in Haral's Overlay. It led around the corner and up another alley to a train terminal. From there, it directed him to a train which left a few seconds after he sat. He didn't realize it until they were moving, but the vehicle had left a full two minutes before schedule and now was going a bit faster than local service generally ran.

QUERY: Have you prioritized my travel?

PullSys Affirmative, the recent intrusion on your home and your current PullGrade automatically changed your existing settings from "pleb-standard passenger" to "advanced passenger," allowing you to wait less and travel more quirkly.

Excellent, thank you. After I arrive at Escamilla's, please return my settings to standard. I'm not used to being treated differently yet. I'm not sure I ever will be.

PullSys Acknowledged.

The trip was short, with the expected remaining time dropping quickly in the corner of his Overlay. Nevertheless, he watched a few minutes of Merit hyping tomorrow's obstacle course. It looked terrifying enough he figured he wouldn't watch, until he remembered he was actually supposed to *run* the course, leaping across the chasm between spars, swooping through hoops, swimming, hopping between platforms, and dodging all manner of swinging, stabbing, and falling things in the process. Haral gave a shudder.

The doors opened and a handful of fist-sized objects flew in, circling around Haral. He cringed at first, but then realized his delivery had arrived. One of the spherical devices stopped to hover before his face.

"Identify, Haral_Adjani, number elided." The message scrolled across the bottom of his Overlay.

"Yes, confirm, I'm Haral Adjani," he agreed. The drone fell into place above his right shoulder. The other three left off scanning others in the train car to find their places, focusing on him at various distances and angles.

"Sorry, folks, first drones. I haven't read the manual yet," Haral quipped. A few riders laughed, but most rolled their eyes or ignored him completely. Shrugging, being used to such indifference, he stepped out onto the platform. He scanned the area below for anything that looked like a florist.

All of the shops along this street were hidden behind the glossy wall of the spar, a constantly-shifting collage of images and text signs vying for the attention of passersby. Here were spas, restaurants, gift shops, a real, physical museum of historical objects one could actually touch… and there stood **Fran's Flowers**, proudly adorned by a white rectangular sign with the corners scooped out, bordered in gold and lettered in a rich green and purple. Some of the letters were stylized to represent flora of various kinds.

Haral followed his purple line through the hologram of an ornate doorway. People couldn't be bothered with waiting for doors, let alone holding them open. Folks of all descriptions strode and shuffled around him as he took in the broad midway dotted with small stalls and a few entertainers, playing music or juggling, pretending to be trapped in boxes. He didn't have time for that, either.

Following the purple line, he came to a shop on the right side that he smelled before he saw. The whole area was thick with natural perfumes. He stepped through the entrance and calm fell. The shop had a sound suppression system which kept the constant hubbub at bay. Three of his drones explored, getting "B roll" footage.

"Greetings, friend," came a humani voice through the jungle of displays, leaves narrow and sharp, broad and veined, tinged with pinks, whites, purples, and wholly green. "How may I delight you today?"

"Um, I'm actually on the way to meet a girl."

"Mm, 'a girl,' so a first date? Someone you don't know well, don't know where you stand, or how invested you are, caught between 'spare no expense' and 'not wanting to seem pushy.'" A bare-headed woman—with a full-scalp tattoo of stylized hair in the same purple with green highlights as the sign lettering—appeared around a stand of especially tall plants with bell-shaped yellow flowers as she spoke.

Haral laughed awkwardly. "Ahh… yeah, and quick at the same time. I only have a few minutes. I know what you're thinking, the same thing Gann says, 'better time management,' but today has been a day you wouldn't believe."

"It's not for me to judge such things," the woman said, though he could tell she was, indeed judging him.

"Anyway, something like you said, not too cheap, not too expensive. I don't know what flowers she likes yet, or colors, although… she did have purple and pink hair. It seems to be trending right now. It's not quite the same purple as yours, maybe a little more blue?"

The woman ran a hand over her scalp and cast her eyes upward, reviewing her catalogue of flowers in her Overlay, no doubt. After a moment, she nodded, turned, and crooked a finger at him. She walked away, and he followed.

At a rack of broad shelves with lights under each, feeding and showing off the flowers below. He immediately spotted the color he was thinking of, recalling his first encounter with Laeua.

"What are these?" Haral asked, pointing to a deep purple bunch of flowers with sharp, striking color that reminded him of the spiked side of Laeua's hairdo.

"Petunias, those are potted, not the usual route for a first date flower," Fran pointed out.

"Seems like it would be a positive sign, though, giving something that can continue to live and not just wither in a day or two," Haral conjectured.

"*My* flowers are not so short-lived," the proprietress snapped. "I guarantee at least a week for my cut flowers."

Haral held his hands up placatingly. "Sorry, you know what I mean, though."

Fran waved a hand dismissively. "Does your female friend know anything about the language of flowers? What they symbolize as used by our ancestors in centuries past?"

"Uh… I really don't know. I doubt it."

"Then you'll be fine. Those will be fifteen."

"Fifteen?" he asked.

"Fifteen hundred Pull." The woman raised an eyebrow. The number was like a slap in the face. For most of his life, that would have been many days' pay. Then the present slammed back to him. He had millions now, and this visit might even pay for itself if he released the video at the right time… Not that he was concerned with that.

"Of course, sorry. Lots of things on my mind." He drew himself back to the present.

"If that's too much, we can look at some lovely faux flowers, cloned and grown in factory farms…"

"No, it's fine, charge it up. Thank you. I've got to catch my train," Haral said, authorizing payment through his Overlay. Clutching the bowl of flowers to his side, he half-jogged toward the entrance and the train platform again. The shop owner started when she saw the name on the payment, starting to chase after him.

"Mr. Adjani! I didn't know. Thank you for coming in today. Best of luck on your date! Please give Fran's Flowers a good review!"

"I will, thanks again," Haral said, stepping back out into the low thunder of the busy mall.

In minutes, he stepped off the train again looking for Escamilla's.

Resume navigation.

A purple curve of light played across his vision, winding up into the sky around a needle of golden crystal a hundred meters before him. He angled his head up and up… Oh! *That* was Escamilla's… Literally a cloud café… Another new thing for this day. Why not? He walked toward the spike and caught one of the small platforms spiraling upward around the smooth crystal spire. As it rose, he became less certain of his choice and grabbed a handle that formed as he reflexively reached for the crystal.

The spar dwindled below him. The River Calamax, between Swanton and Findel, flashed in the sun, sky in evening mode thanks to clouds of nanobots in the middle atmosphere for solar regulation and replication of the day-night cycle humani apparently couldn't live—or at least remain sane—without. Haral had almost come to terms with the amazing height and just how far he could see, how small everything looked, when he arrived at reception.

"Reservation?" A cheery Flexxe asked, pink and blue longitudinal stripes blending into slowly wavering white along their edges. A crystal garden bloomed behind them, the chairs, tables, and various tiers moving up from the center all grown from a single crystal, the roof high above filled with roiling cloud-nanos, from which colored lights flickered. Each table was partly cupped by leaves of crystal emitting light from their tips.

"Res..er..va…tion… I had one, but I… think it might have been canceled? Can you check for Haral_Adjani1773?" Haral asked.

"Sorry, nothing is on the books, sir, but I can fit you in soon. How many?" The Flexxe replied.

"Just me, I think, though could you please see if Laeua_Kio1792 is already seated? I had been invited by her."

"I'm sorry, sir. I'm not allowed to tell you that," the Flexxe said evenly, though one of their rear loops waggled sharply and extended in a particular direction. Haral followed the gesture, spotting purple spikes and pink curls immediately. Laeua was seated with another humani, who was facing him.

"Do you mind if I use the restroom while I wait?" Haral asked, not waiting for an answer. He strode across the crystal floor, trying not to look down, but also trying not to get the attention to the person with Laeua, her mother, if he guessed correctly. He felt keenly aware of his drones, and the idea he might have an audience, at least if he released the video. Nothing to make a first date more awkward like the date's parent being present and unknown numbers of strangers watching on...

Haral followed a path that would have taken him past the table, then turned as he came even with it, looking down at Laeua with a contrite smile. He held out the bowl of petunias. The delicate petals trembled.

"Laeua!" he began, ready to leap into an apology and explanation.

"Haral! You made it! See, Mother? I told you he wouldn't flake out on me!" Laeua grinned smugly.

"I would never, if it was in my power," Haral said. "That... sounded weird, but you know what I mean."

"Flowers! For me?"

Haral nodded. "Uh, yes, Fran helped me pick them. I thought you liked the color, as you made some of your hair that color. But when I tried to... you blocked me. I came here to try to get you to hear my side."

"Blocked? A rising star with such a cute... face?" Laeua blushed a little and slid over on the round bench, waving a hand to get him to sit and then toward the other, who was red far beyond blushing. "This is my mother, Noreen."

"A pleasure to meet you." Haral smiled at Noreen. She stared, fuming, scowling for a moment before tearing the piece of bread she'd been buttering in half, dropping the pieces on her plate.

"Why are you here? *How* are you here?" The woman demanded. "I saw you all over the news, pulling some prank on a train, nearly drowning everybody, the Regulatory Forces after you, and then… diving off the train? How are you not in a hospital? Or in jail? Or both!" The woman slammed a fist on the table, shaking all of the dishes. "I blocked you!"

Chapter Nine

"*You* blocked him, Mother? Where do you get off blocking people on my behalf? Am I still a teen? Less than ten? NO! I'm a grown woman, and I can hang around with, take walks with, and *date* anyone I want to!" Laeua shooed Haral out of the booth now, and stood beside him.

"Don't go!" Her mother said. "You know I don't have enough Pull to pay for this meal on my own."

"I can get it," Haral offered, "Why don't we sit and… and try to…" but both women ignored him.

"Is that what you're worried about? What *you* need? How people look at *you*? What about *me*?" Laeua said to her mother, her voice growing more strident with each phrase. The drones shifted around to get good shots of each face and one went for the broad shot of all of them.

"Everything I've done is for you, dear. He's no good, a hooligan!"

"Corpwage!" Laeua spat.

"Such language!" her mother protested. "Have I treated you so poorly? Raised you without respect?"

"'Respect?' Are you joking right now? C'mon Haral. You've already shown me more respect in the half a day I've known you than that woman has in years. Let's find somewhere else to eat." Laeua hooked an arm through his, pulling him around, striding for the exit.

"No! I couldn't stop you from moving out. I couldn't stop you from meeting one of these influencer layabouts, but I can stop you from walking away from me!" The woman was on her feet and running toward them before Haral knew what was happening. At the maitre d' stand, she held her hands up toward Haral as though to push him away from her daughter, but Laeua shoved him to the side and her mother barreled into her, unable to stop. He fumbled the petunias for a fraction of a second before what had happened struck home.

Laeua fell back against the railing where the elevator platforms docked, allowing diners to step up and speak with the maitre d'. Her arms flailed as she tried to regain her balance, but then the railing retracted to allow the next elevator to dock and she tumbled backward, shock blossoming across her features. Her arms and legs flailed for purchase they would never find on thin air. The Flexxe receptionist slapped a loop around the mother's wrist, hauling her back with a snap and a cry, while Haral and Laeua's mother both watched, shocked, as Laeua began to dwindle in the distance.

Not knowing exactly what he was doing, Haral leapt after her. Wind buffeted him, pulling at his hair and cheeks and clothes like a hungry Rulab in a shallow tank of shrimp. The petunias thrashed around in their bowl, tumbling away and trailing loosed petals. He held his arms close to his sides, as he had seen done in wind-riding videos to shoot through the air faster. There wasn't much point to his having jumped if he couldn't catch up to Laeua.

WARNING!

PullSys_SecurityAlert –
You ap/pear to be
acceeeeelerating to unsafe
speeds and are not in a vehicle of
any *kind.
Would you like to contact Emergency Services?

W˜ARBING!

What are they going to do for me? We have what, a thousand foot fall ahead of us. Could someone catch us in time? Not much use for emergency services after…

"What! Are! You! Doing!" Laeua managed to yell to him as he neared, the wind still roaring in his ears and blotting out most of the sound she made.

"I! Don't! Know!" He answered as loudly as he could. Surreally, his Overlay pinged. Was it Laeua, trying to find a better way to communicate? He glanced at the sender. Merit. For gravity's sake… Maybe not the best epithet at the moment, he reconsidered. His Overlay pinged again a NeuroNet link opening before his eyes against his will. It was Merit.

EMERGENCY

"Listen very carefully," the golden face said calmly but urgently, the warning label flashing above his features, "I'm sending you a link to an app. Click it."

"I really don't have time right now, Merit," Haral said back through the connection, "I kind of have a situation."

"I know. I'm watching. Did you not realize you were broadcasting? Because this is FIRE! We've gotta get you a tutorial on the drones… later. Right now, I'm trying to help you. Click the link!" The spar below was growing larger more quickly than it shrank before, but at least he was only a few arm lengths from Laeua. A link in a long, narrow, box appeared at the bottom of his stream with Merit. Rolling his eyes, he clicked it. It auto-processed and downloaded something into his Overlay.

"What did you do?" Haral asked.

"Something you were going to have to do for tomorrow, anyway. Consider this training!"

"'Training?'" Haral demanded, then a wire frame image of a person, skin stretched out into a flying squirrel suit appeared in his Overlay with a series of check marks after it. "Are you kidding me?"

"Would you rather be spread over hundreds of yards of Swanton Spar?" Merit inquired sarcastically.

"What about Laeua?"

"Like I said, I'm watching your situation right now on your feed. I got you the tandem extension. You can thank me later. Grab her, hug her for a beat, then spread your arms and legs as far as you can." The golden face grinned wide.

"Oh man… I don't know if I can…" Wind continued to whip at his face as gravity pulled at him.

"You have about fifteen seconds, and that's with bouncing off at least one roof. Go!" Merit yelled at him, his calm finally breaking.

"I'm sorry!" Haral yelled over the wind, shifting his body to dive into Laeua's path.

"*You're* sorry?" Laeua asked in surprise. "You didn't—" then her face was buried in his chest. He wrapped his arms around her, then opened them.

"Wider! Legs too!" Merit coached. Laeua began to scream. Haral's body shifted, and clothes with it. His spine stiffened. Skin between his arms and legs, between his legs, and even between his neck and arms stretched out into sail-like control surfaces. The effect was not unlike being a wad of chewing gum pulled one way, then another.

The sudden increase in surface area caught the air immediately. He was a kite with broken string, high enough to ride the sky, but unstable, wobbly. They slewed one way, then another in the air, slowly spinning at the same time. Merit talked him through gaining control and they stopped spinning, then stopped rocking back and forth like a leaf in the wind.

Arms wavering already, he dodged the apex of an especially tall spire moving at what felt like hundreds of mikes per hour. The angular peaks and sharp edges of the rest of the spar structure had never seemed too ominous before. They could end up impaled on any of them…

He kept them skimming over the surface of the crystal tower for long seconds. He could see the fear in his own face reflected there. How was he going to pull this off?

"Nice! Great shot! That should go on your reel," Merit broke in, reminding Haral he was still there in the NeuroNet chat. "We'll talk about optimizing your drone capture for next time."

"Reel? *Next time*? No, never mind. You can tell me later. How do I stop this thing?"

"Stop?" Merit asked.

"Get down safely," Haral answered as calmly as he could.

Merit nodded. "Ah yeah, landing. Well, that can take a few tries to really nail, and with a passenger… Best look for someplace soft. A garden with puffy flowers, or a pool maybe?"

"Haral?" Laeua said from her sling against his chest, voice straining against the still strong winds.

"Yes, Laeua?" Haral replied, a little tense, trying not to get them killed and listening to Merit's directions over his NeuroNet connection.

"I'm sorry about my mom. I didn't know she'd blocked you."

"I appreciate that. I was confused, but not angry at you. I wouldn't have really blamed you after all the weird press I got today. I am trying to land us safely right now. I've never done this before."

"That's not what you want to hear."

"Jokes? We're going almost as fast as a train using an app I downloaded *after* I jumped after you into the sky and you've got jokes?" He asked, then burst out laughing. "You're awesome!"

She joined him in laughing until his arms pulled in from the laughter and they began to tumble. He struggled for a moment, but managed to get them to a smooth path again.

"Sorry, I do that when I'm scared," she said, the laughter fading from her face.

"I get it. It's better than freaking out, which I'm *barely* not doing. Hold on… Or hold still… I don't know. Banking." Haral shifted his weight as advised by Merit who had found a perfect landing spot within range. Laeua squeaked and pinched his chest. "Not what I meant by 'hold on.'" He spotted the rooftop oasis and aimed for it.

"Sorry," Laeua said, but didn't loosen her grip. This was terrifying for him, how much worse must it be for her? They were both relying on someone they had just met to save them, but at least he had a hand in said rescue.

"No, I'm sorry. If it wasn't for my crazy day, you wouldn't be in this mess," he said.

"And how much of this is actually your fault? Getting punched in the face? Going to the hospital? Falling off a train? I saw the footage, that was no swan dive. We're both victims of fate here. I don't blame you, even if we—"

"OK, part of this is going to be slowing down before you get to the LZ," Merit said, "This is going to take some faith. When I tell you, you need to pull up, arching your back so Laeua's on the outside of the 'C,' and lower your arms about halfway. You'll feel like you're falling for a few seconds, but you need to reduce your forward speed while not dropping below the line of the landing."

"Sounds simple," Haral said sarcastically. Haral's Overlay pinged. A new message from Nez. He would have to wait.

"OK, now," Merit said evenly, "Bring your head up a bit to climb for say five seconds. Good." The wind howling past Haral lessened as he hit the top of the incline and brought his arms in.

"What's going on?" Laeua asked.

"Don't worry. I'm getting us down. I have a professional on the line," Haral reassured her.

"What line?"

"NeuroNet chat. I'll explain later." They were speeding up again, aimed at the green space surrounded by bushes full of colorful flowers.

"Is it Merit Lang? Because if there's someone whose fault all this really *is*, it's him! I'd like to give him an ear full!" She shouted.

"OK, wings out again, catch the air, ride it up, and then let yourself come down again like you just did. This is best done in small steps," Merit advised.

"Gotcha, thanks," Haral said. He spread his arms again. They burned with the effort, but not as much as he expected. That was probably part of the app, lactic acid management. Blowing out another breath, he pulled his arms in just a bit, letting himself free fall. It was a moment of peace in an otherwise frantic evening. He embraced it. "We're almost there," he said aloud for Laeua to hear. "The landing zone is seconds away."

"That's great! No offense, but I'm ready to get off this ride."

"You and me bo—" Haral began, but then something struck him in the head, hard. He heard a crackling sound and a hollow drum sound and then drifted away, taking the flowering bushes and swaying grasses of the spar-top garden with it.

"Haral!" Something pinched his chest, but it barely penetrated the thick wool wrapped around his senses. "HaRAL!" The voice seemed familiar, but he couldn't quite focus on it.

"Haral! Wake up man!" A different voice said inside his head.

"Wa?"

"Sorry man, this has got to be done. Hopefully, you'll be able to thank me later," the second voice said just before the world went from warm and fuzzy to vibrating and full of searing light drilling into his brain. The sensation ended, leaving him weak and with the distinct sensation of falling. Then he spotted the golden crystal buildings all rushing up toward him, with one to the side already spearing the sky above. He caught his reflection. He seemed stretched out and all the wrong shapes.

"Snap out of it!" Someone yelled over his NeuroNet directly into his brain. Rude. Someone was yelling outside, as well.

Reality came crashing back through the perception bubble and he thrust his arms and legs out. The impact of the sudden stop nearly knocked him out again. Someone nearby screamed, then cut the sound short.

"Welcome back!" The male voice said. *Merit*. He realized. And Laeua was on his chest. And they were both falling, well, gliding now. "What happened back there?"

"Hit something. Didn't see anything… I don't think..." Haral trailed off.

"Aww… I wonder if it was a hologram projected on a clear wall or dome, not a real garden at all… All right, let's find you somewhere else to land," Merit said.

"Yes, please."

"You're getting pretty low, you lost a lot of altitude free falling like that. That slashes the list of options. All right, cut left about ten degrees and look for a long green sportsball pitch."

"Sportsball, yay…" Haral replied with faux enthusiasm.

"Keep your politics to yourself," Merit snapped. Did the golden boy love sports? Could be, but how many people watching were sports fans? Was that it? He was trying not to lose followers? Pull was his life, more than it had ever been for Haral, but now… He might have to be careful, too. "Haral, you with me?" Merit nudged, bringing him back.

"Right, landing. *Not* dying," Haral reminded himself. He spotted the pitch. "Uh, that's not going to work."

"What? Why? Long, flat, covered in grass and soil beneath. Not going to find a softer, larger place to put your feet."

"It's also full of people. There's a game on, and crowds around the edge."

"Oh! Corptract… I'll keep looking, but there are fewer choices every second."

"I know you don't owe me anything. Thanks for making an effort, here," Haral said.

"Come on, everyone loves a love story, and what's more classic than a girl being tossed off a building and her beau leaping off after?" Merit chuckled.

"Uh… Yeah…"

"Um, OK, I think we're officially… out of options. There's only one choice left apart from trying to slow yourself down enough to land in a street and then get out without being run over…"

"Yeah, that doesn't sound very appealing. Where am I going?" Haral asked, determined.

"You know how to swim?"

"Um, no?" Haral let out a nervous laugh.

"I'll send you another app. You should have just enough time to download and install it."

"What is happening?" Laeua asked, voice muffled but also resonant against his chest.

"I'm not really sure," Haral said. "We're working it out."

"All right, bank it right a solid forty degrees. This is going to be tight, a by a few different definitions of the word."

"Cute. Don't get me killed."

"I'm trying not to. Those last two times were flukes. This will be fine. Trust me."

"I'm trying… Oh pudu! The Callamax? We might be better off with the street."

"It's up to you, man, but I've already got folks looking out for you there and that app is on its way," Merit tried to reassure him.

Merit's app flashed in Haral's Overlay. An install link for SwimSafe popped into the low rectangle along the bottom of Haral's view. He clicked on it and in a few seconds, got the confirmation that his new app was ready. It was none too soon as Merit's trajectory brought him in line with a vast expanse of flowing water. It wasn't the largest in the world, but it was the next tier down.

Massive. Wide, deep, deceptively calm on the surface. In the distance to either side, Haral spotted folk on houseboats tucked against the golden crystal bank walls of the river. A school of something splashed and leapt in the middle distance.

"Get ready, Laeua. We're going for a swim!" Haral said, bracing himself for impact.

"Swim? What? No!" she yelled, but it was too late to turn back. The glassy water shot along beneath them, inches from her back. A second later, she sent up a spray of water fanning behind them for a few meters before they tumbled, the world spinning around them.

The water was cold, bracing. The squirrel suit app retracted his skin, giving him a bit more insulation and freeing Laeua. She thrashed and sputtered. "Which way?"

"I don't know." Haral looked around, spotting a mismatched armada of boats. "Toward them? Merit said he was sending someone to meet us partway." Haral moved his arms and legs without thinking about it. His hands and feet widened into paddles, making each stroke more effective. "Come on. Hold onto my shoulders or neck or something."

"Just don't look," she replied.

"What?" He asked, but then she was on his back, and he couldn't see anything but water and a fleet of small boats and water-adjusted folk racing toward them. He began to swim, clumsily at first, then with more confidence as the app adjusted his technique and increased the mass of a host of muscles. Still, the river dragged them along. He had to angle to the right to keep the oncoming fleet and the houses behind it in sight. His face dipped into the water. His arms swept outward. His legs kicked. Again, and again, he pulled them through water for more than a minute before the others began catching up.

The first, a humani with streaks of blue and green evident in her skin, leaned over from her water ski, offering a hand to Laeua, who fumbled for a moment, but then managed to catch hold. Haral was able to turn now. He briefly saw that Laeua's spikes and curls were both bedraggled, lying flat against her scalp. He looked away so she wouldn't know he had seen, changing his focus to the water ski pilot.

"Can you get her to shore? I'll be right behind you," he said.

"Sure thing. Can't wait to hear the story that led to this. Anyone less prepared could have drowned before we got to them," the woman agreed.

"I've got friends in high places, it seems." Haral laughed.

"Yes, I see, drones. High fancy." Haral spotted them and found himself surprised that they'd kept up, or caught up, with him. Laeua got situated behind the other humani woman, holding on for dear life. The woman turned her vehicle around and they started back. Haral swam after, finding he was able to keep up.

"I just got them, the drones. Today."

"And some hot swimming mods. We're doing like twenty mikes here," the woman said.

"All part of the story," Haral said, "Haral_Adjani1773."

"Laeua_Kio1972," Laeua introduced herself.

"Selee McCram. Hm, your numbers are close… Same age or coincidence, I wonder?"

"Do you have a hyphen or underscore or numbers or anything?" Haral asked. Nearly everyone did. With so many PullSys users, the only the most ancient people, early adopters, or super HighPullers had their name without embellishments for their handle. Even Merit was MeritLang1...

She shook her head. "Nah, we don't go in for the PullSys stuff down here. It's just Selee McCram, all letters."

Haral considered this, "Guess I can't offer you a boost or a guest spot or anything. What *can* I do for you? To thank you for saving us."

"Nah, you were doing fine. Came out for curiosity as much as anything."

"What about them?" Haral asked indicating the dozen or so others riding or swimming behind them.

"They were going to loot your corpses," she said bluntly.

Haral winced. "Ah. Can't say I'm sorry to disappoint them, but honestly, without Merit, we *would* be dead. On the other hand, we'd also be a mike or so that way, all over the street."

"Yeah, Merit let me know you'd be coming. He's a pretty good guy for a PullSys flunky. No offense."

"I don't know that I'm in deep enough to be called a flunky. I've only been on the radar for a day. Well, half a day, this morning. He seems all right. I only met him today, too."

"The story gets juicier."

Haral laughed and then concentrated on swimming. His arms were still hurting after all the flying and now swimming, and he needed to concentrate on his coordination as fatigue slipped back in. While most of his body had adjusted to the water, there was a spot on the back of hand, and creeping up his wrist, that was frigid, like the changes from the app were slipping.

Not long later, they arrived at a flotilla of barges, platforms, and what honestly just looked like ancient-style houses sitting on the water. Some were roped together or had planks of various materials between them as walkways. Selee pulled her ski into a small open space between houses and turned it around, ready to shoot off across the water at a moment's notice. She hopped off onto the platform and extended a hand to help Laeua disembark.

"Erm… Permission to come aboard?" Haral asked, circling at the edge of the collective as more water skis returned and swimmers splashed behind him.

Selee laughed, a hearty, raucous thing. "Are you kidding me with that? How do you even know those words?"

"Well, you know, I get around, from restaurants in the clouds to the surface of Geode's Shell, to the great River Callamax…" Haral joked.

"Come on up and tell us about… did you say the surface? Like… outside where the real stars are? You need to meet someone… or vice versa, possibly both ways… Just get up here and come on." Selee turned and waved for him to follow.

Spotting one of his drones, he had a thought and dove straight down a number of body lengths, then arced back up to emerge at the same spot he dove from, pushing faster and harder with his legs, working them back and forth as one until he shot up out of the water in a spray of sun-catching droplets, going for a front flip and heroic landing.

What actually happened was he overspun and ended up tumbling across the platform in an uncontrolled somersault, landing in a tangle of limbs at Laeua's feet.

She let out a laugh. The gathered crowd whooped and clapped.

"Sorry, that *was* a nice try and would have been quite impressive. These things take practice, even with apps helping you. Perhaps save it for a bloopers reel?" she suggested. He smiled up at her sheepishly.

Laeua smiled and sat with a blanket from one of the riverfolk draped over the top of her head like a hood, covering the damage to her sculpted hair. Selee stood to her side, looking down, shaking her head. Haral unfolded himself, got to his feet, and held a hand out to her as his limbs and core shifted back to landlubber mode.

"Our historian will want to meet you," Selee said, indicating they should follow her.

"Come along," Haral urged Laeua.

"All that and you still want me beside you?" Laeua asked.

"Where else?"

"As far away as possible, I would expect, after almost getting you killed." Killed. The word struck a memory from earlier in the day. The external drones. Feedback. People had died. He suddenly felt terribly fidgety, like he *should* run, but not from these people, who had their own reputation for danger, nor Laeua, but toward Gann and Chopper and whatever was happening outside.

"What kind of date would this be if I didn't see you home?" Haral joked. "Sorry about the flowers. I'll get you other ones if you tell me which ones you like." They caught up with Selee at the first of many narrow bridges of plastic planks laid side by side, connected by ropes flexing and shifting as the group walked across them. "Huh…" he grunted.

"Wow, you must be really… distracted," Selee said.

"What are you talking about?" Laeua asked.

"It took six whole minutes for your boy here to realize his Overlay isn't working."

"What?" Laeua asked, panicked, standing still and staring off into space for a moment. She shook her head once.

"That's not going to help. PullSysy, all outside tech, really, is blocked here. I've signaled someone reliable to retrieve your drones before they float away down the river."

"Uh… thanks. It's eerie. Quiet," Haral noted.

"I can't imagine how noisy it must be usually. Hopefully you'll find it peaceful, this little break in the land of no Big Brother," Selee said.

"Peaceful, or as they used to say in the movies, 'Quiet, too quiet,'" Haral said.

"You are a curious one…" Selee observed.

They passed through textured polymer side yards with potted plants and trees, a few whole platforms with miniature fields of plants bearing what Haral only recognized from movies as vegetables, living, growing. The usual spar green spaces didn't have food, only flowers and bushes and trees for looks.

They continued around one particolor building that reminded Haral of a rubber ball he'd had when he was little, then one that looked like it had been made of all one brand of snack food packaging, melted into bright green panels crowded with the same logo in different orientations and design for walls and door.

His stomach growled. The transformations he had undergone had taken quite a lot of energy, and they'd missed dinner at Escamilla's. He hadn't even gotten to eat that veggie foldy... "Sorry."

"You need to eat. Of course you do," Selee said. "I'll get you settled in with Whip and find you both something. Fish stew? Seaweed?"

"Whatever you have to spare is fine, but something hot would be great," Haral said.

Selee gave him a hard look. "We may not live like you, but we're not inhospitable, and we're not starving. We have plenty because we spend our days working, making actual things, growing crops rather than just ratings."

"I didn't mean…" he began and then trailed off.

Selee laughed again, apparently enjoying his discomfort. She stopped by the door of a small, pale blue, polymer-walled house on a little floating island of its own, two trees giving the house shade and bearing fruit Haral didn't recognize.

"No worries, Haral. Just settle in here and do some listening. Don't start your story until I get back, yeah?"

"Of course, Selee, thanks," Haral agreed, ducking through the open doorway and into a space stacked with books, much larger than the novels Gann kept on his shelves, spines a handspan wide, labeled with what looked like white paper with handwritten text. They seemed to be grouped more or less into pillars by color, dark, somber green here, subdued yellow there, many in shades of blue or gray, with narrow passageways between blocks of pillars like Old Earth cities.

Nestled near the far wall were a truly ancient looking man seated by a heat and light source and a blue parrot the length of Haral's arm.

"Hello, we were told you wanted to see us," the bird said with something close to a humani voice, its black beak opening and moving as it spoke, while its companion's face remained placid. Haral looked back and forth between the two beings, uncertainty creeping in.

"Whip," The bird stated, head inclined toward the humani beside it. "Yes, sit, sit." The man motioned to the pair. Haral looked around, but didn't see a way to comply. The space was entirely taken up with stacks of books, more books than he had ever seen in his life.

Laeua squeezed his hand. He returned the gesture in what he hoped was a reassuring way.

Chapter Ten

"Welcome, Haral Adjani," the bird said.

"Thank you, Whip," Haral said, "This is my… friend, Laeua. We've had quite the adventurous day." Haral brought his free hand over and placed it on top of Laeua's in what he hoped was a reassuring way. Standing here before the man and his bird companion felt oddly like having an audience with a king, a scene he'd witnessed in Gann's movies many times.

The man nodded as the bird spoke again. "I am the man you're speaking to. The parrot, Cracker, is my… translator. An accident damaged the nerves running to my tongue and mouth, so I cannot speak on my own, but my link to Cracker makes his voice mine."

"Ah, so we should look at you," Haral said, turning toward the man. His face and neck were covered in wrinkles and scars, eyes and throat sunken, the memories of tattoos peeking from collar and sleeve of a knit shirt.

"I think I heard Selee was going to get you some food. She's a great host, not that we get so many visitors. A few unfortunates who think they're done with life every year, you know… Loneliness is a great weight upon the humani soul."

Haral nodded, but didn't know what to say. He shuffled his feet.

"Your nanos couldn't heal the nerve damage?" Laeua asked.

"Good, good, you ask the right questions, or at least the ones that will lead you to the right answers, which is pretty much the same thing, no?" The bird laughed. "Sit… oh, there's no room left to sit. You can stack those books up over there, and sit on the remainder,"

Whip offered. "Hmm, how easiest to answer your query…
I don't have any nanos. Never did. My mother didn't
believe in them, and father was killed in an accident from
which his nanos couldn't save him before I was born."

"When was that?" Laeua asked. Cracker laughed
again.

"Oh, must be a hundred seven years by now? I
know, I know, 'But Whip, you don't look a day over
eighty!' I credit clean living and a steady diet of seaweed
and natural fish."

"Nat—natural fish? Like the animals? You *eat*
animals?" Laeua looked terrified, but Haral felt a similar
revulsion stirring in his stomach. The beings of Geode had
used food weavers for centuries. Most people born in the
current millennium had never eaten something formed
wholly by nature, except for the odd child grabbing a leaf
off a bush at a garden or something. It just wasn't done. Or
so they had been taught…

"Soup's on!" Selee said, carrying a tray with three
spoons, steaming bowls, and mugs. Laeua stared at the
bowls for a moment, then back to Whip, then at Haral. She
started to rise from her literary perch, but Haral caught her
hand.

"It's fine. We did this for thousands and thousands
of years. Think of it as an adventure. You just survived
being pitched off the highest place I've ever been, *and*
swimming in a *river!* You've got this," Haral said. Laeua
locked eyes with him, jaw dropping as though she couldn't
believe what she as hearing, but then her stomach growled
in response to the smell of the stew and she nodded subtly.

"Good! Here's yours. Just pretend it's been spun
out of a spider butt like the food you're used to and it'll be
fine. Well… it might ruin you for spider butt food. The
real thing… it's real!" Selee said, delivering bowls to

Whip and Haral and setting the tray on a stack of books, then finding her own book seat.

"Now, tell us about your day!" Selee smiled warmly.

Haral recounted the publicly available aspects of his day: the altercation with Merit, going to the hospital, the train incident, and finally the encounter at Escamilla's. Whip nodded unsteadily through most of it, eating thoughtfully until he had emptied the dish. He stared silently when Haral finished speaking and began eating.

The flavor of the stew was unusual, bold; it had textures and granulations that woven food often lacked or replicated poorly. Laeua made a choking noise but continued to eat. He *had* interrupted her and her mother before the food had arrived… She was likely famished, too.

"A well told half of a story," the oldster said eventually via the parrot.

"Pardon?" Haral's eyebrows raised.

"What about the Shell? Tell me what happened to you… out there" Cracker related Whip's question with a dramatic wing sweep toward the ground.

"Oh, yeah…" Haral trailed off.

"No one's recording here, remember?" Selee pointed out. She was right. For once in his life, he knew he could tell a story—or say anything—knowing only people he could see could hear him.

"So my job is to maintain—mostly cleaning, some repair—the surface systems. Each sector has telescopes and external sensors to know when things(or possibly visitors) are coming and to do research. They map the changing universe around us and expand our knowledge of the stars and galaxies and stuff."

"Wow, I didn't know you did all that. I guess I didn't really know what you did at all," Laeua said.

"Well, we've just met, really, and haven't had a lot of time to talk. I want to hear more about your art, too."

"It's mostly 4D painting. I use-" Laeua began.

"All due respect, Miss," Cracker broke in, "I have a purpose in verifying what happened to young Haral here. It may be time sensitive, a matter of life and death."

"Oh. Sure." Laeua sank into herself a bit, like a deflating balloon. Haral put the spoon back in his bowl and reached over to squeeze her hand. She smiled thinly, but didn't look up.

"Surely what I have to say can't be that important," Haral protested.

"I think you know it is. You've made contact. I can see it on you," Whip said.

"Contact?" Haral asked quietly.

Frustration bled into Whip's tone. "Come on, this isn't Old Earth where we didn't know for sure about aliens and such. You telling me you're not friends with one of those flat fruit strip looking fellas?"

"I know a few Flexxe, sure, and my best friend, Nez, is Xochat. I never denied there was life beyond Geode."

"No, but you're avoiding saying what needs to be said about previously unknown species," Whip pressed.

"What's he talking about?" Laeua asked.

"All right, since you just saved our lives and all..." Haral said, leaping into a retelling of the events around his most recent trip to the surface.

"Are you kidding me with this?" Laeua said more than once as Haral recounted how he ended up in the hospital, his trip up the chute to the Shell and his close encounter.

"No, I think the whole train thing was actually their fault," Haral said.

"Well, I don't know about assigning blame, young one, but their influence on you certainly explains the 'hallucinations,'" Whip said.

"A new species! That's exciting," Selee said.

"Well, there's 'new' and there's 'new,'" Whip said. "These visitors have been here before. We just couldn't understand them. They have no language at all, just the sharing of memories, the forming of images and sensory information."

"How do you know so much about them?" Haral asked.

"Most of what I know was passed to me by my mother. You see, I didn't quite tell you the truth about my father. It wasn't an accident, so much as an incompatibility."

"With the nanos?" Haral asked.

"Clever, didn't I tell you he was clever?" Whip asked Selee. The woman nodded.

"How would you know about me? I'm nobody… *was* nobody until this morning… But that all came down from Merit… and you know Merit." Haral realized as he spoke. "He said he'd contacted someone about helping us get out of the river. He must have told you about me. *You* orchestrated all of this? Meeting Merit, having him drop us in the river? To get me here? Why? How?"

Whip spread his hands. "Orchestrated is a bit… *devious* sounding. I saw an opportunity to steer you to me, and here you are. As Selee indicated, we're dedicated to a simpler, if more demanding, life down here. We study and work, engaging our minds in ways most of you up there don't. I know you work under Gann Surai, who worked with my father, maintaining machinery and electronics. I know that you studied app development but dropped it after a time feeling like you hadn't made enough progress. I know that nearly one hundred ten years ago, these same beings visited Geode, causing terrible problems due to incompatible technologies, though the effects have been largely covered up by PullSys et al."

Haral blinked. "Wow… So, these visitors interacted with your father… who had my job, or one like it… Somewhere where he'd be able to view the outside and be one of very few who knew what was going on. And somehow that interaction messed with his nanos and killed him."

"See? Clever. But…" Whip paused.

"But now I'm in the exact same position, with the gray light," Haral said.

"I'm sorry. It wasn't anyone's fault, but the only way to stop them last time was to blow them up. At least, that was the story," Whip said via Cracker.

"You don't believe it?" Laeua asked.

"It's hard to accept that the only way to stop the alien threat was to kill my father, who then I never got to meet…" Whip trailed off.

"And now they're back for revenge?" Haral asked.

"My contacts tell me the visitors have disabled surface cameras and sensors for sectors in every direction," Whip said. The pulse they sent that knocked you out and killed those others was just a test. It wasn't efficient enough, which is why they infected you."

"Infected?" Laeua asked, setting aside her empty bowl. "What does that mean?"

"It means that what happened to Whip's father a century ago is going to happen to me," Haral said, stricken. He looked to Whip. "How long do I have?"

"A few days, if you follow the same pattern as my father," Whip said.

"What can we do?" Haral and Laeua asked at the same time.

"I have no idea, but I brought you here to try to work it out," Whip said.

"How? Are you a scientist? Without nanos?" Haral asked, incredulous.

"Knowledge may be easier to access through the Overlay, but it's also heavily monitored and edited. The library around you is tailored to the specific problems at hand. Mother always knew this day would come, and despite my handicaps, she trained me in the sciences and other areas to try to help the next time," Whip replied.

"These are all…" Laeua began, but then let the words die off as the scope of knowledge around her struck home.

"You can only fish and farm so many hours of the day. Why not fill the rest with reading?" Whip said. "At any rate, tell me all about your experience in the ship again, every detail, and anything about this gray light you can recall. Any and all of these could be useful, but we've been distilling and condensing the information for decades.

"I suggest you take that one, yes, the yellow one, with conclusions of my father's autopsy, the neurological changes, immune response shifts, etc… the thinner black one containing my fahter's own observations… and that pair of greens there. They have information about the progress of my father's disease, with data from his own nanos, with all the erroneous data and artifacts and such caused by the incompatibilities and what we were able to determine about the aliens themselves. It may not amount to much, but it's all we have to go off."

Whip studied Haral and Laeua before continuing, "Unfortunately, we don't have any laboratory equipment here, no way to reprogram nanos or test their reactions to different treatments. Also, I'm fairly sure PullSys flunkies will be here within the hour. They always show up after someone's gone into the river, but I just had to meet you and pass on the relevant books. Take them with you and find Gann. He should be able to get you to the equipment and facilities you need."

"Thank you… that's a lot. How are we to carry them?" Haral asked.

"Bam!" Selee said, holding out a gray satchel with a long, broad strap and a main compartment that looked like it would carry the required tomes. Haral's drones hung in a mesh pocket running along one side.

"You are having too much fun with this," Haral said.

"If you're not having fun, what's the point?" Selee said with a smile.

"When you say things like that, you remind me that you're really from up there," Whip said. The smile vanished from Selee's lips. "Theirs is a world dominated by 'fun.' Ours is led by survival, struggle, maintaining our identities," he reminded her.

Laeua and Haral were escorted to an undercut in the high bank of the river, where the riverfolk had a hidden passage into the undercity.

"Are you sure about this? We could get lost," Laeua said.

"Not a chance," Haral said. "I've spent years and years down here. My primary workstation is on one of the middle levels and Chopper, the mech friend I mentioned who helped me get to the surface in person, works in a storage space in one of the lowest levels. This is my neighborhood as much as any place up there."

"You'll be fine, and you'll have Overlay back as soon as you pass that stanchion there," Selee pointed to a steeply-angled vertical section of spar understructure which had been painted black.

"Thank you for all your help. I'll be back to talk with Whip," Haral said.

"Sure thing. Maybe come down this way instead of diving in next time, but don't let me tell you what to do." Selee smiled.

"Thanks, I'll try. Take care."

Haral and Laeua walked along the passage between alternating top-heavy and bottom-heavy trapezoids created by the underlying crystalline matrix of Geode. Great diagonal pillars—the roots of the spars— rose before them, leaving enough space to drive a bus through. Between the actual flat path before them and the varying sets of upper and lower corners, the space was massive, echoing with flat hard surfaces, and almost alien in its own way. Light traveled down from above along the crystal, except where it was painted black. Still, it was nothing like caves in Gann's movies.

A cascade of pings assaulted Haral's Overlay as it picked up signal and reconnected him to the world. Haral gasped. In the same moment, his drones came alive, swinging around him as they wriggled free of the pocket to return to their preset relative positions.

"Are you all right?" Laeua asked.

Haral nodded distractedly. "Just a flood of alerts. A few from Merit, a few from Nez, a handful from Gann, my boss at… Oh! I've got to get these books to him and get them all scanned in so we can use this information against the visitors."

"Has something happened?"

Haral squinted in concentration. "It sounds like they reestablished communications with the silent sectors, but they… tried to defend themselves and keep the fragments away from the visitors."

"From your tone, I'm guessing it didn't go well."

"People died. A lot of people. This isn't something we can keep to ourselves anymore. This can't be a secret. It's history… maybe… war." Looking back on it, nothing of deep consequence had really happened in centuries. No wars or major unrest, no natural disasters or tech failures. These last couple were partly due to his own efforts and those of thousands like him around Geode, maintaining systems and keeping an eye on the outside, just in case.

The biggest news on any given day was an upset in the top follower counts in various categories and the release of new PullSys-backed apps repped by folks like Merit. He wondered briefly if he showed up on any of those, but shoved the thought away. New menu items developed for exclusive restaurants he never paid attention to because he couldn't afford to eat there, and all kinds of other content he couldn't get access to or wasn't interested in before were highlights of some peoples' weeks. He also realized, looking back, that he had been disconnected from the tides of fame and fortune, his or anyone's, simply because he never dreamed he'd be able to compete.

That wasn't true anymore. He glanced as his latest updates from PullSys. Video of the skydive and splash landing in the river had nearly doubled his Pull in just a few hours. A number of messages in his inbox were from reporters. These ones he had actually heard of, unlike the one that had cornered him on the train. This was getting serious, if you could take *any* of it seriously, especially in the face of what he could only think of as interstellar war breaking out far beneath peoples' feet. And they didn't know a thing about it.

But they needed to.

"If only we could get a taxi down here…" Haral said, thinking aloud of how long it would take to get to Gann on foot. Flying had been terrifying, but at least it was fast. They had to crack these books and get into the Inter-Sector-Messaging System as quickly as possible.

"Right?" Laeua agreed. "It's already been such a long—what is that?" She cut herself off and pointed ahead. A light had come on, playing across one of the massive crystal ramps as it turned toward them. "Are you… Kidding me?" she asked as Haral's Overlay pinged.

PullSys - Transportation request processed. Your car should arrive at your location in thirty seconds.

"PullSys…" Haral said.

"So now you're voice ordering cars?" she half-laughed.

"It looks like… I'm not complaining." He grinned.

"Me either." Exhausted, they both nodded. The car rolled up to them, a bulbous, rounded hood curving down toward the floor, ending with half a foot of clearance. It was bounded on the left and right by two smaller bulbs which housed arrays of lights vaguely like flowers, with central round faces and petals all around. The side bulbs swept back, tapering down and running under the edges of the doors and then back up over the rear wheels. It was all in black with strips and whorls of silver.

The front doors opened on their own, inviting them to sit. Once inside, the seats moved up and down, forward and back according to the size of their occupants, making them comfortable, the doors shut, and safety belts automatically deployed. The area before them was a rounded wave of featureless gray.

"I've never actually… been in a car before. Just buses and trains," Laeua said as though sharing a big secret.

"Neither have I." Haral shook his head.

The inside of the windscreen came alive with a friendly mechanoid face, humani enough to seem friendly, but not so much that it was creepy. "All is well, my friends. I am Personal Conveyance RD3427. I can drive myself. Where are headed tonight?"

"Sector Monitoring Hub, please," Haral said. "As quickly as is safe. We're on a number of deadlines."

"Ah, of course. Everyone's always in a hurry," the car replied.

"I'm sorry, but we really are. I have only a few days to live unless we can figure this very complicated problem out, and you know, the entire world is in danger from alien forces," Haral, trying to sound matter of fact. RD3427 took a nearly imperceptible beat.

"I was going to ask if you needed to go to the hospital instead after the first part. Now I'm sure that's what you need," RD3427 said.

"No, it's really true, all of it," Laeua said, "Though I wouldn't have believed it six hours ago."

"Me either," Haral confided.

"Corroboration accepted. This time. Just kidding! If you're fine, I'm fine! Let's roll!" The car turned a tight about face and sped in the direction it had come from. "Anyone need a drink? A snack? I don't have a food weaver onboard, but I do have some pre-created snacks, guaranteed to be restocked at least weekly." RD3427 offered. That claim pinged a memory of Haral's, of one of the other people in an undercity workers chat room claiming to always be flush with snacks as a perk of his job.

The gray curve of plastic before them rolled back, revealing a display of gel fruit snacks, chips, crackers, cookies, dried and fresh fruit, and bottled drinks, including waters, juices, and adult beverages. Haral and Laeua looked at one another and nodded, reaching for snacks. Dinner had been different, adventurous, but not enough given the events of the day.

As they broke into the food, they shot by what Haral saw was a depot of dozens of vehicles being cleaned, fueled and otherwise maintained. He spotted a zone designation on a stanchion and recognized it, though he'd only been on lower levels of this zone. A mechanic in a jumpsuit not unlike Haral's usual outfit, but with this zone designation, waved at them. He waved back.

"You know him?" Laeua asked.

"Nah, but he waved. Why not? He's my people."

PART II: THE RIVER

Chapter Eleven

As they rode, PullSys prompted Haral to use the internal cameras to accept a NeuroNet call from Gann. He did so and was met with a massive silver face occupying the middle of the windscreen where RD3427's face had appeared previously.

"Where have you been?" Gann demanded. "The hospital was weird enough. I thought I'd lost you for at least a day when you got knocked out, but then you're back on your feet and gallivanting around the spar jumping off trains and restaurants and swimming in the river… I have serious concerns about your mental health following your accident."

"I appreciate those concerns, and yours, and I share them to some degree," Haral said, trying to sound businesslike, "But seriously, it's been one heck of a day. You wouldn't believe most of it. I'm on my way to you with some books that need to be scanned into databases."

"Books?" Gann's eyebrows, or the ridges where they would be if he had any, rose with interest. "What kinds of books? Gifts for me to fend off threats of a lost job?"

"You could say they're gifts, but not from me, and not specifically for you, though you need to look at them. Did you know our… visitors have been here before?" Haral asked.

Gann rolled his eyes. "Not this again… Chopper wasn't the sanest of mechs before whatever happened when you went down there. If he's off on another alien jag —"

"You haven't heard this from anyone else?"

"What? Aliens? Certainly not," Gann scoffed.

"Well, they're here, they've been here before, and they're not playing nice. The pulse that hit me was a straight up attack and…"

"And?" Gann prompted.

"I'll fill you in when I get there, which will be…" Haral glanced at PullSys pulling up a standard traffic app. A small map appeared in the lower part of his view, showing route, speed, and expected remaining time. "About sixteen minutes. I really need you to get the scanner prepped."

"Excuse me?" Gann asked.

"Please," Haral pleaded.

"That's not really how this works," Gann said.

"We've been coworkers for—"

"Ahem."

"Fine. I've worked *for you* for years now. You trained me, and watched me improve many of the techniques that had been in the manual for ages. I've been reliable and constant. I like to think I've earned a bit of trust and the extremely serious situation overrides seniority or titles."

"I don't appreciate that just because you've had some random spike in followers you can order me around," Gann said, his silver face a stern mask.

Haral threw his hands up in exasperation. "For the love of crystal, I'm not. I'm just asking you to help me not die."

"Die? That's not funny."

"Agreed," he replied steadily.

"If the families of one of those two workers who did die hear you throwing that kind of phrasing around, you'll be out and there will be nothing I can do," Gann warned.

"I'm not throwing anything around, and if you get on the ISMS, you'll find the numbers are a lot higher than two."

"What?" Gann asked flatly, the spiral he'd been building himself into suddenly disintegrating like morning mist in the sun. "I… I've got to make some calls," his superior said, vanishing from the window.

"So that was my boss. Sorry I didn't really get a chance to introdu—," Haral began before the window popped back open, showing Nez, tentacles quivering, tympana rolling, colors muted. Nervous.

"Haral! Finally! Where are you?" His voice wavered more than usual.

"In a car, on my way to the Monitoring Hub. I need some of the equipment there. How are you? How's Chopper?"

"We're OK, well *I'm* OK. I'm not sure about Chopper. The tech team cleared him, but he's still talking jibberish about flying metal leeches and aliens. I guess it's not far off from his usual rants, but he seems especially disturbed today."

"What do you mean 'jibberish?' You were there. I went to the surface in the exosuit. An alien grabbed me, cracked it like a candy egg, took me onto its ship, and then dragged me and Chopper back down the chute and into the warehouse. That was the leechy bit. Then it stole, or like… *ate*? The fragments he'd shown us in that crate and went back up the chute."

Nez replied, "Well, you took the suit. I remember that. Chopper followed you after he got some strange readings. The consoles went a little babonk. But then you were back, both of you. Chopper's going on about the fragments, but I never smelled or heard or felt anything. It was just an empty box. I never did figure out what you two were talking about.”

Haral paused, “Huh, so you couldn’t sense the alien, or the fragments of the old alien… At all?”

“No. I think maybe you should get checked out again,” Nez said.

“Oh, I definitely should, given what I’ve just been told. Can you meet us at the Hub?”

“Chopper’s calm for the moment, chatting with his peers in other sectors, so I guess he’ll be OK,” Nez said.

“Excel, I’ll see you in twelve.”

Once again, the call screen bounced closed and open again. The pain of popularity. A familiar golden face appeared in the windshield.

“Haral! Look at the rising superstar! I started out thinking I’d need to hold your hand through all this, but your whole flipping the ‘waking up a king’ thing on its head shows me you’ve got this. Of course, the more Pull you have, the more desirable your co-streaming will be, so you’re going to be getting a bunch more offers, if you haven’t already. I just wanted to say ‘dibs!’ Ha! But seriously, I know you’ve got some stuff going on, your own story you’re trying to tell, but if you want to collab, you’re officially on my whitelist. Call any time.” This one appeared to be a pre-recorded video message rather than a live NeuroNet connection, as it cut out and a little circle arrow hung in the middle of the screen.

“Wow…” Haral said in awe.

“‘Wow’ barely covers it. That’s amazing that someone as famous as Merit Lang is sniffing around you like a fanboy,” Laeua said.

"I don't know how this day could get stranger." Haral sat up straighter, hearing the words having come from his mouth. "Oh corp, why did I say that?"

"It's like you've never watched a scripto before," Laeua agreed.

"I've seen hundreds…thousands… Gann has quite a collection… So let's talk about something else, totally unrelated. You said you were an artist. I never really got to ask about that," Haral prompted.

She looked at him in surprise. "Me? All of this stuff going on and you want to talk about my art? Um, OK, well, like I said before, my primary medium is 4D painting. I love showing how like flowers and things grow…"

The next ten minutes were full of lively discussion of current art trends, how art fit into PullSys ratings, and balancing trend-chasing and really expressing oneself. RD3427 pulled around a corner and rolled to a stop. Haral's drones dropped like stones over the dashboard and in the back seat.

"Hey! The Overlay just wen—" Laeua started a fraction of a second before Haral opened his mouth to point out the almost unheard of anomaly.

Ahead of them was arrayed a veritable army: dozens of armed and armored humani, Flexxe, even a few Rulab and Xochat, though these latter didn't carry weapons that Haral could see. The force stood to either side of the Hub entrance and swept around to both sides.

As he turned his head to take the scene in, Haral noticed more figures closing in behind.

"RD3427, get us out of here." The vehicle didn't respond, in words or movement.

"I don't think he can. I think they completely cut us off," Laeua said. "It's just like being back at the river village." Haral nodded.

"Haral Adjani and Laeua Kio, exit the vehicle slowly, hands in the air. Leave any devices, belongings or weapons in the vehicle!" a stern voice that brooked no discussion demanded over an amplification system. "You have fifteen seconds."

"I don't see any other options," Haral said.

"Do not speak!" the amplified voice added. Ducking his head in assent, Haral fumbled with the manual handle and opened the car door slowly. Having similar difficulty with getting through the oddly shaped door, he stood. "Close the doors!" the voice ordered. Haral turned and pushed the door closed. As soon as he did, he heard a flurry of footsteps behind him.

"If this is because of the train thing, that was not really my—gfwrlth!" A tube was jammed down his throat and a thick white pad of fibrous, pillowy, material closed in from either side, hugging him, immobilizing him, and blocking out all light. He heard the zipping sounds of webbing straps being pulled tight and a moment later felt the padding constrict, pinning his arms to his body and his legs together.

"Haral Adjani," the voice from before now spoke calmly, quietly, in his ear, "You are the subject of a control warrant. This is not a criminal arrest, though any evidence revealed during investigation and interview may be used to support criminal charges which may have been leveled, or may be leveled in the future. You will be transported to a secure facility. If you attempt to escape or resist in any way, your confinement wrap will constrict until you pass out."

Haral stood until he was tipped on his side. He felt the sway of being carried by someone walking. He was jostled, then moved steadily for some time. As far as he could tell, he had been walked a short distance and then laid into a vehicle. He wondered what had happened to Laeua. How could she have had any charges against her? No, he couldn't think of a way. They had probably just escorted her to a vehicle for questioning or put her back in RD3427 for a ride home.

The steady sensation of motion was tinted with angles this way or that for some time before the vehicle bumped over a perimeter ridge or speed bump and soon came to a stop. He was hauled from the vehicle and stood in place for a seemingly endless time. He went through phases of reactions to his predicament, from trying to figure out how to get the Overlay back, how to get himself out of the padding, how to tip and roll himself out of here, maybe into one of the smaller rivers, or down a hallway while no one was looking.

Of course it was ludicrous.

He was trapped.

Hours later, it seemed, bereft of messaging system, videos, or even a room to look at, Haral heard a sizzling sound. He began to panic, feeling like he couldn't get a breath, that he was being constricted as though by an ancient serpent. A sharp smoke entered the breathing tube, choking him. He coughed and jumped involuntarily. He heard someone yelling outside. The voice became clearer by the moment.

"…have choked him. If he sues, you'll be on the block!" the voice Haral recognized from his capture said.

"Yes sir, sorry sir." Seconds later, something struck the tube, wrenching it in his throat. He tried to protest but couldn't make a sound.

Over the next few seconds, light became visible through the white. The pressure let off and then a seam appeared before him. Hands pulled apart the batting and slid the tube from his throat. The attendants fled with the confinement materials trailing behind them, leaving him alone, standing before a wall of gleaming vertical poles crossed with flat pieces of metal, reminding Haral of an Old World prison cell. A door of similar design slid to with a heavy metallic clang, reinforcing the finality and futility of his situation.

"Welcome back to the world. I trust your time alone was used wisely and you have considered your options," the first voice again, the person in charge of… whatever was happening here. A few bright lights beamed down from the low ceiling, but only touched the floor in tangential circles on the gray-blue plascrete. The speaker stood with the shiny black toes of their shoes barely sticking into the sharp-edged cone of light. They were clearly military, based on Gann's old movies, but Haral hadn't seen anything like that in real life. Their form and face were hidden. Others lurked nearby, furtive but busy shadows.

"That would have been easier to do without a pipe down my airway," Haral croaked, stopping and rubbing his throat. "Can I get some water or something?"

"Mm, yes, an unfortunate side effect of the control process. Had to get you here, though, didn't we?" A figure standing in the shadows of the larger room waved a hand, sending one of the other shadows running. "But here you are, with nary an incident."

"You sound surprised."

"In the capability of my team? Never," the figure replied.

"Then in the design of the control get up? The wrapper? The cage…? You've never seen this thing work, because what's happening now has only happened once before, and you didn't have these fancy toys… What is it supposed to do, anyway? Why did you take me prisoner?"

"It's not so much you…" the other said.

"What is that supposed to mean? Where's Laeua? Don't you think this is a little overboard for a few stunts? No one got hurt."

"Tell me about the train," the shadowy figure said, avoiding his question.

Haral frowned. "What about it? Some kid stole my hat and I went to get it back, but before I got halfway to the door, I heard him screaming. He'd fallen over the railing or something and was barely hanging on. That had nothing to do with me."

The figure tutted. "Our records show something happened *before* you got outside to the boy."

Haral thought back. "Oh, the guy? I didn't touch him. He got in my way, thought I was going to hurt the kid or something? I don't know. I… ran around him." A gray light twinkled along the bars of the cage, but before it could run together, it sparked, sending gray motes arcing around the space.

The interrogator stepped farther back into the darkness. He whispered something angrily to the shadow at his side. It fled like the previous one. Or perhaps it was the previous one, returned from the last errand. It was hard to concentrate.

"Come now, Haral, we're all friends here…" the other said evenly, stepping forward again, but remaining hidden. "You can tell me the truth. You know that's not what happened… *I* know that's not what happened…"

"Ok… I don't actually *know* what happened," he replied.

The interrogator seemed pleased. "Ah, there, you see? A bit of honesty. In return, I offer you… a seat."

Haral looked around and saw that immediately behind him was a metal chair, the welds recent and unfinished, straight legs connecting to a flat platform for sitting, and armrests which connected to the mostly vertical back. He also noted the whole thing was fused to the bare metal floor. He did feel exhausted, but decided to sit on the floor, which looked equally comfortable.

The figure continued, "Have it your way. Now, tell me everything you remember about what you saw… What you felt… When you were faced with this man, twice your size, more, standing in your way?"

"Well, at first, I was annoyed, but then maybe a little upset. I would have gone back to sit except I'd heard the boy by then, and knew he was in trouble."

"And had you seen this boy before? Or the man?" the voice pressed.

Haral shook his head. "Not that I know of. I mean, I wasn't so far from home. It's possible we'd been in the same place before."

"We're veering off topic here," the sharp response came, "The confrontation. Your feelings. Your… memories?"

"How…? Yeah, okay, for some reason, I remembered the water park I went to when I was a kid, the wave pool sending a huge one toward me, lifting me right off my… No…"

"I believe, yes," the interrogator said, "your memories are being hijacked to create expressions unlike the kind of language we are used to. There are no symbols, no interpretations, just sending of memories, experiences, from one mind to another."

"Sure, okay…" Haral said, realizing that his encounter with the visitors had been centered on the same memories, that water park, going down the slides, the wave pool…

"A bare human mind *might* be able to survive contact, but mechanicals, nanos, anything relying on programming languages, or people over-reliant on their nanos… Well, they're just incompatible."

Incompatible. Exactly the term Whip had used. That wasn't a coincidence. These people knew exactly what had happened to him on the Shell. But how? He felt Chopper nodding in the back of his mind as the shadow threads of a hidden military with access to everyone's information feeds—public and private—even the sensor arrays on the surface solidified into an unpleasant picture of societal structure.

"That's great, but I don't see—" Haral began.

The other cut him off, "I think you *do*. I think if we could crack your brain open right now, we'd see every little neuron firing toward one realization… That as I said at the beginning, *you're* not the prisoner here."

"I *feel* like a prisoner. I see a cage and not much else. I'm being interrogated."

He could hear the smile in the military man's voice. "Ah, no, Mr. Adjani. This is just the meet and greet, a chance for all parties involved to gauge one another and understand the situation. The interrogation will come when your rider fails to reveal itself and cooperate."

"'Rider?'" A gray light now shone from his fingertips, rolling across his hands and up his arms. "What's going on? What is that?"

"That's what we're here to find out, Mr. Adjani. Turn it up." The last was clearly to one of the shadows rather than Haral. He felt a kind of pressure inside his head and down his back. His limbs began to buzz from the inside, as if bees had taken up residence in his bones. The gray glow slowed its advance up his arms, but he felt the cool dryness on his feet, sliding across his shoulders and cheeks. "What does it feel like? Is it fighting back? Is it *angry*?" The figure pressed eagerly.

"The light?" The questions were incomprehensible to him. His awareness slipped into a memory of a bird he had seen once, no bigger than his hand at the time, when he was maybe ten years old. His family was at a green space. They had ordered a handful of wriggling beetle larva to entice the birds closer, to witness them up close. The bird had flutter-hopped down from the low-branched tree and then hopped gradually closer, turning its head aside to inspect the waving tan thing in his palm. It approached to a few inches beyond his fingers, then hopping up to sit on his fingertips. Its head darted forward, snapping at the larva, but stabbing into his palm, drawing blood. The memory faded as the pressure in his body increased, the buzz reached toward his skin, making his muscles twitch.

Was that how that encounter had happened? Or was the memory changed for some reason? Sparks flew across the inside of the cage as his awareness returned to his surroundings.

"What did you see? What was its message?"

"'It?' 'Message?'" Haral asked, dazed, having as much trouble discerning the words as he had with the imagery he'd been shown.

"What did it tell you?"

"Not every action that does harm is an attack. Sometimes, we don't know what effect our actions will have on others." The words flowed now, though he wasn't sure how much hand he had in choosing them. He felt something on his hand and looked down. At the center of his palm was a small bead of blood.

Chapter Twelve

Haral felt light and distant from his body. The buzz, which had begun to cause him physical pain, seemed far away, like rain on the outside of the spar while you're safe in your apartment.

"Yes, why is it here? Your rider."

"'Rider?'" Haral asked again, feeling like it was something he should know, but there was a wall between him and the information.

"Its hold is too great, General. He's not going to tell you anything," one of the shadows said. "But these books he brought back are a trove. It's inconceivable that this kind of information was leaked."

"It's not really a leak when the information sits there for a hundred years. We knew she stole some records. We didn't realize she had so much," the first speaker, the "General," said. "I suppose it leaves us ahead of where we were, even if this one tells us nothing. When the host dies, we'll do a dissection right away."

"Yes, sir."

"Dissection? How do you know I'm going to die? *Why* am I going to die?" Haral asked, his voice shaking.

"An acute lack of cooperation, it would seem," the General said with a wry edge to his tone.

"What? *Cooperation*? You kidnapped me—" Haral pointed out, indignant.

"Arrested," the General cut in.

"Potatoes."

"Pardon?"

"Never mind. The point is you can call it whatever you want, but you abducted myself and my friend, wrapped me up in cling wrap like an old sandwich, and

149

now you're telling me I'm going to die because I'm somehow not cooperating?"

"You're only harming yourself. My people estimate you have under seventy hours left. If we can get your rider out of you, you may survive," the General said.

"'Rider' again. What is that, even? I didn't know anyone on that train. No motive, no grudge, no connection I'm aware of at all."

"And yet, the rider was there, with you, in you."

"*In*? Why are you forcing me to sound like a broken record? Just tell me what's going on."

"You mean Whip didn't tell you everything? That's too bad. I'd hoped he would have put the fear of death into you."

"You know about Whip?"

"Obviously. One doesn't just *let* an anti-technology cult go about its business without close supervision, especially when it has connections to outside forces. Outsiders that are even now mounting attacks on Geode."

"Attacks… the other sectors."

"What do you know about that?" The General asked.

"The thing… You haven't talked to Chopper?" Haral answered a question with a question.

"Your mechanical friend may be functional enough to return to his sorting and cataloging job, but he's not exactly firing on all cylinders. You can thank your rider and its friends for that."

"Meaning what?" Haral pressed.

"That pulse your hub recorded that sent you to the hospital for a few hours wasn't just an energy jolt. Some might say the incompatible were the lucky ones."

"Incompatible? As in the people who died? You think because I survived, something went into my brain?"

"Brain, spinal cord, yes. It's riding on the electrical currents or metawaves or some such. I'm not the science guy. I'm the—"

"Kidnapping guy?" Haral threw out. One of the shadows snorted, froze for a fraction of a second, then went back about their shadow business as if nothing had happened, or at least they hoped the General would not be able to ID them.

The General was less amused. "Well, have fun with your nanosystems as the rider fries every one of them, causing nodes on your nerves, destroying your memory, your mobility, and eventually, your ability to breathe. Don't worry though. Such diseases in Old Earth would run for months or years. *You'll* only have to endure a few dozen hours. Shall I have my people put up a clock on the wall?"

Haral snapped. "What do you even want from me? If I'm infected with an alien, why haven't you just dumped me in an incinerator?"

The General paused, considering. "Good question; solid thought. I would, but my people seem to think they can get it out, study it, perhaps learn what it wants, how it works, how to kill it…"

"Ah, death delayed for more death. Weirdly poetic." Haral chuckled grimly.

"If you like. I'm not one for poetry, except a good limerick. You have any? No? Ah well. The thing we really 'want from *you*' is anything that you have observed that could help with prying the rider off your central nervous system."

The light built up at the edges of Haral's vision again. Darkness fell across the middle. It quickly resolved into a vaguely curved horizon limned in the same gray light which illuminated radio telescope dishes and hundreds of other bumps and nodes across the visible surface. Haral recognized it as Geode's Shell.

The light advanced, drawing over the raised shapes. Suddenly afraid, Haral turned, but the growing wave rolled toward him from every direction. Still walking, dazed, he stumbled upon something. Segmented fragments of metal, or something like it. He stood, taking the fragments and stuffing them into the front seam of his suit as though it were a simple jacket.

The gray light converged on him, obliterating all else from his vision.

In the wash of pale light, Haral thought he saw movement. As the seconds passed, wavefronts and streams, always shifting, but rolling in particular ways, a pattern, almost, swam through the gray miasma.

"Is that you? Are you trying to communicate? Tell me something? Make a deal? I don't want you to die, but I kind of don't want me to die more. It's a quirk my people have."

Haral slipped back into the memory of the wave pool, being gently lifted and lowered by slow swells. It was a moment full of joy and comfort. People all around were smiling, laughing. The sun shone on the water. Across the top of the water, peculiar narrow ripples twisted, forming arcs and S curves which existed momentarily before transforming. His mind recognized patterns from the gray light.

"Well?" the General demanded, "What did you see this time?"

"What?"

"The cage sets up a field, allowing us to see when the rider is active, but we can't translate its activity into the images you see."

"Just water at the pool, floating, everyone having fun."

"Empty promises, trying to lull you into complacency," the General warned.

"Maybe, but it's better than a metal cage. Or maybe, it's trying to communicate. Isn't that what you want?" Haral challenged.

"No, I want *you* to communicate. I just want the rider to leave."

"When did we become so hostile to other species? What about the Rulab, Xochat, and Flexxe? Especially given you have some of them on your 'team?'"

The General mocked, "I thought *you* were the history buff. 'When did we become so hostile,' indeed."

"Gann's really the history guy. I just get a lot by osmosis," Haral quipped.

"The observation stands. It's always been about ingroups and outgroups. It was language, skin color, income, so many things over the span of civilizations. When aliens came along, they either integrated, became part of the ingroup as much as possible, or…"

"Just how many species have we 'or…'d?" Haral asked, his chest tightening.

"I couldn't say, but we harvested thousands of Extra Terran Objects to get the material to build Geode, maybe millions if you count every moon, every asteroid, wiping out the Oort Cloud…" The General said. This revelation stunned Haral more than the idea that an alien entity was riding in him like he had ridden the exosuit to the Shell.

"So you're afraid of it," Haral said.

"Damn right." The General agreed. Mumurs of assent rose from the shadows.

"Because you've seen its species before," he pressed.

"Mmm," the General agreed noncommittally.

"And you shot it down rather than communicating with it," Haral continued.

"Couldn't communicate with it. We tried every form of communication available to us or our integrated species: language, math, colors, and pure music. They were just cutting a swath of destruction, killing citizens with their pulses."

"And now they're back, maybe for revenge, or maybe just recover their lost ships or survivors—"

"There were no survivors," the General cut him off.

"You sound proud of that, General" Haral accused.

"I saw good beings die from their pulses, riders, other effects. They started this war." A steely edge entered the General's tone.

"I don't think *they* think it's war. They struggle to understand us as much as we do them," Haral said, willing the General to see reason.

"So they're not intelligent? How did they get here? Where did they get ships? Killing off some other race?"

"I tell you we're the same and you leap to them not being intelligent… Hmm…" Haral said, disappointed.

"Have they destroyed other races?" The General pressed, ignoring his barb.

"I don't know, but I don't think so. Maybe it's like… you know how when you see signs or books in a dream, the words are just incomprehensible squiggles? Or blurs?"

"So they're just dreaming of reaching us and that barrier blocks coherent communication?" The General asked.

"I don't know. I'm no expert, but I think it's been trying to tell me… for lack of a better phrase… they come in peace." The General laughed out loud at this, turning and walking away through the shadows while his team kept working at a series of consoles in the dark dim readouts twinkling off wet eyes, and giving just enough ambient light to catch movement.

After a minute of Haral steeping in his thoughts, the shadows moved again. One came close to the light, the rough reflection off the flooring and cage giving a ghostly grayness to their black form.

"I think you're right. I don't think they mean us harm. We don't, either, most of us, mean them any. We're all scientists pulled from our projects by the General and his goons. I'm a food chemist for crying out loud. How am I going to help decipher alien technology or physiology?" The shadow said.

"Do you know anything about other prisoners? Laeua? The girl I was with when I was captured?" Haral asked quickly, voice low.

"I don't, but I can try to find out. I know you don't have much time, but this might help. I've been scanning in those books you had with you. All kinds of information we either never got or was so heavily redacted as to be useless." The shadow backed away, completely disappearing. Something small and metallic shot out of the darkness, pinging off one of the bars and coming to rest a few feet away, just to the other side of the chair.

"What do I do with this?" Haral whispered. There was no response. He turned toward the bars and walked along the perimeter of the cage. After a circuit, he took another round a pace in from the edge, spiraling inward until he could kick the object toward the chair. When he came to the chair, he finally sat, then waited for a time, trying to surreptitiously look around. Was anyone watching?

Undoubtedly. Could he get the object without drawing attention? He was about to find out. Pretending to fiddle with his shoe, he took it off and set it down on the object, rolling it over just a bit so that it fell to the floor to one side of the metal thing. Then he took his other shoe off and dropped it to the other side. He made a show of inspecting his feet, then grabbed the shoes, pinching them together to pick up the object. Watching all those old prisoner of war movies with Gann was again paying dividends.

Object dropped into his other hand, he studied it for a moment. It was roughly the size of the last knuckle of his pinky finger with a picture of an ear inscribed lightly in the surface and a small arrow pointing to the place where the sound entered the ear canal. It seemed clear enough, but could he trust the shadow who threw him the device? Perhaps it was just a ruse to get him to plug in some sensor or other device into his own body rather than having to drug him or wrestle him down. He didn't think they would hesitate much in that case.

In the end, it seemed to Haral that little choice. Either A) he didn't put it in and it was a ruse, he would then be drugged or held down, having the thing forced on him, or B) if the other was trying to help, the window for that help could close. Holding the object between his first and third fingers, he hid it with his second as he pretended to scratch his ear. It slid in easily enough. He brushed his hair in front of his ear and settled in to wait.

"Don't look around," a voice said in his ear. "If you subvocalize, make the words without pushing air from your lungs, the device can read them and I can hear you, more or less."

OK, Haral tried.

"Good, now listen closely. We think holding you here is a mistake. You're one of only a few who have survived the initial pulse. We have to wonder if there are any parallels between you and the others," the voice continued.

I assume we have the same or similar jobs to be exposed in the first place. Mechanics, repair workers for the Hubs.

"Good guess. Most people exposed were likely mechanics, though. Many died. We need to know more about those who lived, perhaps figure out why they did, at least initially. Do you enjoy any unusual foods? Take any chemical drugs or have any drug-replicating apps?"

No... Haral said. *Nothing like that I can think of. As far as I know, I'm a pretty average guy, watch streams, work, eat, sleep. I go to theme parks and immersion exhibits, but not more than normal.*

"How about language? They don't seem to have any language like ours, spoken, written, etc. as the General said. But what about you? Do you have any language difficulties? Or abilities? How many languages do you speak?" The voice pressed.

Interesting question. I speak humani, obviously, and Xochat pretty well, Rulab and Flexxe poorly... Again,

I think that's pretty normal, though some people resist learning any they aren't born to and other people really go all in and can talk to just about anyone alive right now without Overlay. There's something intimate, better for making connections, in speaking to someone in their own language.

"Ah, I will keep thinking."

Well, there are the ancient 'landguages' of Old Earth. Each area had its own language, or its version of another language. I wouldn't say I know them all, but I've been exposed to dozens through old movies and series.

"Hmm, and you've uploaded language databases for these?"

Haral nodded. *Yes, some from every habitable continent of Old Earth, but there are hundreds, and many in which there aren't but a few entertainment or educational pieces.*

"That is certainly a place to start," the voice replied. Hope brightened the tone. "It's possible that your language centers, or your Overlay's libraries, have been expanded enough that the rider's attempt at language are partly interpreted and not just a chaotic assault on your brain. Oh, I've got to go. Meeting. Don't do anything."

Me?

"We've all seen the clips, but there's no leaping from spires and downloading a squirrel suit in time to save yourself here," the shadow retreated.

And then Haral was alone with his thoughts again. He considered what Nez might be up to now. Normally, they would be bringing up ridiculous scenarios about alternate endings of stories, or who had the best voice for certain kinds of characters. The Xochat version of the Overlay did work to allow them to experience vision-based media, but it was imperfect to say the least… It *was* imperfect… What had Nez said about the alien when it dropped them back in the warehouse? Something about Haral and Chopper "reappearing," but not any excitement over having seen an alien… because he *couldn't* see. He could only interpret when the Overlay gave him as substitute visual data.

Can you hear me?

Nothing. It was possible the shadow food chemist was too far away to receive his signal, or that they couldn't answer because they were in the meeting, surrounded by others, under scrutiny.

Don't worry about answering. I get you might not be able to, but I hope you can hear me. I thought of something. Not about me, though, about my friend. Nez wasn't able to see the alien at all. It zoomed right by him, not ten feet away. It dropped Chopper and I off, moved around the room, and then shot away. But Nez only wondered how we had gotten back. He's a Xochat. They can't see at all. I wonder if the invasion point is the eyes or the visual lobe or whatever.

Haral heard a noise from another room. Was that confirmation the other had heard? Or coincidence? He had little choice now but to wait and try to see if he could think of anything else. He felt as though he were sitting for a test for which he had dreamed he had studied but woke to find himself not knowing a thing on the subject. He poked and prodded in various directions inside his brain, trying to dredge up memories, stories that might apply. How would he get out of here? And if he did, where could he hide?

Gray light shrouded his vision again, this time showing him something other than the water park. But there was still water, a lot of water. It twisted in great pillars into the sky, joining what seemed to be a deeper, darker green sea and a paler, bluer sea encased on one edge by ice. Regardless of color, everything had an edging of gray light, making it look like an artistic rendering of an impossible scene.

But no… Not entirely impossible. At the poles, the gravity created by Geode's spin, the thrusters and river jets, mainly, waned, to the point that architecture, landmasses, even the flow and surge of water, was much less Old Earth and more "alien biosphere." Nonetheless, the remaining animals were largely relegated to these regions as unsuitable for the average humani or other citizens. A semblance of what they called an "ecosystem" back on Old Earth existed here. Plants clung to rock pillars or small islands, some in the water, some in the space between the waters, drawing energy from the sun and continuing to produce a baseline food supply for small animals, and those small animals for larger, up the scale.

As he watched, a wave rolled along, rising and rising until it drifted off the surface of the water, floating in a constantly evolving reverberation of waves. The view zoomed in to the water globule, showing Haral rippling lines and fronts it had been showing him all along. Was it a memory from the rider? A message about why they were there?

The view shifted again to a very recent memory of his, of crashing into the river and spiraling out of control for a moment. The scene shifted directly to another gray-limned view of being drawn into tunnels, being shunted along by pumps firing out water, and finally being launched just outside of a bay-side spar, the kind of spar reserved for those who enjoyed or benefited from the slightly lower gravity but not the mind-bending freedom of the poles.

Chapter Thirteen

Haral sat in the cell again, staring at his hands, waiting for something to happen. Would the shadow return to his ear? Would the General stand at the edge of the light and demand more answers he didn't himself have?

What could he do? Even if he escaped, the people here knew science, had Whip's books and equipment, and… where would he go?

Gray light impinged on his vision again, recalling a rectangular grate in a floor... no, a wall with water flowing through, a strong current. The point of view slid past the bars into a dark tunnel, a pipe, maybe, its inner wall smooth and round.

"There's talk of moving you to an even more secure facility, one you'll have no chance of escaping from. " The shadow!

You don't think your team can get the rider out of me? Haral subvocalized.

"I honestly don't know. There's a lot of data in these books, even more we've gotten from you, with our up-to-date machines, but it takes time to formulate responses to the challenges the rider poses to our technology, our physiology."

So, you need time. But you told me I don't have time, Haral said.

"You don't," the shadow agreed, "but we're going to end up dissecting you, either way. That's what the meeting was about. Apparently, someone far more important than you, even with your recent fame, is infected. You're the guinea pig they're going to try out whatever we find on, and then vet the method by some very… Invasive tests. Go, now. I've turned off the dampening field in the cage. You should have Overlay any second, but only while the field is down. Can't give you more than thirty seconds."

While the shadow spoke in Haral's ear, his Overlay flicked back to life in his vision. He tried not to react outwardly, searching quickly for a polymorphing app to allow him to slip through the bars. All the general ones were super expensive, still out of reach above his PullGrade. Couldn't have too many citizens turning themselves into eagles and flying around the spars, he supposed. A gray edge grew over his Overlay, interacting with it.

The shapes of the fish, bird, and spider in the banner depicting the use of the app turned the familiar gray, stray diagonal lines flickering into existence through them. Characters of the text flipped orientation and changed to other symbols like someone dragging a spoon thorugh a bowl of alphabet soup.

Haral's body began to hum, then shudder. The bees which had inhabited his bones before now spread through his flesh as he receded like a piece of paper caught in flame. He began to cry out, then fell out of the chair onto his side. Beyond the bars, an alarm rose up. Shadows spoke excitedly to one another. Red lights flashed from the top of the walls, revealing the height of the heretofore unseen ceiling. Struggling to rein in his body, Haral spotted a drain grate like the one the rider had shown him.

"Run, Haral, run!" The shadow shouted in his earpiece.

The cage seemed to grow larger around him, the bars drew farther apart. He tried to push himself up, to crawl toward the open space, but found he had no control over his limbs.

Gah! What is that? Haral exclaimed.

"It looks like… a fish!" another shadow observed.

Or perhaps, he didn't have any limbs that could reach the ground. If only fish could run. The thought rattled around in his brain as he flopped and thrashed, ever closer to the bars.

"Get him! Don't let him escape!" the General commanded. But then he was at the bars, his head clearing as he learned to control the form, he lunged forward on his side, then rolled and pushed the outside of the bar with a turn of his head to pull himself through. From there, it was half a dozen flips and flops. Heavy shoes pounded across the dense floor, sending shock waves up his sides with every crash. He saw the General's face, broad, distorted by eyes not used to seeing out of water. Then he flipped one last time and jammed his head between the even smaller bars.

Think thin!

He felt himself narrow and elongate further.

Rough hands grabbed him, but the eel's slippery skin and slime coat deflected the predator as it had done for eons on Old Earth. In seconds, he was swimming free, or at least splashing in the remains of the flow which had been here before the chamber behind him had been commandeered by the General. He heard the echoing roar of order after order as he slid gently down, finding deeper water where he could actually swim.

Down and down Haral fled, along steeper and easier slopes by turns, joining larger and larger waterways. Rarely, light from a maintenance hatch or spar root which reached all the way down here shone, filling a space, but there was nothing to see but flat walls and curved pipes.

He checked messages, and saw that while his Pull had fluctuated in the face of the day's events, overall, he was higher on the board than he ever had dreamed he could be. But he turned away from these notices to look for messages from Nez, Laeua—if she had actually escaped, or had been released—Gann, Chopper, even Merit. There seemed to be notes from each, save Laeua, not the best sign. There were also a few from names he recognized from his own stream watching, or from the catch-up watching he had done to know Merit better after their agreement had begun. A spread of friends, teaming up for this event or that, often worked for these people. He might do well to ally himself with some of them "against" Merit, in their "feud." Still, responsibilities were responsibilities… and he had larger problems than Pull at the moment.

He clicked into Gann's earliest unread message and received a jolt as though from electricity. He had a hard time focusing on the text. Silver static roved across his vision in broad, soft-edged diagonal bands. Moreover, the disruption wasn't purely visual. He felt it itching under his borrowed skin, prickling his muscles.

He tried to read the words hovering before him again, only to bounce off them as hard as he had bounced off the invisible wall he had thought was a roof garden while flying. The digits and letters swam, incomprehensible.

That's you, isn't it? Somehow my trying to read is crossing paths with the areas you're sitting on my nerves. We're joined, now, aren't we? It's not just that you don't understand language, but that it somehow… hurts you… Haral shut the Overlay and immediately his muscles relaxed. Swimming became easier. For a time, he did simply that, a moment of calm in a day filled with chaos.

The dark was all-encompassing for long stretches of time between deeper spar roots. Unable to really communicate yet with his "rider," Haral thought idly of how to make that connection. A simple name wouldn't do any good, as it would be composed of sounds and symbols familiar to him, but painful, even damaging to the rider. How did one begin a conversation with a language-averse creature? Think happy thoughts?

A rumble crept into the edges of Haral's senses as he wriggled along, trying to figure out how to break the ice now that he'd, in the vaguest of ways, realized what he had to do to communicate with the rider. He envisioned a series of vehicles: Old Earth cars, bikes, buses new and old, boats, planes, skateboards and surfboards. This last made him chuckle, mentally, anyway. Nothing physical really happened to his eel body when the thought came over him. It was a bit sad that eels' bodies weren't equipped to laugh.

The rumble graduated to a roar, more demanding of his attention, and a gray edge began to creep over the curved pipe wall. Then the gray rose up and bubbled, shooting away in streaks and the sound grew louder and louder.

A pump! He felt some static from the exuberant, loud word inside his mind and backed off, taking a more reserved stance within his own mind while setting his long, narrow body to writhing as fast as it could toward the pipe wall to get as far from the pump and its jet as possible.

The sound only grew louder, the water rougher. Currents Haral didn't expect rolled him even as he neared the place he deemed safest. A gray gleam appeared, showing a low ledge, just above the water as another spout appeared in the near distance. Not far from here, the water would become impassable or tear him apart.

The rider's vision showed a very liquid mass of gray light hopping up onto the ledge, spreading itself very flat, long and low to keep from falling back into the turbulent water. It was how the previous alien had escaped the pump when it had come through here. But how did his rider remember what happened to another of its kin?

Moreover, could his eel body even do it? It would certainly have a better chance than his humani form. Giving all of his effort now, all the coordination he'd found in this body, Haral swam toward the ledge and drew nearly parallel with it, then dove down. Again, he was spun and battered by the churning water, but he managed to leap up, bouncing off the wall just above the ledge.

As smooth as it was, the plascrete pipe scraped through his slime coat and his thin, delicate, skin. He could smell his own blood in the water almost as soon as he landed back in the roiling black. He struck something. It couldn't have been the pump. He was sure he hadn't launched himself that far away from the wall. But still, it was larger, and had a convex curve to it. Some kind of detritus that had somehow become stuck in the plascrete? In the maelstrom, there was no way to tell.

Haral, feeling his strength wane, lined up and launched again. This time, his tail struck a hard, unyielding, object just before he cleared the water, but he rolled up onto the ledge and lay, heaving for breath for a moment.

Then something touched his tail fin. It had to be his imagination, surely. He lolled the end of his body, rolling it away from whatever piece of detritus he'd laid it down upon.

A few seconds later, something scraped just behind his rear side fins. He arced his body to view it. Towering about him in the gloom was a white not-quite sphere. It was nearly the size of a humani head, if his guage was right. At the base of the sphere, a ponderous, slow mass of muscle writhed and slid, now partially wrapping around the curve of his body.

Another scrape. He wriggled farther away, risking falling back into the water with every movement. As he watched, the broad foot settled back to the plascrete ledge, partly over it on the water side, and slid forward another inch, then another. As it came, something swayed and danced at the front of the mass two, no *four* somethings. Tentacles… no wait, Haral recognized the general form as another rose from the water, following the thin trail of his blood along the surface of the plascrete.

Snails!

Giant… Cave… Pipe? Snails!

Snails that were hungry, for him. He frantically wriggled on, slipping back into the water and immediately being swept into a strong current, bumped and even launched above the rest of the water as he passed a pump. He tried to right himself, but another pump caught him, then another. If he could have drowned, he would have as he traversed the pump field, being knocked along one current after another, up out and then back down into the surge.

Dazed, bruised, all but unable to swim, Haral finally came through the field, leaving the thunderous waters behind.

Some help you were, Haral said inside his head. The vision of the bird approaching his hand came to him again, but this time, it nestled in his palm and nibbled the morsel he'd held out. *So, what? You like me now? Is that the message? Great.*

He wondered idly how far he was from Swanton Spar, from everyone he knew. On the other hand, er… fin, he was also farther from the General and his shadows, and hopefully difficult to track. As fitness returned to him, Haral felt the first telltale rumble of another pump array in the distance. How would he get past them? And the snails, or whatever other predators might be down here? Hmm, he considered other forms available through the app, such as a bird to fly over that section of the underground river, or the spider to climb the walls.

A gray memory appeared in his mind. A snail slithered up the plascrete pipe, rasping tongue reaching, scraping the residue from the surface, then him before he managed to ooze away. No, not Haral, the rider… This *was* the way the previous visitor had come, sucked down into the river system and shot out into the sea!

Gingerly, Haral tapped into the Overlay, sustaining some fry as he got to the map program. It showed him a wide shot of this quadrant of Geode, a blinking cursor where he was and his relative position. He was millies, no, whole *degrees*, away from home, moving around the equator. If he was going to follow the previous visitor's path, which he felt he was meant to, his current rider *wanted* him to… He would have to angle south at the next intersection.

Haral swam, mentally exhausted, uncertain as to what he needed to do, afraid for his future. The rider kept flashing him comforting scenes from his own memory: green spaces, rolling waves in the wave pool, people singing, their words blurred into meaningless melodies, and rider's memories of the polar region.

"I get it. I get it. We're headed that way." The next gray memory began, and he focused, trying to counter with a memory of his own choosing.

He walked along a path through a green space toward the lifts, which were kind of like Old Earth escalators, but whole platforms instead of stairs shifted up one side and down the other. It was easier for Rulab, Xochat, and others who had or had chosen non-legged forms to traverse than steps. Someone called his name, now just a sound that lit up with recognition, but confusion as he didn't know the voice. He turned and saw Laeua, with her purple and pink hair, heavily reflective eye makeup, and smile pulled slightly to one side.

Rider showed him a series of ripples intersecting and rolling over one another in a gray expanse.

Was it meant to be the same kind of interaction? Meeting someone? He had the sense of family, saw flashes of his mother, his father, or maybe… wholeness? Completion? His own part of the vision shifted to the last time he had visited his mother. Rider pushed their version. The ripples resolved into an embrace as the two meetings overlapped and became indistinguishable.

Indistinguishable. Yes, that was the feeling. The rider's people were individuals when they needed to be, but their standard state was one of unity, of all the personalities and individualities melding. That's why they hadn't needed to develop language. There was no barrier to block knowledge from passing between them. They never had to break down ideas and try to convey them via gestures or sounds, at an *evolutionary level,* never had to.

The beings that had been attached to the crashed ships weren't just lost members of their society for whom they would do anything to regain. They were parts of their own greater self. The concept was emotional, intimate in ways which with Haral didn't have much experience. The world moved so fast. Everyone was as occupied as they wanted to be, getting their surrogate human contact from the Pull personalities they followed, sometimes obsessed over.

The riders' collective plight seemed to Haral like homesickness, a topic that came up in Gann's old movies a lot, in between making one's fortune and winning the partner one chose. It seemed that most people were struggling toward, or away from, something their whole lives. Now he was, after a fashion, doing both, in running from the General and his shadows, and seeking the other portions of the rider.

A flash of gray accompanied by the impulse to turn yielded a solid crash into the wall. No, not a wall, a closed off channel. They came to the edge a few seconds later. Confusion washed over Haral, though he identified what had happened, and who had made it happen, almost immediately. If there was one thing they knew about the General, it was that he had the Pull, or other influence, perhaps, as an actual PullSys worker, perhaps? He could have gates opened and closed.

The shadows had figured out where Haral was going and cut him off. He knew from his brief look at the map and his experience with these systems that another side-river would be along in just a few hours. He spent the time wondering if it, too would be closed, or if, having confirmed Haral's path by his impact on the gate, it would be lying in wait like an ambush predator, mouth agape, or surging open at the last second, drawing them inexorably in.

Haral tried to convey this image from nature videos he had watched in his youth. Rider's concern grew. In return, he got a gray-washed vision which was a montage of various animals looking in one direction, then another, or looking over their shoulders, or up in the sky.

That was it. Up. There were other ways out of the river system, smaller maintenance hatches, pressure feeds that sent water up to… It was insane, but given the last day, or days, he couldn't even be sure anymore how long it had been since "meeting" Merit…

Chapter Fourteen

Haral kept an eye out for what they needed and found it in short order. Most household water was shunted to local facilities to be cleansed and made ready for use, but these facilities had over-fill lines which led to the river system. It wasn't meant to be a regular flow, but the pipes were there for emergencies. To Haral, it seemed this was emergency enough.

One would expect a wastewater pipe to be a dark, unpleasant place. One would be right, but as Haral ascended, more and more light filtered in through the thin pipe material and from above. He emerged into a space above a massive holding tank which was, as far as he could tell, largely empty. He reached with his narrow eel body along the surface only to encounter inch-thick sludge clinging to the whole surface.

He found no purchase and fell for long seconds to splash into the thick soup at the bottom. He was thankful for his current form not the least because while he could smell the accumulated, fermented, mess, it didn't seem distasteful to him. He writhed himself over to a ladder and, thoroughly covered in sludge, began working his way up, spooling around one rung, then the next.

After a few loops, Rider sent him a gray image of himself as he had been for most of his life, the kind of form the ladder was meant for. Haral considered it, but then decided that it might still be easier to sneak around as an eel, and he really didn't want to smell this place with his normal nostrils. Nez might not ever talk to him again if they got a whiff of this on him. He paused on his climb to send an image of the Xochat recoiling, tympani pulled down, tentacles hidden, whole body turned flat gray, though he wasn't sure if that last part would come through. He saw Rider's images through a gray lens. Was that how they saw? Or was there some loss from the transmission and translation process?

There was a gurgle and a liter or so of fluid fell from one of the openings near the top of the chamber. At least the ladder itself was clear, which was good for anyone who had to come down here. Haral passed more rungs at a slow, steady, pace. If he was humani again, he'd be able to reach the inside of the hatch at the top of the ladder. Only a few to go. Another liquid choking sound was followed by an odor that made it past Haral's clamped-shut nostrils.

A thin beam of light shone from a small dome at the underside of the hatch. It passed from one side of the ladder to the other, only a few inches out from the rungs. Uncertain, Haral slithered out of its way. He was almost immediately certain this was the wrong move when, the moment the light completed its transit, a small alarm went off just outside the tank and a grinding sound issued from below.

Haral had a bad feeling about this change in activity. The grinding continued, neared as Haral managed the last couple of rungs and lay pressed against the hatch. He wasn't going to be able to get it open like this…

He opened the Overlay again, immediately receiving a shock as words and symbols bored into his optic nerve, upsetting Rider. Bees in his bones. *Just gotta…* He got back to the shape-changing app and focused on the humani form. He immediately felt himself begin to spread and branch. He slammed his Overlay shut and breathed a sigh of relief, or tried to, choking on the absolutely invasive stench trying to push every "eject" button for his stomach at once. Luckily, or un-, he hadn't eaten in quite a while, and nothing came up as he struggled to hold onto the top rungs while choking and retching.

"Do you hear something?" Someone said outside the tank, muffled, but understandable. "I think someone's… in there."

"That's ludicrous," another, deeper, sharper, voice dismissed.

Meanwhile, Haral focused on controlling his breathing and turned to pat around the hatch and on it. There had to be a release in here, right? What if someone fell in? Then it occurred to him that's what the laser had been for. It was making sure the ladder was clear of people. The grinding from below grew slowly. The stench seemed to be increasing, as well, despite his efforts not to breathe through his nose.

Rider sent him a vision of someone clapping.

Great. Hilarious. Didn't expect sarcasm from an alien who doesn't even understand language.

Rider sent another vision of louder, enthusiastic, clapping.

No, not applause, hands slamming together, like the gesture he had thought had been a primitive rite to ward off insects at first, but Gann had told him the insects were bothersome and the humani were trying to slay them between their hands. Because they were so small. And humani hands were so large and hard in comparison…

Haral looked down into the gloom and spotted tiny flecks of light, almost certainly closer than they had been… No, it was just his imagination. But the sound…

No, it was definitely moving! Coming to clap him. *He* was the insect! Haral pounded on the inside of the tank.

"Help! Help me! I'm stuck in here!" Haral yelled.

"Shesh! You have to have heard that! Stop the press!"

"It's just solids getting broken up. This tank is pretty low flow. It's entirely possible they've dried up enough that they'd snap and fly around, hitting the walls as the floor pushes up and they hit the rungs of the ladder," the deeper voice argued.

"No! I heard words!"

"Listen to her!" Haral yelled.

"Oh, get out of the way!" the first speaker cried out. Haral thought he heard an impact like someone enthusiastically striking a button, and the grinding wound down.

"Don't be ridiculous, Dell. You're putting us behind schedule." The grinding wound back up again. "Get back! I'm going to have to report you if you don't calm down and return to your station. NO! Not like that!" the second speaker cried out as the hatch opened with a hiss.

A surprised humani woman's face, round, freckled, framed by an auburn bob, peered down at Haral.

"Uh, thanks!" Haral said. "Excuse me?" Sludge pressed up against his foot and the feeling of it sent a wriggle of disgust through his entire form. Dell turned to the side and vomited. He took his chance and crawled up and out, collapsing on the floor at her feet.

"My word! It's inconceivable!" the other wastewater technician hollered. He was a male humani, tall, square-jawed, with a gray fringe hugging a tanned, bald, dome, looking as though he was about to faint.

"Thanks again," Haral said, standing unsteadily, one hand on the top of the pale blue tank, which stood about waist high in this room, though it must have been twenty or more feet deep below them.

"No worries, just stop… touching things…" Dell, nearly face to face with him, looked down at his naked, waste-smeared body, then quickly back at his face, eyes wide, and very focused on not looking down again. Haral covered his genitals with his hands. "You… should really get cleaned up."

"Do you… uh… have facilities for that?" Haral asked, looking at her smeared and smudged coveralls. All the marks looked new, wet. She had been pristine before he came up from the tank.

"Of course, let me show you the way." She turned away crisply, head high, pointedly staring out the door. "We can get you some clothes, too." Haral looked over at the other technician, who just stared, not believing his own eyes. Haral smiled weakly and waved with one hand before realizing what he was doing and putting his hand back down before his groin.

"That would be great, clothes, thanks," he called after Dell. To the other, he said, "Sorry, I had… A bit of an accident."

"And then flushed yourself?" the other wastewater tech suggested.

"Something like that."

"So, I have to ask…" Dell said as they walked down a long hallway, keeping her eyes trained ahead, "how *did* you get in there? The only way that's big enough for a humani is the hatch you came out of." They stopped at an open doorway without a door. He could see lockers and benches. The walls were lined in white tile.

"I got this new app…" Haral began. Official news programs always blamed new, poorly developed or malicious apps for minor disasters.

"Ahh, gotta be careful of those shady back-alley apps. You never know what security risks you're opening yourself up for, or if the programmer's even qualified to be messing with your nanos," she warned.

"I guess you're right, thanks, Dell." Haral held out a hand, then realized he was still covered in muck and withdrew it. "So… through here?" he said, peering through an open doorway into a long, tiled, room with a number of shower heads at a few different heights.

Dell nodded. "Yep, just have your Overlay turn it on and adjust temp. The no-download localized app should pop up right off. I'll find us some coveralls. Mine seem to have become soiled, as well, somehow…"

"Uhh… Sorry again. Thanks again. Is there any way you could turn on the water? My Overlay seems to be having issues."

"I told you…" Dell began to chide him again.

"I get it, I do. Won't happen again, but until I can download a reset…"

"Of course." Dell stared off into space for a moment. "I've turned them on in a range of temps, cooler is nearer the door, hottest by the far wall." Her pleasant tone had cooled a bit. He must have been asking too much. "Hey, how did you know my name?"

"I heard it through the tank wall when I was climbing up and you and your friend—" he began.

Dell interrupted, "Co-worker, and barely that. He thinks he's my boss most of the time. Cash is his name."

"You and Cash were arguing about whether someone could really be in there and all. Thanks for sticking to your guns. I owe you one."

Dell sighed. "Alright, no need for all that. Just get in there and clean up so we can all breathe easier. Are you hungry? Drastic form changes often exact a toll on the body, especially in energy reserves."

"I… don't know… It's hard to think about food when I literally smell like the end product," Haral tried to breathe through his mouth to avoid his own stench.

She nodded. "Fair. I'll get you some clothes and then we can hit the lounge, just two doors down."

"That would be great. Thank you again… again. I wish there was a way to repay you."

"I just want to hear the story that led to you being in that tank." Dell scoffed, making her shoulders bob. With that, she turned and left him in the locker room. A thin steam was already issuing from the showers. Haral heaved a sigh and trudged into the tiled enclosure.

The first shower was too cold by far. He could hardly imagine anyone enjoying a shower so frigid. He imagined he felt his skin hardening under the chilling torrent. He hustled through, slipping and nearly falling trying to get past. The next few were gradually more bearable, but he really wanted a steam cleaning after the day he'd had and the thought of waste all over him. The last one was a little too hot for his usual tastes, but he could endure reddened skin for the freedom from the stench and bacteria that in Old Earth would have made him terribly ill.

"How's it going in there?" Dell called from the locker room.

"Oh! Hey! Great. I feel so much better," he yelled back.

"I'm glad. I've got some clothes for you. I'll just leave them right here on the bench and wait in the hallway."

"Perfect, thanks again," Haral said. "You can turn off the water." The showers all ceased at once. He watched the dense bubbles of the soap he'd used slide down the drain. He'd been down there, and didn't want to visit again any time soon. In the locker room, he found a set of white coveralls with a pale blue logo to match the tank he'd come out of reading "Hygienic Hydration Operation". The last word formed a circle, and the other two branched off at the angle hydrogen atoms sit to one another in a water molecule. *Two "Hs" and an "O," H_2O. Clever.*

Dressing quickly, Haral stepped into the hallway. Dell waited there, but wasn't alone. Beside her, a Flexxe in shades of brown slumped against the white wall layered with blue waves, palest at the top, and gradually darker values at each uneven stratum down until the dark blue merged with the color of the floor. Before he could speak, Haral's stomach rumbled.

Dell laughed. "I was going to ask if you were hungry yet, but I guess we've already heard the answer. Feel better?"

"Tremendously. I don't even have the proper words. It was… like a world of filth down there, and I felt like I brought half of it back with me. I hope your drains can handle it."

"I'm sure it'll be fine. If not, we have the best plumbers around, right, Ffna?" The Flexxe rolled up off the wall, standing at a height between Haral's and the slightly shorter Dell's.

"Unquestionably," the Flexxe said, holding a loop poking from the end of a coverall sleeve toward Haral. "Ffna Rundo."

"Haral Adjani," he said reflexively, only realizing afterward that perhaps he should have made something up.

Blast, he had wasted all that time in the shower just getting clean, not plotting or planning or anything else.

"Oh yeah! Recognize you!" Ffna suddenly exclaimed.

"You do?" Dell and Haral asked in completely different tones. She was impressed. He was concerned. Would they turn him in?

Ffna continued, "Oh yeah, most of my job is waiting around for problems to happen, so I'm what they call a 'superviewer.' I get some media before the general public, and do reviews and reaction videos all the time. I also have hundreds of hours of flight simulators in a dozen different models of old school airplanes and helicopters."

"Oh yes, you *have* to meet Chopper, and maybe Gann…" Haral said.

"*That's* why your apartment is so much nicer than mine," said Dell.

"Well, that, and I have better taste. I decorated it all myself. I've had three different higher PullGrade guests do segments with me for their design and trend feeds," Ffna said.

"You learn something new…" Dell said. "Let's go learn about today's menu!"

"I hear that!" Haral said, using a phrase that had trended earlier that year.

"Ha! You're lucky that's come back around after making the circuit of the recognized senses," Ffna said, "Or I might not be able to eat with you."

Real chefs stood by each food weaver, taking special requests. The air was full of spice and savory scents of seared flesh, fungus, and vegetation, all created by the weaving stored chemicals, applying heat and enzymatic activators and Haral wasn't sure what all. The scents and puffs of warm air brought Nez to mind. He saw in his mind's eye the Xochat standing beside a food weaver in the mess station before he had left for culinary school, awed by the skill of the chef and pointing out to Haral the techniques the other used, like a sports play-by-play.

Another memory chased the first. Nez had been down about a relationship not working out. Then he recalled one of when the Xochat had comforted Haral in the same situation. He remembered enjoying a green space they didn't have enough Pull to really be at, but Nez had followed his olfactory senses to a certain cluster of flowers. A dozen other memories flooded over him.

"Are you all right?" Dell asked.

"Hmm?" Haral asked, his brow furrowing.

"You're crying," she said.

"I'm… just missing my friend, I guess." Haral sniffed and wiped at his face, finding tears on his cheeks.

"Well, we'll figure out how to get you back home soon. Food first," Dell insisted. Haral's stomach loudly agreed. Dell chuckled.

"You are quite far away from home… Swanton Spar is something like five degrees from here," Ffna noted.

"Five degrees? Whole degrees, not millies?" Dell asked, eyes wide. "I've never been half that far from home."

"I was told I should travel." Haral shrugged.

They all laughed. They ate, ravenously. Ffna seemed very fidgety.

"What's on your mind, Ffna?" Haral asked, dragging a fork through the remains of sauce on his plate.

"Am I that transparent?" the Flexxe asked.

"Even I could tell, and I've been distracted catching up with Haral's exploits." Dell indicated her eye with a finger. Not having his Overlay available buzzed like a fly at the back of Haral's mind. He missed the constant contact with his friends and feeds. In a world where they were as natural as breathing, he was forced to hold his breath.

"I've never dined with a fugitive before. Nearly derailing a train, jumping out of a sky restaurant, squirrel-suiting through high-population areas." The Flexxe admitted.

"Yeah, fair enough. I think events got a little exaggerated, but it *was* a wild day."

"It must be if they're still looking for you days later. Something about damaging property, interfering with critical operations…" Ffna said.

"They made that up… but I know *why* they would say that…" Haral decided to bite the bullet. How could he expect them to trust him if he didn't trust them? "I saw something."

"Like what?" Ffna and Dell leaned in.

"An alien." Ffna leaned back out a few degrees.

"That's not what I meant. I'm not one of those throwbacks that thinks if you're not humani you don't belong. I mean species you've never seen, never heard of." Dell gasped. Ffna seemed dubious still. Haral continued, "Look, it's my job—was my job, probably now—to maintain external monitoring systems, communications between sectors and such, but also looking—" He paused to point down through the table. "Out there."

"I knew it!" Ffna exclaimed, then quieted his voice. "I knew we were keeping an eye out. It would be madness not to, don't you think? But they hardly teach anything about space in school anymore. Even old science shows are hard to find, practically contraband."

"Oh, Chopper would love you," Haral smiled.

"'Chopper?'" Ffna asked.

"A friend back home. He always has a… less intuitive answer for everyday oddities."

"Ah, you mean he *knows* things." Ffna dipped one side of his uppermost loop, the equivalent of a wink or a knowing nod. "So… what's happening… outside?" he asked more quietly.

"It's all bits and pieces. I don't have time to tell my whole story, but… We have visitors. There was a crash about a hundred years ago, and now others of their species are here to recover their kin."

"That sounds like an easy win. Hand over the captives… or their bodies, though that would be harder to explain… We must have learned everything we could from them by now, anyway," Dell suggested.

"You would think, but it gets more complicated. You see, their technology, their entire being is incompatible with our tech. Makes nanos go nuts."

"That *would* make it hard to communicate," Ffna agreed.

"You have no idea."

"You've met them?" Ffna was engrossed. Dell squinted at Haral, trying to tell if he was pulling their legs.

Haral nodded. "You could say that. I went to the surface to check on our sensor arrays. Every one in our sector was wiped off the Shell, completely gone."

"No!" They both exclaimed.

"Then…" Haral let the word stretch, creating tension. He had learned a few things about storytelling from his feed.

"Yes?" They leaned in closer.

"Then they picked up my exosuit and peeled it off me like the rind of a fruit."

"Whoa!" Ffna had flushed a greenish color and could hardly hold his quasi-humanoid form he was so excited.

"I'm sorry, you're telling me you, you *personally* have made contact with an alien race," Dell said, cocking her head and raising an eyebrow.

"That has messed up my nanos," Haral agreed. Dell just stared for a moment before comprehension dawned on her face.

"You're either very, very good, or… That's why you couldn't run the shower for yourself."

Haral nodded. "Or check my feeds or messages, let anyone know I'm all right… *if* I'm all right…"

"And you need to keep a low profile because some shady PullSys operatives are after you," Ffna suggested. Haral nodded slowly.

"I've got to get to the southern polar region. I think… I think one of them from that first crash has been surviving there all this time, hiding out."

"Imagine… hiding for a century…" Ffna said, attention drifting away as though he was trying to cram that whole period into one daydream.

"Can you help me one more time?" Haral asked.

PART III: THE SOUTH

Chapter Fifteen

Simultaneously, Dell said, "No!" and Ffna said, "Of course!" They looked at one another and demanded, "'Of course?' Are you mad?" and "'No?' Are you heartless?"

"Shh!" Haral said, then looked down at his plate. "I understand if it's too risky, or if you just don't believe me. I appreciate the help you've given me so far. I just ask if you feel it's your duty to turn me in that you give me a head start."

"No one's turning you in," Ffna assured him, "*Right, Dell?*"

"I… I don't know what your game is, if you're just pranking us, or you're off your meds, or what, but this is all just too much. Aliens? That's just… a bridge too far as my great grandfather says." The wastewater tech twisted her napkin into a ratty spindle, eyes everywhere but on Haral.

"I don't know how to convince you right now, and I can't spend time waiting here to try. The General could have agents on their way here right now. I can't stay anywhere until I've met up with this alien and work things out."

"So aliens *and* you're the ambassador for all of Geode? A trillion plus people?" Dell scoffed.

"I understand. It was good meeting you, Dell, Ffna, but I should get going. Could one of you point me toward the south? Without my Overlay, it's so easy to get lost."

"I get that," Ffna said, "in the Flexxe genome, there's a recessive gene that pops up every once in a while that makes those individuals that get the triple shot intolerant to nanos. No Overlay, no morphing, healing, navigation, music and video feeds… It's truly sad, like they're stuck in the past."

"I'm sorry to hear that, but I know what it feels like now," Haral said.

"Come on, Haral, I'll get you to the seashore," Ffna said.

Dell looked at him in horror. "Ffna! That's hours away. We're in the middle of a work cycle!"

"Seven hours, according to Overlay. I've got time off saved up," Ffna said. "Let's go."

"Thank you so much, Ffna. Sorry to intrude on your day, Dell, but thank you for your kindness."

Haral and Ffna returned their trays and utensils to the sanitizer and headed out the door.

"Do you mind if I get a few selfies? Maybe a short interview I can shop around to some friends?" Ffna asked.

Haral nodded. "Of course, just don't post anything until I'm away, all right? For your safety as much as mine. These people are deadly serious. I still don't know what happened to Laeua…"

The Flexxe looked at him. "Laeua Kio? Your new girlfriend? Apparently, according to her feed, they scanned her and interrogated her and let her go. No doubt she's living her life under active surveillance, bait for if you go to her." A wave of relief flooded over Haral. They might not have known each other long, but he had jumped after her when her mother threw her out of Escamilla's. There was clearly a connection between them.

"Thank you for that. I would love to, but she's safer without me," Haral responded.

"That is most likely true for the moment," Ffna said, not unkindly.

"What about you? Aren't you worried?" Haral asked.

Ffna replied, "A little, but I need some adventure, and if this all plays out how I hope, maybe I won't ever have to go pipe-diving again."

"Pull isn't all it seems, but it was nice for the first day. I'm sure it'll go better for you," Haral said. As they spoke, Ffna recorded and they threw up all kinds of signs of greetings from peace signs to heart thumbs and unity salutes.

"Wait! Wait!" Dell yelled after them from the other end of a long passage. She hustled to catch up. Haral looked at Ffna who looked back at him and nodded. They waited for nearly a minute for Dell to arrive, breathing heavily. Haral looked out over the unfamiliar spars. They didn't seem that different. "OK, I'm in. This is crazy, but I don't know… I *shouldn't* believe you. It's all way out there, but for some reason, I do…"

"I can appreciate that. It's all new and scary to me, too," Haral said.

They continued south to the HHO corporate rail, smaller but faster than the public train.

"It will get us there, and should be empty, unless someone else from the company has business in the south," Ffna said.

"What's going on? What happened to 'empty'?" Haral asked. The terminal was crowded with casually dressed folk of all kinds. The Flexxe shrugged, an exaggerated movement of the loops comprising his "shoulders."

"Oh wait! It's Last Drop Day! We peons just get the chefs to make lunch, but the upper management get a trip to the coast, a full three days of HighPull experiences and a party train to get them from their offices to the highest concentration of wealth in the world," Ffna replied.

"Is it true they don't even have proper spars down there? Everyone has their own personal mini-spar, fully customized, and not even required to be solar-film coated to generate their own power?" Dell asked.

"Absolutely. The rich have always had the best toys, the best food, the best everything, and once every revolution the middles get to play in the riches' world to keep them motivated to deal with the stress of being in charge of so many workers," Ffna said.

"OK, but how do we get on the train? They're all in sparkly dresses and costumes," Haral pointed out, "We'll stand out."

"Unmissable," Dell agreed, "Especially since you don't have anything on underneath your coveralls."

"Look," said Ffna, "I think those are changing booths." The others turned to see a row of cloth-walled cabanas with short lines of folk in more everyday dress or business suits leading to each. "Shall we?"

Once again, Haral was smacked in the face by the reality of being unable to use his Overlay. He stood in the booth, cloth walls puffing out and pushing in with the wind like the whole tiny building was breathing, standing on a circular pad with a sextet of smaller pads around the edge, trying to figure out if there was a manual control.

"All right in there?" Someone called from outside.

"Yeah, uh, just having a hard time deciding," Haral lied.

"Train leaves in fifteen, so you'd better make up your mind or you'll be left behind. I wouldn't want to miss the party."

"You're right," Haral agreed, "What are you going to choose?" But apparently, the moment was over, because he didn't get a response. "Hmm…" he thought aloud, remembering what Ffna had said about a certain population of his people not being able to use the Overlay. He was certain he had heard of others like that as well, like a fraction of Rulabs. It made a degree of sense, seeing as the tech was largely developed by humani, and they were pretty self-centered, if less than in previous millennia.

Still, a Flexxe outfit modeled after a humani form would work perfectly, if the changing pad was set up for the nano-intolerant. But how to access it?

"Need some help?" Dell. Haral sighed. It wasn't fair to her to have to rely on her help with every little thing.

"I can do it… if you happen to know how to get into handicap mode."

"Ah, right, no Overlay. Should be somewhere along the edge of the main pad, I should think. Mind if I come in?"

"I suppose. I mean, you've already seen me naked," Haral joked.

"What would Laeua say?" she asked with a laugh.

"Ouch, touché. Sorry, no more jokes. Help me, please?" He asked.

Dell entered the small tent with a flash of daylight from the door flap. "Like I said back in the lounge, I've seen some of your videos, and your current rating. That

Merit Lang fellow is searching for you. Apparently, he's keeping your memory alive. Your rating is—"

"Tanking? Rising?" He shook his head to dispel the thoughts. "Never mind. I don't want to know. This isn't about Pull, none of it. I'm just trying to survive."

"And Merit is just an empty sack? Not a friend?" She pressed.

"I'm not really sure he *is* my friend. I knew him for a day. If he's searching for me now, it's to synergize more Pull."

"If I could show you his feed, you might think again," she said.

"He's probably a really good actor. He's been HighPull his whole life, grew up putting on a show."

"All right, enough. Just let me pick something for you, or we'll miss the train. I don't have a plan B for getting to the coast. Do you?" She asked.

"No… Fine… Thank you…" Haral said, defeated by circumstance once again.

A gray-lit memory impinged on the moment. Small flashing things cruised through the water, around irregular rocks and past larger forms, into shadows and back out into the sunlight, keeping their place in the mob of hundreds, twisting and darting as one.

"Haral? Hello?" Dell again.

"Yeah, sorry, daydreaming, I guess. What were you saying?"

"Something called a fire-man, or a cow-boy. Both look nothing like you would expect from their names, but at least they come with full sets of clothing. Many of the female counterpart ones have… considerably less material."

"I—I don't know…" But then he realized he *did* know, again thanks to Gann. He had gone through a Westerns phase some years ago, watched hundreds of movies and some connected series centered on the riders of the Old West, which was apparently part of but different from Old Earth, as a square was a rectangle, but a rectangle wasn't necessarily a square. "Cowboy. Please." Funny thing, many of those movies had been produced in shades of glowing gray… Hmm…

Ffna had chosen to lean into his flexibility and was some kind of ancient sea creature with a bunch of legs and a large head. Dell had gone with a very colorful outfit of knee-high boots in rainbow bands, a shiny black skirt and vest, and a puffy purple shirt that billowed around her arms and rode low on her chest, along with a pile of metal necklaces. Her very tall spiked teal hairdo reminded him of Laeua, at least in spirit. Haral's outfit was in mostly browns, but with a red fringe along the seam of the arms and along the edge of the body of the shirt. He also wore boots that clanged with small bells on his heels at every step.

"We look great!" Ffna said, sliding up close to the others and using a longer loop to hold up his card and take a groupie.

"Wait, don't—" Haral said, reaching for the card.

"And sent!"

"Oh… We should probably hustle out of here. Tell me you didn't get the train in the picture," Haral pled.

"I don't think… nope, why? Oh… I'm… Oh. I forgot… I'm sor—" Ffna stuttered.

"No, no, no, not your fault, we just need to be on this train and long gone before they get here. Does it make any stops? Like at other depots where we… Or at least *I* can hop trains?" Haral asked.

"I don't think so. I'm pretty sure it's a straight shot charter type thing. Unless they need to pick someone up from an outlying office…" the Flexxe fell silent for a moment. "No, I don't see any. There *are* a couple of other party trains headed to the coast, though, from a few different offices. Looks like they're all scheduled to arrive at the same time. Well over a thousand middle-managers dressed for—" Someone nearby whooped so loudly, Haral lost the rest of what Ffna was saying, or perhaps he stopped when the wave of sound rolled over him.

"We should get on the train. I think that was the last bell you might say." They all hustled, pushing past a few stragglers and finding the nearest cars to be standing room only. They continued on, moving up car after car as the crowd slowly thinned.

In minutes, the train was soaring past spars Haral had never seen, farther south than he'd ever been. He was in Alagain's sector, and there was very little call for inter-sector travel for work. Most of what he had done was via drone, after all. It made him wonder, though. Had Rider's people been somewhere down there, searching for their missing explorers? Or were they hovering above the Shell, trying to find a way in even now? He had no idea how to ask his rider, nor any idea if the other would answer if he could.

The crowd quickly spread throughout the train, increasing the density of the car they were in, but reducing the density overall, making it traversable. People drank and ate and sang and danced and all manner of images and

193

clips played across the ceilings, the seats, and the floor via surface displays.

Even the simple things, like a clock, were beyond Haral's reach given the Overlay that would probably kill him in another day or so, anyway… Maybe it had been the continued use of the Overlay that had led to those others' quick deaths. How long could he go without breathing? How long had Whip's father lasted? The others? How much had each used their Overlay after getting a rider? How long until they figured out what the problem was? Answers to all these questions were in the books the General had taken from him. He sighed.

A gray veil fell over Haral's vision, wiping away dozens of Geode denizens dressed up as people and creatures and even a tree and a signpost. Everything was awash in rolling waves of barely discernible height above a surface of pale gray. Rider again, showing him their own world, which appeared to be featureless and covered in just them. How did they eat? Everything had to eat, right? Perhaps they gained energy from the sun like Geode's tech and plants. There had to be some overlap, right? For there to be interference… Rider pulled his attention back to what was happening, even though he didn't understand what he was seeing beyond the most rudimentary observations.

I don't… He began, but knew the other couldn't translate his words any more than he could translate movement in their fluid body. What memory could convey confusion? This one, tomorrow, he thought to himself, but focused, trying to reach back through the years.

Haral stood in Gann's office for the first time, before the other had adopted the silver face. He had

looked like an average humani, nondescript, but already
carrying four arms. He had some financial allowance for
adjustments that would help him with his job, not real Pull
itself. He stood before a bank of flat screens of a style
Haral had never seen before, tapping buttons and keys on
replicas of ancient keyboards. The whole thing looked like
a mixed-up museum exhibit.

Something crashed into him, knocking him from
the memory and direct contact with Rider. He hoped his
message had gotten through. He came back to his senses
with a man sitting on his lap, laughing and spilling a drink
on himself and Haral.

"Tha's a great hat!" he said, standing with the help
of the back of the next seat and staggering off.

Haral tried to wipe away the liquid, but it mostly
soaked into the cloth of his tan shirt. He looked around for
Ffna and Dell, finding them at the minibar, talking, one of
Ffna's costume tentacles wrapped around Dell's hand.
Haral was rethinking bothering them when Dell looked
over, waving him forward with her free hand, barely
rescuing her drink as a mechanical hand reached from the
minibar to clear it away.

He rose and walked to them with a stiff gait. His
body felt somewhat less responsive than usual. Perhaps
the breakdown from Rider was coming whether he used
the Overlay or not… They did figure it out, that's why
Whip never got the nanos, but when had they figured it
out? After everyone was dead? Maybe not using the
Overlay would save him, but he couldn't like a normal life
like that. The train swayed around Haral as he worked his
way to his friends, his body becoming less and less
responsive.

"Are you all right?" Dell asked.

"I…" Haral managed but pitched over before he could get another word out.

"Too much already? How did such a lightweight get to be a manager?" Someone observed, inciting a round of laughter. A long flat loop zigzagged against his body, pulling him back up to his feet. He tried to thank Ffna, but nothing came out. The walls flashed red, then yellow, then back to red, solid blocks of color for a few cycles before the General's face appeared.

"Haral Adjani, you are the subject of a criminal arrest warrant. Failure to cooperate may result in injury to yourself, your companions, or bystanders. Remain in place. Agents are on their way to take you into custody."

"Ggg!" Haral grunted.

"What's this all about? He doesn't look like everyday PullSys Regs," Dell said.

"Gen-ral!" Haral managed to get out through the paralysis gripping most of his body.

"General? That's a military rank. We haven't had a military for centuries…" Ffna said, "Except for the secret Geode Defense Force."

"It's no time for conspiracy theories, Ffna," Dell said.

"It's not a conspiracy. You can see him right in front of your face," Ffna argued.

"What would we need a defense force for? Who would they defend us against?"

"Aliens?" Ffna said as though the question was so blatantly obvious that it didn't bear asking.

Dell scoffed. "It's all just stories. The only sapient species in light years are here already."

"As far as you know… I thought you believed Haral," Ffna said. Haral felt his muscles tighten further. Actual breathing was becoming difficult. Was he breathing at all? He began to panic, but the only one who knew was Rider.

The General's face was replaced by Haral's all over the car.

A cacophony of voices reached him:

"Hey, I've seen that guy! He's one of the new HighPullers. Leonardo Sperra met with him a few days ago! Zero to 5 mill in like a day?"

"And Natalie Tattle-y interviewed him on a train. Is he here?"

"Haral Adjani's here?" a woman squealed. "Where? Don't you think he's just the cutest?"

Far from locked down, the car seemed animated now, everyone peering around for Haral to try to get a selfie in before he was arrested. Being the last person to take a picture with someone while they were still famous was worth something in some circles, even when the subject fell off the charts.

Chapter Sixteen

We've got to get you out of here," Ffna said, "but to where?"

"What? I mean, I feel for the guy, too, and this has been fun and all, but… What are we going to risk for him? Our freedom? Our lives?" Dell asked.

"Now who's being dramatic?" Ffna said, "*Lives?*"

Could be, they held me in a cage, talked about dissecting me, Haral thought.

"What?" Ffna asked, shocked, his grip loosening on Haral, who dipped before the Flexxe exerted himself again.

"*What* what?" Dell asked.

"Say that again," Ffna prompted.

When they captured me and Laeua, Haral said inside his head, experimentally, *they put me in a cage in an emptied-out river section. That's part of how I really ended up in that wastewater tank.* Haral hoped that it wasn't just his imagination that Ffna had heard him.

"What are you talking about? This is not the ideal time to go crazy," Dell said to Ffna.

"He's talking to me, somehow, inside my mind," Ffna said.

"Who? The General?" Dell asked.

"Haral," Ffna replied.

You can *hear me!* Haral rejoiced.

"How are you doing that?" Ffna asked, astonished.

"Ffna, this isn't fu… nny… Oh my…! What *is* that?" Dell demanded.

I'm not sure. It might have something to do with… Well, I'm not really sure what it's called. But the general calls them riders. I have a suspicion that "they" aren't so much a "they" as an "it."

"Not making yourself clearer," Ffna said. Dell grabbed Ffna's loop, bypassing the costume.

"Look!" Dell insisted, staring out the window.

"Oh no!" Ffna exclaimed. Haral followed their gazes as best he could. At least half a dozen dark gray, boxy troop carriers were converging on the train.

They're here for me. I can't put you all in danger. Just um… throw me out into the water. Draw them away.

"What?" Dell asked. "Now *I'm* hearing things."

"I think somehow I've tapped into Haral's brain channel and you're listening in through me. Don't let go," Ffna said.

"Damned right I'm not letting go of you," Dell said.

I thank you both for all you've risked, but they have weapons, the kinds of things that can kill you and other bystanders. Just let me go, get rid of—

"Wait, what's happening?" Dell asked. "Everyone out here is… They're all Haral!"

What? What do you mean?

"There was a kind of gray cloud that fell over the whole car, and then everyone kind of morphed into you! Ah! Even me!" she said, looking down at her free hand, which was a lighter shade of brown and somewhat broader than before.

"Ahh! There he is!" A riot of calls and demands rang out through the car.

"Can I get a selfie?"

"Haral! Over here!"

Rider… The gray light thing happens whenever it shows me a memory. Its people don't seem to have language, any language, numbers, words, symbols as we know them. Everything is shared via sensory experience memory.

"Fascinating. I mean, I thought humani languages were strange, especially in their variety, versus only the two Flexxe languages, which are by needs very different, if based on the same thought process, but no words…?" The Flexxe trailed off.

"Who's this 'Rider?'" Dell asked.

The simplest way to put it is that when the visitor, the alien, got here, it sent itself into our sensor array. Anyone who was connected to the systems at the time got… injected with a part of the alien consciousness. When I went to the surface, I think it completed the job in a way it hadn't been able to with anyone else. The General called it my "Rider." Without words, or probably names of their own, I guess it's kind of become its name, the creature "riding" my nervous system.

"And *that's* interfering with your Overlay, because of the language thing," Dell concluded.

I think so, yes. The scientists were sure it would kill me, but I think I'm learning how to deal with it being there and not getting my brain shorted out. Rider must *be the one projecting my appearance over everyone.*

"So that hides you, but what about this paralysis? Where do we take you and how do we get there? I'm not just tossing you in the ocean when you can't even move," Ffna said.

"Sir, they're *all* Adjani," a clipped voice said nearby. Two flying personnel carriers had docked with the end cars of the train, which had been halted in mid-air. Soldiers streamed through the doors and along the length of the train.

"*We're* all Adjani, sir!" another soldier said, pointing to his comrades.

"Look for the unconscious one. We had an agent drug the target. He'll be passed out for another twenty, easy."

"They're confused for the moment, but I don't see this ruse lasting the twenty minutes that voice claimed, and I'm cut off from my Overlay. No messages, no searches, nothing," Dell whispered.

"Probably part of arrest protocol," Ffna said. "But I have an idea… Follow my lead." Ffna stood, visibly dragging Haral behind him. Dell helped support the paralyzed repair tech and they moved toward the door.

"Nobody in or out. Each car is to be searched for the fugitive," the military man who looked just like Haral said sharply.

"Got him right here. Bringing him back to the transport," Ffna said, replicating the other's tone.

"You sure, soldier? Lots of look alikes around here. No doubt the invader's doing."

"This is him," Ffna said with reassuring certainty. "Move aside so I can get him on the transport." The other held up a scanner which he passed over Haral's face and arm. The device beeped and a green light shown on the front.

"Good work, soldier. We'll hold down the fort in case he has allies that try to free him before he's fully secured. Shame there's not enough room for a wrapper in here."

"Shame," Ffna agreed and pulled Haral through the door and onto a short gangplank with rope grapple railings.

The transport was about the size of the train car they'd just left, but with only a narrow horizon of window at the front and numerous panels, which Haral imagined hid weapons and manipulators, along the sides. Within, the pilot remained at his post and an operator, like Gann, sat before a bank of screens with a headset to help isolate the sounds from the feed from the noises in the vessel. Neither were looking at the door when the trio entered.

"Three's company," Ffna said as he let Haral drop onto the bench seat and turned toward the operator. In a second, he had anchored himself to the supports of a nearby bench behind the humani, wrapped loops around all four of his limbs and his throat. In the next second, the headset cord pulled free of the console and the whole soldier sailed through the open doorway, catching an arm on the rope railing and tumbling away into the sky beneath the floating train track's maglev beacons. Two and a quarter spins in, the operator came to and loosed a scream that faded over long seconds.

"Hey!" the pilot hollered, roused from her daydreaming by the operator's inarticulate cry.

"'Hey' yourself," Ffna said, hauling the pilot from her seat and launching her out the door as well, then slapping the gangplank retraction command on her console. The ropes snapped from their anchors and slithered back into sockets to either side of the door.

"What the undercity goblins was that?" Dell demanded.

"They'll be fine. I'm sure they have morphing suites for every environment, and distress beacons. They might not even hit the water, if others are on their game," the Flexxe shrugged.

"What's going on over there, SCD-003?" A voice came over the operator's communicator, defaulting to speaker mode since the headset was gone.

"We're all fine here," Ffna said into the console's mic, slamming down the channel button to cut off the conversation. "Let's go!"

"You know how to fly this thing?" Dell asked, incredulous.

"Of course! You know all those simulators I play. I've worked my way up to max skill level, which is modeled directly off of commercial cockpits and controls. I assume all this stuff I don't recognize is like guns and things."

"'Stuff you don't recognize?'" Dell asked, not sounding at all reassured.

"It'll be fiiine," Ffna said, elongating the word 'fine', while dragging a control to one side. The transport leaned in the same direction, pulling away from the train. "Where are we going again? Ah yeah, south. That covers a lot of area, but the farther south we go, the smaller the area is, and the less likely they are to chase us."

"'Chase us?' Do you hear yourself?" Dell yelled.

"Calm down, sweetie. I've got this," he replied confidently.

"'Calm down?' Did you seriously just tell me to 'calm down?'" She demanded.

"Or you know, familiarize yourself with the weapons console. I think it's this one." As Ffna spoke, bolts of radiant energy zizzed past the transport into the sky. Haral hoped it would lose power by the time it reached whatever spar was unlucky enough to be in its path. Geode was a closed form, after all.

"You might be having a little too much fun, my friend," Haral said, "How about no more shooting unless we have to."

"Seconded," Dell agreed.

Ffna banked and wove, trying to present a more difficult target while distancing the GDF forces from the train and the private islands they were passing over. A number of irate HighPull folk or their representatives raised voices and shook fists from the screen just below the narrow window, blocking out parts of the external view Ffna was working with.

Haral, wholly out of control of his body still, edged closer and closer to the brink of the bench seat where Ffna had left him and was thrown back a number of times by the maneuvers. It couldn't last forever, and he fell hard onto the floor, back first. Pain blossomed across his shoulders and up his neck.

For a few minutes longer, he slid around beneath the seats, observing crude carvings and wads of something beneath the benches and careening off support poles. Finally, as he had hoped when he'd overheard the discussion of his poisoning, he began to regain some control over his limbs and managed to wedge himself between two rises in the flooring near the back wall.

"Whoops! What did that do? We didn't blow up…" From Dell was followed by a seam of bright light playing down over Haral and air tore over the opening with a whistling roar, creating all kinds of frightening pseudo-vocalizations.

"Guys!" Haral tried to say, wishing Ffna had thought to leave him a bit of loop to talk through, but his voice was weak and the wind was strong. The rear wall continued to angle outward, letting more wind in. The roar deepened and broadened and pulled at his clothes. The cowboy hat, on the floor between a couple of the bench seats, rose up like an early movie flying saucer, wobbling and zipping around, then exited with a small "woom!"

"Guys!" Haral tried again.

"Oh, sacred signal! That wall's a door?" Dell cried out, slapping the board before her. With a grinding noise, the protrusions Haral had seated himself between rolled away, tearing his vest, but also revealing a folding seat which held him awkwardly sideways, and a curved windscreen, below which was a small console and two-handled yoke arrayed with colored buttons. Red crosshairs appeared in the windscreen. Two other transports appeared in the growing field of white and blue before him. Dell said something else, but it was lost on Haral as the whole chair jerked slightly, placing the reticule automatically on the rightmost transport.

"Oh no…" Haral said, trying to summon enough strength to wrench himself out of the seat, which had auto-formed around his body as a safety measure. His arms were pinned and still weakened, his legs flailed ineffectively. Then the whole assembly rose from the floor and swung out through the doorway into open air, firing at the first ship. The pilot evaded, barely, and then the two transports he had seen and another coming in at an angle began firing steady streams of light pulses.

Get us out of here! Haral yelled in his head. Words were useless. Ffna was occupied. Haral crammed his eyes shut, trying to focus on fleeing, a memory of running, at the very least. Amid the rushing air and *knowing* the sea was unbelievably far below them right now kept returning him to his leap from Escamilla's. He fought it at first, but then realized if Rider could help him get the squirrel morph back, he could distance himself from Ffna and Dell, saving them by leading the General's soldiers away, and continue to head south once he hit the water and changed again to a fish form. It was the closest thing to a plan that had gelled in his head for some time.

As if in acknowledgment, a gray light filled the space behind his eyes he felt his body slide and loosen. In seconds, he was free from the molded seat and falling. Haral opened his eyes and pushed his arms apart. The air caught him a bit, sending him end over end until he pushed his legs into position. Then he evened out, gliding at a downward angle that would have sent his stomach into flips just days before. Now, though, it almost seemed natural. Almost. At least control was easier without another person strapped to his chest. This led him to think about Laeua: wondering how she was, what she thought, what PullSys was allowing out into the world about the current situation.

A hot blast of energy seared the air just inches from Haral's face, baking into his cheek and throwing off a pressure wave that bowled him over to the side. He spun chaotically, feeling distinctly less comfortable than he had moments before. He struggled to straighten his limbs and regain control of his fall even as bulky transports moved in to either side and behind him.

Perhaps this had not been the wondrous plan he had envisioned.

Mechanical grippers emerged from panels, reaching toward Haral. He spun away from one only to be gabbed by another. Squirming, he managed to pull free, tearing part of his skin-wing with a spray of blood which hung in the air for a moment, gleaming globules of bright red, before being scattered. Metal fingers grasped him from both directions and he was drawn toward the yawning maw at the back of one of the transports.

No! This can't be it! He struggled. Even falling would be preferable to capture, the torture and death the shadow had predicted before helping him escape. In the sea, he'd have a chance. Thoughts of the waves far below brought a familiar sensation, casting his vision in silvery grays again.

Before an image began to form, Haral took control and reached for his encounter on the alien vessel. He saw the exosuit tearing around him, metal shredding to some unseen force. The claws fell away in pieces as the now blunt ends of the arm swept at him. He closed his eyes, pulling his limbs in to try to get them to heal faster under the nanos' influence.

Something grabbed him around the waist, pinning his arms. This wasn't another metal grasper, though, but a gray and green-outfitted soldier with helmet and polymer armor plates on his torso and limbs standing on a small glider. Haral tried to squirm, but the other was strong, enhanced by nanos, no doubt, the best and most advanced for the GDF, no Pull required.

"Let me… grr…" Haral demanded, but the other squeezed harder, pressing the air from his lungs. He looked up at the other's face, focusing past his own reflection in the other's goggles to stare into the soldier's eyes. Gray spread over both of them. Haral saw a picnic, on a blanket, in a greenspace, but not one he recognized. This wasn't a school trip or his family or Nez. It dawned on him that it was the soldier's memory.

He saw the man and his wife, a child, too young to guess its gender, barely sitting up, reaching for every smaller storage container their parents drew forth from the basket.

"What are you do—?" The soldier asked, his grip weakening a few degrees. One arm released Haral entirely, swatting at something on the control arch to his side. The clamps holding the soldier's feet in place released. "Ants! I didn't know we still had ants!" The man muttered as he stepped back, tipping back off the glider, swatting at himself.

"Nice one," Haral said, then tried to send Rider a happy thought. The first thing he thought of to show his appreciation for the aid was a man in a large room, surrounded by others clapping while he danced a dance full of jerking elbows and knees from one of Gann's movies.

"Now, how do I work this thing?" Haral said to no one as he fit his cowboy boots into the bindings and looked over the array of controls on the crescent of metal at his side. Before he could figure anything out, the craft began moving on its own, shooting right toward the open bay of the ship that had tried to grab him with mechanical arms. "Ugh, should have figured that…" He sighed, trying to pull out of the bindings.

"Give it up, Adjani," the General's voice stabbed at him from the console, "there's nowhere to go and no way to get there. Just sit back and enjoy the view. You're going to be a in a metal box for the rest of your life unless I can get that rider out of your head… and even then, you've given me such a hard time, you might anyway."

Haral hauled harder at one foot, then the other, using the console for leverage and managing to free one foot from its boot. As he worked, though, the glider swooped toward the transport.

"Come on! Or… off!" He demanded of the boot, finally making progress as he passed the opening at the rear of the craft. Desperate, he grabbed onto the edge with both hands, bracing for the wrenching of his ankle as the glider tried to go on and he tried to remain. The pain that flooded through his foot and ankle made him think he might have lost the appendage entirely. He gritted his teeth. Tears streamed down his face. Stars swam in his vision. He fell onto the lowered back wall of the transport with a thud and scrambled toward the edge, intent on flinging himself to freedom.

A net fell over him as his left hand cleared the edge of the wall, already ascending. He tried to grip the edge and pull himself up, but there were four healthy soldiers who hadn't been on the run for days, sleep deprived, half-starved, and fearing their imminent deaths at the other end of the net. He was quickly immobilized, lying on the cold metal floor. Rough hands lifted him.

A metal chair had been welded to the flooring. This one had straps which were wrapped around his torso and limbs before the rear wall was back in position, bringing relative silence.

"I'm disappointed, Mr. Adjani," the General said solemnly. "You could have been a good citizen and told me what I needed to know, helped yourself to boot. Instead, we have to do all this," he waved one arm from the elbow to encompass the situation, "just for you to be back in the same, exact, position."

"Nng!" Haral struggled against his restraints, gaining no ground. He closed his eyes and tried to envision the waves in the wave pool rising up and washing him off his feet.

The General laughed. "Nice try. We thought you might have gained some control over the creature."

"Asking for help is different to having control," Haral spat. "It's not a monster."

"Oh, let me read your mind for a moment, since it seems to be the hot thing, 'I'm the monster,' right?"

"If the uniform fits…" Haral spat.

"Lower the device," the General said. A transparent bubble lined with wired and black protrusions descended over Haral's head, encapsulating it entirely. The air within buzzed. "*You* are in the same position, but *we* have a much better hand. You see, those books you brought us held quite a wealth of information. They described from a variety of perspectives exactly what happened to the infected subjects one hundred years ago. With our advances and a larger team having an idea of what they were looking for, we hit upon a remedy in just a couple of days. Then you popped up. Well-timed, I'd say, for the safety of Geode, anyway, not so much for you… Sadly, while we were able to extract and isolate the enemy, stuff the genie in the bottle, as it were, we were too late to save the host…"

"It's not the enemy, and I'm not infected!" Haral growled. "Let me go! I can end this without anyone else getting hurt!"

"Mmm, or I can end this with only one getting hurt and everything being firmly under my control. I think I'll take choice B. Pump him." The buzz increased in intensity and pitch. Haral's vision went gray again, but he could feel it sliding over his back and his shoulders as though a cape was being pulled off from above.

"Rider! No!" Haral shouted.

"You didn't even learn its name? Or give it one? How sad," the General mocked.

Haral snapped, "It doesn't have a name. They don't have language, not like anything we know, no symbolism, just memories, shared."

"Something so different, and you're protecting it over your people?" The General asked, eyebrow raised.

"Are you an example of 'my people?' Then yes," Haral said.

"Suck it out of there," the General ordered. The machine's hum intensified, accompanied by crackling. Haral's hair stood up. A few strands hit the nodes, incinerating immediately into wafts of a sharp, harsh chemical-smelling smoke. Before he could speak again, or figure out how to resist the machine's pull, the gray tint to his vision vanished. A pressure he didn't realize had been there released like a balloon losing air.

"Extraction successful, General," someone said, "Rider seems to be intact and contained."

"Excellent. Dump the ballast. Another sad case of some kid getting too much Pull too fast and not being able to handle it." The General turned and walked away. Others scrambled in, hands all over his body, rolling him over, then again, toward the back wall.

"What? You're just going to throw me in the ocean?"

"I don't see why not," the General said nonchalantly.

"And you? You're just going to do it?" Haral asked those actually manhandling him.

"Orders," one of the rollers shrugged. The other didn't respond at all. Once he was propped against the wall, the soldiers retreated and someone hit a control which started an alarm and let the roar of wind back into the cabin.

The first muscles he gained control over again were his trunk and back muscles. He twisted his body, trying to roll away from the door. Focusing, he managed to extend one arm, changing his center of gravity and tipping. Pulling or pushing was right out, though. His whole body felt like he had been asleep for days, muscles forgetting how to tighten, how to move his weight around. He couldn't make a fist, even if he'd known how to throw it to good effect. The grating of the floor dug into his face, his knees.

A chill carried in on the blasting wind, sending a shiver of adrenaline or some other panic chemical through his body. He jerked and bent his head forward, managing to finally fall onto his side, then his back. His Overlay flickered back to life. It surprised him, as he'd started getting used to not having it. He strained to pull his legs up to his chest and roll partway over again. Message alerts streamed into his consciousness, a warbling tone of hundreds of pings blending together. Focusing past this, he could see the device where they held Rider, a clear jar of swirling gray fluid streaked with bright blue glowing fractals of energy.

"Somebody get him out of here and close the door. The wind is making it hard to adjust the controls," one of the team members in long blue lab coats demanded. None of the others looked up. Nobody wanted to be the one to *actually* kill him, to be singularly responsible, he guessed. He rolled over onto his knees and hands, got a foot under himself and pushed. It was easier than it would have been back home, so high were they, the gravity lessened, but also more difficult, as his body was still adjusting to the change of Rider being gone.

"Anyone ever tell you you're a real pain the ass, Adjani?" the General asked, turning toward him and pulling something from a holder on his hip. It was black, roughly "L" shaped. Haral's eyes widened. He'd only seen a gun in Gann's movies before all this. He didn't know they even still made them. Seemed like a bad choice. Haral pulled himself all the way up with a hand on the wall, while wind pulled at him from behind.

"More than once."

"I'm not surprised." The General lifted his weapon to point at Haral.

"Sir! What if someone links the damage to your weapon?" The blue-coat who had called for his more immediate death said.

"No one will find the body. The fish aren't going to report me," the General said calmly.

The General pulled the trigger. The sharp report of the weapon overwhelmed the cacophony of the winds swirling around Haral.

Chapter Seventeen

Fire flashed at the opening of the gun. A heavy blow struck Haral's chest like a burning fist. His feet left the deck of the transport. His arms raised before him, a conductor beginning a symphony. He spun away from the General, caught once again by the wind. Clouds and the ever-present sun wheeled above him as he came around to face the other ships.

They had continued to fly south after they caught up with Ffna's stolen transport. Haral could feel gravity waning and spotted one of the famous waterspouts in the distance. Rider glowed brighter in its container, whether from nearing its missing part, or from concern for him, or something the scientists were doing to it, Haral had no idea. The blazing jar flashed past his field of vision one more time before he fell below the level of the transport.

Pain burrowed into his chest, radiating out like roots of burning ice, some alien plant he knew was actually death blossoming. This couldn't be happening, could it? Nobody *died* anymore. How Old Earth was that? Would Gann throw him a funeral like in so many of his movies? It would have to rain, and everyone would wear black and throw flowers on the box where his body was. There wasn't really any soil, though, except in greenspaces. He supposed that could be worse. Eternity in a greenspace, even if he didn't actually get to witness it…

Come on! He urged himself. *This isn't it. You've got your Overlay back. You can do this.* He opened his Overlay search, ignoring the red "new message" dots stacked up along the left side of his HUD like a gaudy necklace. Dozens of lines of flashing subjects insisted their information was the most urgent. He searched up and clicked the download for an upgrade for his healing nanos, only to find he'd been blocked from downloading anything during his arrest. They probably wouldn't bother to reverse that in the next couple of minutes…

Still, he had the squirrel suit… He accessed the app directly, but gray blocks and blotches stood in the way of the interface and his clicks didn't go through. Residual damage from Rider? Of course, gliding wouldn't keep him alive as his heart stopped… The pain had faded into a dull ache across his entire torso, just starting to reach into his limbs. The cold at the center of his chest had only deepened.

Not knowing what else to do, Haral opened a new message share, adding his parents, Laeua, Nez, Merit, Gann and Chopper to the direct send list, leaving forwarding open in case there was someone he'd forgotten in his distraction.

"Hi guys," he began, "I don't have a will. Never thought I'd need one, never had anything worth passing down, anyway. But I did want to say goodbye. I've learned a lot from each of you, and called many of you friends and loved ones for many years. For newer friends, I'm sorry I didn't get to know you better or spend more time together. I hope PullSys lets this message be sent…"

He was drifting downward now, still spinning slowly, but managing to at least stabilize a bit even without the sails of skin from the morphing app. No flaps, no changing into a bird, no healing or expelling this pulsating frozen sun lodged in his chest. Only stabs of pain every time he breathed and imminent doom amid the waves. There were a hundred, a thousand ways he could survive this if only he could access his apps library or the store. So many times Rider had saved him, but ultimately, the visitor would be what killed him, bullet or no.

"Need a ping, buddy!" Merit said in Haral's Overlay, static disrupting some of the words, and a snowstorm of shifting gray spots obscuring his face. Others crowded around him in the frame. Laeua, Nez, even Chopper peered at him.

"Ping? Nothing's working. I can barely hear you. Downloads are borked. You can't save me with an emergency app. They've thrown me off the transport. Rider's gone," Haral said, defeated.

"Good! Excellent!" Merit said.

"No, it's terrible! The General shot me, and I have no access to apps. I'm going to die, pancaked on the surface of the ocean and eaten by fish. Who knows what tortures they have ready for Rider."

"Just keep talking. I've got something better than an app," Merit said.

"A parachute?" Haral asked, becoming dizzy from the pain radiating from his chest.

"How about a ride?" Before Haral could question what the PullSys star meant, something white and gold and blue with broad wings and a narrow nose slid into view below him. Moment by moment, it grew closer. Haral cringed, turning his face away as it neared, but then he landed with the merest of bumps on the flat surface.

A moment later, the golden face of Merit Lang peaked up over the spine of the plane. He walked across the wing toward Haral.

"How?" Haral hollered into the wind.

"Magnetic boots!" Merit announced, directing Haral's attention to his feet. Indeed, the star's footwear was anything but couture: blocky, gray, serviceable. Merit knelt beside him. "Can you walk?"

"I'll damn well walk out of here," Haral said, quoting one of Gann's movies. As they trudged back toward the edge of the wing, he continued, "I got blood on your plane…" and crumpled in Merit's arms.

Haral dreamed of swimming in gray water that moved and pushed him around, of rolling over and twisting, observing the sky, a mass of stars and a few moons, and an arc of scattered sunlight they called "day" back when day and night were natural things, before Geode.

Silver towers reached up from the midst of rivers and ponds of gray fluid, which were all interconnected, a single… *unity*.

And yet, Haral could tell it was incomplete, there was an ache, indefinable, unplaceable, but an absence, like missing a loved one, and an uncertainty you would ever see them again. He felt the reaching, urgent mass rising up one of the towers, creating its own tower, higher, higher, until it fell back like rain. It recollected, then raced up, up, and out of the planet's gravity well. The mass flew into space, where it shifted and molded itself… into segmented armor and a motivator he didn't understand the workings of. The armor soared through the infinite black toward a place it remembered there being a light, like so many other lights, in the sky. The place where a fragment of itself had gone and not returned. Still, it could feel it, reaching out on its own, persisting…

"Haral!" The sounds were odd, alien, hard and sharp, painful, but he felt they had meaning. "Haral! His eyes moved, they flickered open!" The voice, yes, it was a being making the sounds, said, incomprehensibly. A warmth touched him, pressure, but pleasant. He drifted.

A red shape appeared before him, open, with overlapping other shapes, filled in, or containing scribbles of some kind. Each shape tried to press itself into him, become part of him without fitting. It was other, invasive. A scatter of gray marks lay across the red, but as he watched, they vanished, one by one. He drifted.

"Haral?" The voice returned, more concerned than relieved as the time before. But still nearby, nearer than anything else he could sense. "You've got to come back now. Your Overlay has been purged. We had to get into some deep code to dig out the corruption. You should be fine now. Chest all healed. Come on back."

Despite himself, he opened his eyes. The first things they saw were rows of purple spikes and pink curls framing a face.

"Fa..ce..."

"Haral! It's good to see your face, too! We're almost home. Well, almost to shore. We were really far down there," the voice replied.

"No... Not home... Help Rider..." Haral's thoughts organized themselves as he spoke. "They're going to kill him, use him to find the others and kill them, too."

"Who's getting killed?" Nez rasped, sliding slightly rough tentacles over Haral's hand as he spoke. Nez. Hadn't expected to seem him again...

"Rider, the... visitor that was stuck in my head for..." Haral tried to recall how long it had been but gave up, "I can't feel them anymore."

"That must have been the residue we found all over your nervous system. It was tough to clear out, but I don't think it did any permanent damage, though... There are a few morphological changes to your brain and spinal

218

cord I want some real doctors to look at when we get back. Two trips to the hospital in one month!" Nez said, excitedly.

"I *am* a real doctor!" said a face in Haral's Overlay.

"Of course, of course…" Nez said, making a sweeping motion. The face vanished. "Power of attorney, remember? In case you did something crazy and needed medical help? You said it would never happen, but… Here. We. Are."

"Yes we are, but… Where's the fluid? Gray? Maybe moving on its own?"

"How did you know?" Nez asked. "It's in a canister over there, in case we needed to study it to fix you."

"I'm… fine? I'm something… I don't know. But we need to go south! Turn the plane around, Merit, please?"

"Turn around?" Merit asked in confusion. "When Laeua contacted me, told me where you were, what had happened in the undercity when you left Whip, I could hardly believe it. But then Nez, Chopper, and Gann backed her up. We took off at once. Then I find you and you're… You've been practically in a coma for hours. We've just broken a dozen navigation laws, including more than doubling speed limits in some places—"

"Tripling once!" Nez said, grabbing onto a tall, padded, white seat back as though he were about to fall over. "Gave me vertigo. That just doesn't happen to my people…"

Merit ignored him. "Suffice to say we—*I* burned a chunk of Pull getting to you. You're welcome and all, but don't you think we should be done? Head home? Rest up?"

Haral frowned. "I can't. Thank you. I know it cost you and I'll do what I can to help you get that Pull back, and more, whatever stunts it takes, but we've got to get back there, stop the army… the *General*."

Merit let out a short laugh. "Stop them? They have the guns, the law on their side, numbers."

"It's not about numbers, or words. It's about doing what's right," Haral insisted. "Rider needs us."

"Maybe that's it," Laeua said. "We can't force them to do anything. We can't overpower them, but maybe… we *can* use numbers… Pull."

"How so?" Merit asked. "I'm the highest Pull person here, and I have no chance of ordering around the military, which most people don't even believe exist."

"They don't believe *yet*," Laeua said with a sly smile.

Laeua outlined her plan. Merit turned after dipping down to the shore area to pick up a new set of camera drones for Haral and a charge of fuel. Haral caught up with everyone he had been missing.

Haral smiled. "I'm so glad to see you all—especially you, Nez, Chopper, my closest friends forever… I'll tell you all about my… adventures once we're *all* back home safely, Rider included."

"You had us so wo-wo-worried," Chopped said, a digital tone interrupting his words.

"I'm *still* worried about *you*."

"Nahahahah… I'm fi-i-ine fine. Golden," Chopper said haltingly.

"He's not fine," Nez whispered with his tentacles.

"Yeah," Haral said, rubbing his fingers back in Xochat. He felt bad for his friend, but wasn't sure what he could do at the best of times, let alone away from all his equipment, flying south as quickly as the plane would go.

Plan in place, Haral and Merit stood in the center of the cabin while Laeua directed and the others watched. Autopilot shot them south as quickly as it would go.

Merit addressed his audience, expression brightening, stance shifting as he looked into one of his drones, "Hey, Team Merit! I'm coming at you with this live, unscheduled, unrehearsed, but absolutely critical stream today to ask you for a little help. Some of you may remember Haral from a few days ago. We had a dust up, and then he was all over the news streams, jumping out of restaurants, off moving trains, all kinds of 'don't do this at home, kids!' kinda stuff. He's a pretty wild guy, it turns out… or *is* he? I've gotten to know him a little, after visiting him in the hospital, and after his dive into the water slides over at the Discotech. The tale he has to tell is far wilder than a few stunts. Haral?" Merit turned toward Haral, inviting him to say his piece.

His mouth suddenly dry, Haral stared for a second into the nearest drone. "Uhh… Thanks, Merit. Some of you might be wondering how we're standing here, not enemies, but friends, trying to get your help. Well, I'll tell you, and as they used to say, I—uh, hope you're sitting down…" Haral went on to reveal everything that had happened to him, trying not to loop back too often.

He didn't hold back: from learning of the problems outside the Shell, to being blasted by the alien signal, going to the Shell itself, the discovery of Whip's books, which he said came from a hidden cache a mysterious tipster led him to. He didn't want to create more problems for Whip or Selee. He paused in his retelling after his capture by the General.

Laeua nodded, giving him the cupped hands sign to encourage him. Stats on those watching scrolled at the bottom of their Overlays. The numbers were slowly increasing, just passing ten thousand. While that number seemed unthinkable to Haral, for Merit, it was nothing, only those who happened to be flipping through their feed. This was unscheduled, after all. No one knew they should be watching.

"Whoa, this 'General' sounds like a shady character," Merit said. "Isn't 'General' an old military term? All those wars we got into… with ourselves… He can't be a good guy."

"He's not," Haral agreed, reading from the script Laeua had fleshed out as he told the first part of his tale, except the parts that involved her, when she stood beside him. "He's a class-A corpslime. This 'General' is apparently part of the only army left on Geode, a secret army."

"A secret army? Are you sure that's not just a conspiracy theory?" Merit prompted. Twelve thousand. The numbers continued to rise.

"Sure, your crazy uncle," Haral glanced over at Laeua on this bit of script. She shrugged and waved for him to continue. "May go on about the Geode Defense Force abducting people and stealing certain technological advances. We've had those stories for centuries, since Old Earth, men in black disappearing people who had seen too much or dared to dream of something other what *they* want you to dream about… but this army has a specific purpose: to deal with aliens from outside our society," Haral said.

"There are *other* aliens? Besides my neighbor?" Merit asked. Everyone on the Sky Cutter laughed. The numbers spiked over fifteen thousand. That seemed to happen more with Merit than Haral, though that might be expected, with the difference in experience in doing this kind of thing. A week ago, Haral had never done a stream, aside from a couple of video games in his school years.

"It's been understood that in such a vast universe, even within our very galaxy it was more than likely that there were many more intelligent, even technologically advanced, species. But this idea that we need an army against these distant neighbors is a holdover from the ancient movies of Old Earth. I'm here to tell you my own story of an alien encounter." That got a solid spike to seventeen thousand. Numbers rose steadily for a few seconds while he let the phrase settle in. Laeua messaged that she was looping his last few words with effects. He should stare off into the distance, thoughtfully. He did so for what seemed like half a minute before she made a rolling sign with her hands to get him going again. Nineteen thousand.

Haral continued his tale. "So you know that the visitors' signal knocked me out for a time, and later I was pulled into their ship, but that's not the end of that story. You see, the General kidnapped me because he was certain that the alien, a creature of no real physical form, had somehow… invaded *me*!" Twenty-one thousand. He was starting to get a reaction, too.

"What we learned from those books, stashed away by some knowing seeker of truth years, maybe decades ago, had made me scared. I almost went along with the General and his army of shadow scientists hiding in the back of the room where I was held, but then one of them told me Laeua was free. Their leverage over me was broken, so *I* made a break for it, with the alien's help!" The numbers spiked again, to nearly twenty-four thousand. Apparently aliens were good for viewership.

People did still have imaginations and understood on some level that space was still out there, nearly endless and full of who knew what.

"I overcame the problems with my Overlay and got out of the cage where they held me." Laeua summoned a cage into the stream, enclosing him again. Some people were disturbed and numbers began to slide. Just over twenty-three. They couldn't lose a thousand. Momentum had been great.

"And for a long time I swam through the dark rivers, deep underground. I was cold, hungry, scared, and missing my friends. But more, I could feel that the alien, that the General and his people called 'Rider,' felt the same. As we went along, it shared many memories with me. Language, words, can be twisted. They can lie and trick us, but memories… It showed me how some of its people had come here earlier, a hundred years ago, and met with the General's army. They had been attacked, their ship destroyed, the pieces stolen, along with… prisoners." The numbers climbed. Twenty-five thousand.

"In time, some prisoners escaped, other were killed. Others were stowed away in vaults, unable to even hope for escape. But then this second ship came to check on the lost. And again, the General can do nothing but point guns and destroy."

"That's one heck of a story, Haral," Merit said. Twenty-six thousand.

Haral nodded grimly. "If only *it* was just a story, Merit. I mean, uh, 'if only it *was* just a story.' After spending days trying to communicate with Rider, I learned some things about their people, their world, but even more about our own. So many of us feel unheard, unseen. In Rider's society, there are no bosses, no HighPullers. There is true unity and equality. That may not appeal to some of us, but should we attack and kill beings who don't even come here thinking they're better than us, let alone bear us ill will?" Twenty-eight thousand.

"That sounds like Old Earth, the world we left behind when we joined together and created Geode," Merit said. Another bump in numbers. Thirty thousand.

"Exactly. The same should be said for the military. So what can you do? What do we want?" Haral asked. Together, they read the next lines, joined by Chopper and Nez and Laeua.

"We need *you* to vote 'NO' now to stop the General from killing innocent visitors from another world!" Merit, as the highest Pull member of the stream, sent the dialog box allowing people to sign the petition to override the General's orders. Numbers immediately began dropping. People wanted to see drama. They didn't want to be drawn into it, to *have* to act or take responsibility. Twenty-seven thousand. Twenty-six…

"What do we do?" Haral asked. "Please don't turn away. Stick with us and we'll show you shots of the south region like you've never seen them!"

"It's true!" Merit said. "We're on our way there right now, chasing down the villainous General to keep him from using Rider to discover their kin and destroying all of them. Don't you want to reach out to these new people? Learn about them? Tell them about us?" The numbers continued to slide. Twenty-five thousand. Twenty-four thousand.

"Oh! You like winning things, right?" Haral vamped, "How about, if we can save these visitors, one lucky viewer gets to spend the day with me—"

"And me! Great idea, Haral. We'll choose one of you at random. In fact, what do you think about picking one winner for every hundred thousand votes?" Merit suggested. The number seemed astronomical, but he also saw an immediate reaction in both the viewer numbers and the votes. Twenty-seven thousand viewers. Twenty-nine thousand. The chance to become part of the celebration motivated people more than the consequences of failure, it seemed.

Haral agreed, "Uh, yeah! That sounds great! Thanks for putting your time in on this one, Merit! I'm sure glad we could resolve our differences like we did when our peoples built Geode! And I know just the chef to make food for the event! My pal Nez here has just completed a rigorous culinary course." The rates increased slightly. Thirty thousand.

"Oh right! You remember Nez from Haral's first appearance, don't you, folks? Come here, buddy!" Merit wrapped an arm around Nez, drawing him in. "That's one special memory from that day, the amazing smell of that burger you made for Haral. And I know just the chef to make the sides, old-style fries and brownies, eh crew? Let's get my old pal, master chef, and owner of Geode-renowned Le Jeunesse Affamée restaurant, J'mal on the stream right now and ask for his help!"

Nez faded, turning gray. Haral rubbed his fingers together, telling him, "It's going to be great. Haven't you always wanted to work beside world class chefs like J'mal?"

"Of course, but me doing mains while he does sides? It's a slap in the face. He'd never agree, and I'd be embarrassed to give him orders, even if he did," Nez responded.

"Then you can work side by side. The important thing now is the story. We'll do what we need to in order to make it work out later, all right?" The color began returning to his friend.

A moment later, a Xochat with six noses radiating from his central core, a deep purple hue along each bridge and the edge of his tympani appeared in the stream, beaming his visage in from his own kitchen on Geroo Spar.

"Merit! It's so great to see you again my friend. To what do I owe this visit? Aha! I am kidding, of course! I've been watching your stream. Of course I'll help you out with your incentive lunch! The peoples of Geode came together all those years ago with the idea that we should all have a safe place to live, to learn, and to build the lives we wanted. How can we turn our backs on visitors because they're a little different? Are we not all different? Different tastes? Different senses? We must not reject the rest of the universe just because we've created a cozy home for ourselves. There's always more to learn!" The numbers soared. Fifty thousand. Fifty-five thousand. Seventy thousand. Merit was in the solid fifty million pull region, but J'mal was well known across much of the world, at over two billion Pull.

Chapter Eighteen

Nearly two hours later, after contacting a few other HighPullers and expanding the festivities into donations of advanced apps, virtual reality experiences and more, a PullSys alert crowded into Haral's Overlay just above the graphs tracking views and votes.

PullSysVoting Has processed your request to address the issue, "Order General of Geode Defense Force —Stop Pursuing Alien Visitor." Due to internal PullSys policies, the threshold for revising PullSys representative orders has been increased to five billion. Current vote count is one billion, two hundred thousand, seven hundred twelve.

"Are you kidding me?" Haral interrupted Merit, who was having a rousing conversation with J'mal and Nez about menu choices and course order.

"Pardon?" J'mal asked.

"I'm sorry, chef, I've just been alerted that our required votes to calling the General off is… significantly higher than we expected," Haral replied.

"I'm seeing it now," Merit said, "Yeah, we'd need to really call in the big accounts, people literally everyone on Geode knows. No offense, J'mal, you're a legend, but it looks like we need a *team* of legends."

"Or something… outside the system…" Laeua said under her breath. Haral heard, but everyone else missed it, or pretended to. "Keep them happy," she said to Merit and pulled at Haral's hand, drawing him to a corner of the cabin. "Send them away."

"Merit and J'mal? They seem like huge allies—" Haral started.

"No, the drones. I want to talk in private," she said. Haral nodded his understanding and sent his drones to take shots out the front window and of Merit.

"What's up?" Haral asked, looking into Laeua's eyes.

Haral walked back into the main cabin area. Merit slapped him on the shoulder.

"Good news, bro. J'mal and I have reached out to a few other HighPullers who are going to join the brand-new Extreme Food Festival as headliners, bringing their fans into a Geode-wide event in support of our new friends," Merit said aloud. Meanwhile, Haral also got a message from him on the Overlay.

MeritLang1 - README

Hey Haral, here's a list of people I need you to follow right away so we can organize this festival.

The rest of the message was an impressive list of names, most of which he'd not only heard of, but could barely imagine anyone *not* having heard of. There were fashionari, culinari, artists, actors, streamers who counted their viewership in spars rather than individuals. How would he be able to get through the flood of requests they no doubt got every day?

Haral popped over to the contacts tab of the Overlay and right at the top of the list, prioritized automatically by PullSys, were those hundred plus names, inviting *him* to follow them, no searching, no gatekeeping. Could it be? He began clicking his way down the list of starred names. He imagined he could feel his own Pull increasing with every connection, like a training montage in one of Gann's movies, getting closer to his goal with every step he ran up, every piece of equipment he mastered.

He laughed aloud when he saw names he recognized from the meeting where Leonardo Sperra gave him the medallion for getting to five million viewers: Clieth, Tyla, Zan-DAZ. Duran Doran! Hadn't Sperra said something about them being the advertising exec?

Haral accepted their request and immediately sent them a message.

Hi, Duran Doran! Thanks for the invite to follow you. I gather you've been watching my stream with Merit and J'mal, or are at least aware that it's going on. It is imperative that we help these visitors to our world and connect with them as the originators of Geode would have if they were close enough when it was being designed. We should try to live in harmony with all beings, don't you think?

What kind of advertising advice can you give us to get the word out ASAP, as they used to say? Rider has been captured by this General and is being used to track down others who have lived here peacefully for a century. I know that doesn't seem as long as it once did, given our lifespans these days, but it certainly counts for something.

Anyway, thanks for reading, I hope to hear from you soon,
-Haral Adjani

"Heads up!" Laeua said from the pilot's seat, "The transports are on the long-range sensors or whatever they're called."

"'Long-range sensors?' Very sci-fi," Haral said with a note of appreciation.

"Keep it in your holster, cowboy," Merit said with a wink and went back to chatting with J'mal. Haral could feel his face turning pink. The numbers bumped up a bit. People loved mild embarrassment in others. He guessed it felt good to see people on their feeds feeling the small, normal feelings, too, not just the grand heroic ones. He crossed the space to stand at Laeua's shoulder.

There were, indeed, three vessels before them flying in formation, with a fourth hanging off to the side at some distance. Ffna? Had they stayed with the General?

"Can you contact that fourth transport? The one off to the side? Hanging way back? I think they may be friends," he said.

"Friends on a military transport?" she asked, skeptical.

Haral nodded. "That's a stolen transport. Ffna and Dell helped me escape the General back at the train, and they helped me before that, a lot."

"All right, let me try," Laeua said, scouring the controls for a moment before relenting and pulling up a manual in her Overlay. At least, that's what Haral assumed she was doing, given her surety in the next moment, of pushing buttons and spinning knobs. "Geode Defense Force transport, this is…" Laeua quieted her voice, looking up at Haral. "What's the name of this ship?" Haral shrugged.

"Merit, what's the name of your vessel?" He asked across the cabin.

"The Sky Cutter!" Merit shot back, barely looking up from his virtual conversation. Haral could see in the feed that half a dozen extremely famous folk were gathered around. One famous actor was extolling the ancient virtues of peace put forth by something called Buddhism.

"This is the Sky Cutter," Laeua completed her introduction.

"Hail, Sky Cutter. That doesn't sound like a Geode Defense Force vessel designation," Dell called back.

"It's not, we're a private vessel. We've got Haral on board," she replied.

"Thank the signal! He's alive!" Dell said, not into the mic, but still picked up and transmitted.

"I told you he never reached the water," Ffna said, quieter for his distance from the communicator.

"Yeah, yeah, you're always right, blah blah." Dell turned her attention back to her conversation with Laeua. "That's great news, Sky Cutter. We've been sticking with the General. They're keeping to a mostly southerly course. They seem to have a destination in mind."

"The General sucked Rider out of my body," Haral said, leaning over Laeua's shoulder, "and dumped me like a dirty napkin."

"Xenophobia *and* littering? The abomination!" Ffna exclaimed dramatically. Haral envisioned him leaning over Dell's shoulder in the same way he was standing by Laeua.

"Uh oh," Laeua said, pointing at one of the readouts. "More company, and from the tight, maintained formations, they're not a pleasure expedition."

"GDF…" Haral said.

"Thanks for the heads up. Any idea how many? How long it will take for them to get here?" Dell asked.

"No time. They're overtaking us now— Laeua's response was cut short.

"Private vessel Sky Cutter, prepare for emergency inspection," a new voice boomed.

"There's no place to land out here, uh... Please advise," Laeua said, looking up at Haral.

"Everyone on the Sky Cutter will strap into seats and you will open the port hatch," the voice demanded.

"Is that safe?" she asked.

"It's safer than not complying, Sky Cutter," the voice replied in an even tone.

"What do we do? They're here for you, aren't they?" Laeua asked.

"I'm afraid so," Haral agreed, mind already spinning on the problem of how to save his friends.

"What will they do?" she asked, worried.

"Not a damn," Merit said angrily, storming toward them. "This is *my* ship, operating in free skies. We're not stopping for anyone." A heavy clang rang through the cabin.

"I've lost control, or at least the controls aren't doing much. I think they've clamped onto us somehow," Laeua said.

"No! This isn't right! I'm HighPull!" Merit said. Nez buckled into one of the Xochat-optimized seats. Chopper locked into a clamp on the wall.

"Like Laeua said, they're here for me. If they don't find me, they might let you go," Haral pointed out.

"How is *that* going to happen?" Laeua asked, brows furrowed, cheeks pale.

"'My destiny is the sea!' as a ship captain from one of Gann's old movies said." Haral scrolled through his shape options in the now fully functioning body morphing app. Yes, that would be good for a start. He went to the starboard side and accessed the bathroom. Once inside, he heard the clank and hiss of the other hatch open. Wind screamed into the cabin. He started tapping on the small console before the toilet, finding the menu he needed within seconds. He hit the last command and the confirmation code, then did the same on the app loaded in his Overlay.

Water rolled down the sides of the toilet bowl. He jumped in even as his form shrank and twisted. He felt like a towel being wrung out. The emergency venting protocol, to get rid of especially foul emissions or, as he'd seen in a modern movie, a bomb, dropped the entire contents of the tank beneath the toilet out into the air. Once again, he was falling and once again, he was covered in waste. This was surely a once in a lifetime week… He could only hope.

Wind roaring around him again, his new form, of a small bird, was buffeted and flipped in turbulence as the Sky Cutter zipped away, three ships in solid formation around it. Haral spotted other ships continuing south as he regained his orientation and began to fly, albeit much slower than the transports. But then, his goal wasn't to fly all the way there.

He angled toward one of the many upspouts caused by subsea pumps that kept the sea from drifting back toward the equator and flooding the spars. It rose hundreds of feet into the air, hanging there, creating a slow, tumbling body of water like nothing in Old Earth. Long, rippling, transparent, limbs hung in the air, light from the sun bouncing between then, illuminating the fish and other creatures occupying them. Occupying, but not trapped, as a pod of dolphins demonstrated, leaping from their otherwise barren sky sea to the next with flourishing flips and spins.

When the dolphins arrived in the second sky sea, they immediately homed in on a school of fish which glimmered like a sheet of living jewels in the sunlight, capable of penetrating the whole body of water due to its relative shallowness. The dolphins quickly rounded up the fish, then ate as Haral flew by. He took his time, enthralled, until he barreled into another briny bubble, where the app immediately gave him a more apropos form. He slipped into the shape of a dolphin as well. Shimmying through the water, he popped up enough to get a breath of air, then shot forward in pursuit of the GDF ships and the Sky Cutter.

Only when he heard clicking and squealing did he realize the other dolphins had spotted him and leapt from their sky sea to his. He half-wished he knew dolphin and could talk with them, but at the moment, he had bigger problems. How would he catch up with the ships? And how would he execute the other part of his plan?

The water before Haral rippled gray and he pulled up short, swimming in a tight circle, then hanging in the water, drifting to one side as he concentrated.

Hello? He thought at the wave, then remembered the language barrier. He focused on a memory from Rider, the gray sea of ripples back home. The returning vision was of humani meeting on a pier, extending hands toward one another, then another meeting where two others embraced.

They did understand one another.

Haral sent a memory of being on the Shell, the stars above, of grippers tearing apart his suit and pulling him inside the vessel.

The other shared a memory of coming through the underground rivers and being spat out into the sea. Just the same memory Rider had shown him at one point, in telling him which way to go to find the lost expedition members.

Haral shared his own memories of that water conduit, the snails and jets and darkness. He quickly shifted off that to a newer memory of Rider, the bit of Unity that had been inside Haral, captured in a large glass vessel studded with electrodes or some such. He got a sense of alarm at this news, and urgency. Even without words, Haral got the message: "show me."

Haral pictured the transport ships, then the Sky Cutter's radar viewer, with the three main ships and the one off to the side he tried to convey were friends, trying to stop the others. The broad, soft-edged wave of gray rearranged itself into a dolphin beside him. The other dolphins clicked, surprised by yet another stranger in their hunting ground.

When Haral and the other swam off, they gave chase. As they went, the Unity dolphin cavorted with the others. Perhaps Haral was the only intruder here. After all, the Unity fragment would have had to survive here for over a century. It made sense it had made friends. How many fragments were scattered across the poles of Geode? Why hadn't they re-collected into a singular form? Perhaps it was easier to care for smaller bodies spread over the area than one gargantuan mass? There could only be so many apex predators, after all. Smaller pieces would hide easier, as well… Yes, he could see the strategy there…

Haral's Overlay alerted him to a string of important messages.

PullSys - Your vote, regarding...
MeritLang1 - You're a legend, man...
Laeua-Kio1792 - I hope you get this...
Kylerstomp - HighPull visibility override
message: Hey! Rockin' showing...

Your vote, regarding issue: "Order General of Geode Defense Force—Stop Pursuing Alien Visitor" has been suspended at three billion, two hundred sixty thousand, three hundred eight votes. Further inquiry into this matter must be addressed with your local PullSys office within seventy-two hours. Failure to inquire within this time will be taken as acceptance of the ruling. No later recourse will be available.

Awesome. Someone inside PullSys had pulled the plug on the legal route. Even if Haral had a means to take his grievance to the PullSys office, he was certain he'd never be seen again. The only way through was forward. Haral opened the next message:

You're a legend, man. I don't know anyone who would have turned himself into something so small and stuffed himself down the toilet to save his friends. If we get through this, we're definitely reaching for the sun. Gonna get you in a penthouse with your own pool and whatever you like. I hope you're still there, man. -ML

Haral couldn't help but immediately respond to Merit's message.

Hey Merit, I'm sure I didn't do anything crazier than one of those adrenaline streamers does every other day. Of course, my heart almost stopped, but these last few days have been more "exciting" than I ever expected my life to be. Thanks for coming to get me and for chasing down the General with me.

Sorry to say PullSys told me the vote was suspended. If you can get away, do it. Say what you need to about me to get yourself out of trouble. You've been a good friend since I've entered this whole other world that's barely recognizable to me.

Thanks for everything. I hope we all survive this, too.

Haral reached for the send button, but then wondered if sending a message might be confirmation of his survival, if the General's people were still watching, or had an automated alert on him. Instead, he saved the draft and moved on.

I hope you get this message. They're still on the ship. Three transports are locked around us like the jaws of a predator. They're watching all around in case you come back, so don't, unless I send you the right message.

Good luck.

I hope you're still alive. -Laeua

Was what he did *that* dangerous? He hadn't thought so. Perhaps they were considering the surrounding of the Sky Cutter by GDF ships, that they would somehow shoot him out of the sky as soon as he appeared. But he was here, getting their messages.

PullSys pinged another message through. Nez.

Hey Haral, they've taken Chopper away. I think they think that he's acting weird because there's still one of those Rider things in him. I don't know if that's true, but I figured you would have known? At any rate, they're sticking round, carrying weapons that remind me of machine guns from Gann's movies. We're all just trying to stay calm here, but they're escorting us further south.

They haven't said anything, but I can feel gravity lessening. This place is as weird as it looks in the vids: water jets, sky islands, sky rocks completely coated in water. I wouldn't call them islands, but I don't know what else to call them. I guess what I really wanted to say is I'm scared. Everyone is scared.

Please don't be dead. -Nez

Haral's heart felt heavy. Everyone was so worried for him, and they were still in danger themselves. He *had* to keep swimming south and try to get the Unity part that was pretending to be a dolphin in contact with the new part which had ridden with him. Surely, given their combined knowledge, they could find a way to stop the General. He had to believe. Curious, he opened the last new message from today. He didn't recognize the username.

Hey! Rockin' showing over these last days, my man! Way to burst onto the scene like an incendiary, lighting the place up and causing maximum destruction to the status quo. I saw your and Merit's stream and I'm totally in for any event you all want to hold—live, recorded, in person, multi-streamed, whatever—to make sure we become better galactic citizens. It's only a matter of time before we draw the attention of even more races, and we can't go punching out everyone who comes to our door.

Keep me in the loop, Kyler "Stomp" Rambo

The positive message heartened Haral. He swam faster. The other dolphins kept up, swimming in paths that wove around his own. Was he expected to try to add something to the pattern? Understand it? Was it some form of language? Not wanting to "say" the wrong thing, he kept on his path, due south, toward the area he was sure the General was going. One of the dolphins came to swim beside him. It clicked and squealed, and a flicker of gray slid across his vision.

He tried to think a greeting to the dolphin—a memory of meeting hands with Merit, and another time, Nez, and even Gann, when they first met during his interview for the maintenance position. A series of clicks rose and fell, then again the same pattern, quickly. A flipper grazed his own. Coincidence? Or mimicking what the other might have gotten of his projected memory?

Before Haral could tell if the other had understood him, or the contact had been unrelated, a shadow bore down above the tiny floating sea they traveled through.

Chapter Nineteen

Beginning to panic, Haral prepared himself by taking a deep breath from the surface. As he did so, though, his eyes broke through the water and he could make out a large whale, much bigger than the GDF transports, paddling through the sky between seas. The vision stunned him and he soared up out of the water he'd been in, leaving himself largely helpless. Haral's panic returned as the awe wore thin. Still in dolphin form, the heat outside of the water baked into his gray skin.

A blue shadow fell over his view. He saw a gray cloud in the deep and endless water, the sea below. Curiosity. Intuition. The whale approached the gray cloud, viewed the rolling waves within it. The cloud fascinated the whale, creating images within its mind, and reacting to memories, and images it had created in its mind to go along with stories it had been told, songs of its ancestors and of creatures who swam in ancient seas and walked on land.

The gray cloud began to disperse, to be pulled apart by the currents and its own fatigue. Understanding somehow its need, the whale swam through the cloud, inviting the other into its nervous system. The refugee became a rider.

Haral reached back to a memory of gratitude, of a special gift his mother had given him one birthday, a carving she had crafted using real tools, not just a matter spinner from a catalog of templates. It was a small statue of a bird that he always kept beside his bed to remind him of her though she was what he *had* thought of as far away, at the other end of Swanton Spar. Now that distance seemed laughably small.

And they had millies to go to catch up with the military transports. The whale turned in the air, slow, but far from clumsy. Without a specific memory entering his mind, Haral knew it meant to come with him. He touched on the memory of unwrapping the silly upside-down puffin carving and immediately loving it again.

Haral watched the dolphin-shaped cloud as they swam. What made it different? How could it exist outside of something with a nervous system? Why didn't it have to ride like the other fragments? But he was no scientist. He didn't have the answers. PullSys notified him of more messages.

PullSys - Congrats on reaching 10 million followers!
MeritLang1 - Add Ffna and Dell! T...

Ten million people wanting to know what Haral was up to, what he had to say, or even finding him somewhat entertaining was mind-blowing. But then, he was currently a dolphin, swimming through a floating swath of ocean accompanied by dolphins and a whale, some of whom were basically possessed by fragments of an alien consciousness. His bar for surprise had been lifted significantly. Skipping the PullSys alert, he went into Merit's message, though he could see the intent from the subject line.

Add Ffna and Dell! They've got updates. -ML

Well, all right. Updates were probably good, right? Better than "developments" or "news." Haral went over to

242

the contacts tab. There were thousands of folk of high enough pull to think they could approach someone of his alleged stature, which was amusing. Who was he, after all? No one. Some were likely responding to Merit's call to arms.

He put Ffna in the search feature and quickly found their account, approving them, and using their friends and followers list to find Dell. Having accomplished this, Haral skimmed through the list of requests to see if anyone he had heard of was trying to add him. He recognized a few people from school, some neighbors, and a handful of streamers he had looked up to for a while. He clicked through and added most of them.

FfnaRundo99718 - Things are heating u...

Haral opened the message.

Things are heating up down here. I really hope you're still around and on your way with an underground army or something. We've arrived at some kind of massive pool built on top of one of the floating islands. More ships have arrived, most of them GDF, is our guess, but not all. Some look... normal? If you have a master plan, this is the time to reveal it.

A master plan? He had never had a master plan in his entire life. He had spent so many days, weeks, months, years living day to day. The most planning he did was figuring out when to hang out with Nez and how long it would take to get through Gann's current play list so they could actually vote on what to watch next. Nevertheless, he figured he should respond.

243

Hey, Ffna, I can't claim a master plan, but I am on my way with more allies. More ships? Can you give me an idea of how many? Or tell me more about this pool?
Thanks. -Haral

Haral took another breath as he leapt between shimmering globules of water the size of medium sized spars, water sprayed from a dozen other blowholes catching sunlight like stars against the deep gray of the whale's flank. His worries fell back in the presence of such beauty. He swam on, learning more about the Unity fragments' plights since crashing on Geode a century before, trying to decode messages from all manner of seagoing memories.

As they swam, more dolphins and a second whale of a smaller species—but still majestic and awe-inspiring —joined them, turning the otherwise thinly-populated sky seas into bustling travel lanes. Hanging plumes of seaweed and clouds of plankton were consumed or thrashed out of the way by dozens, and eventually, hundreds of flippers.

Ffna replied:

Haral, the ships are continuing to trickle in, but there have to be at least thirty out there. We've been keeping the transport hidden amongst sky islands, but given how the ships are coming from all directions, I don't know how much longer we can remain unnoticed. I'm not sure all the arrivals are

Yes, hope. Perhaps that was the point of streamers who did all the crazy things one dreamed of doing as a child, before reality set in. They—perhaps he, now—were the exception to the rules of reality. On the one hand, he could have done without the seemingly endless hours in the dark of the underground river, but on the other, he knew more about his world now, and met Ffna and Dell. In fact, the whole of his time since Rider had splashed down into the calmly flowing stream of his life had been beautiful chaos, and more living than he had done in all the years leading up to that moment.

The General and those he was working for within PullSys were trying to wipe that all away, to prevent any more splashing around in the dull little pond they had made for themselves to be the big fish in. But the world, the universe, was wider and wilder than Geode. Being safe at home was all well and good, but if one sealed oneself away and didn't look outside, pretended "outside" didn't even exist, that didn't leave anyone prepared for anything.

One of the lead whales let out a booming call. A flash of alarm ran through the massive pod, a clash of gray and blue overlaid memories of worry and excitement washed over Haral's mind, followed by another of a grand sky island. It was a veritable mountain inverted, with the broad base carved out in a round basin. In it was collected not water from the sea or rain, but gray fluid crisscrossed with rolling waves. Haral recognized it immediately as a larger fraction of the Unity he had seen in Rider's memories of home. The local fragments had once gathered here, or perhaps did so regularly.

He spotted a small cluster of stationary dark spots in the distance. Ships. Seemingly unmindful of the humani machines, the whales and dolphins undulated on. Haral tried to send memories of warning, of wariness, but got confidence in return. The initial fear was gone now. This was some kind of final showdown between the General's GDF and the Unity and their allies. The sea mammals had chosen a side, and he supposed he had, too. He hoped the others would stand with them. He felt they would. But still, what was the plan? Could someone who could not form words even devise plans?

Plan or no, the lead whale, the largest one, drove straight toward one of the transport ships as though it were prey the creature could simply devour. The rest of the pod peeled off to the right, starting to encircle the sky island. Haral spotted other groups of ships—three here, ten there—more than Ffna had reported. They must still be coming in. A group of five dropped out of position and began chasing the line of cetaceans.

Haral stuck with the lead whale, wanting to see what happened next. Too late, the transport began to pull forward. Had the pilot broken? Or had the captain of the ship given the order, screaming at the last moment, sweat rolling down his face? No, not a captain, the General. Haral could see him in a fuzzy-edged gray window in his vision. Bright blue-white light reflected chaotically from a number of courses, but Haral couldn't really see the source.

But he remembered.

The capsule.

The whale was heading straight for Rider.

At the last moment, the General already having "blinked" by trying to get away, the whale soared a few degrees up and over the ship, giving it the merest of nudges. The ship's tail end noticeably swung down toward the water. It poured on speed, angling back up over the sky island. As it passed over the floating mass, the whales and dolphins and ships circling below the lip rose up, creating a screen of moving bodies and ships. As they did, two other groups of ships left their positions, spreading out, covering the top of the wall as it closed into a dome, then rotating counter to the others' paths at about twice the radius.

They *did* have a plan! And for all the world, it seemed to be working. But what was next? Trapping a transport ship with limited weapons was one thing. Keeping it there against unknown numbers of other ships and armaments was another. How would they get Rider back? How would they escape without armed conflict Haral felt sure they would lose? After all, he hadn't seen anything like a weapon, or any memories including anything that seemed like a weapon. There had been no war, no fighting between themselves, because of course, they were all one will.

The dome closed in, tightening the grip on the transport, forcing it to risk impact with them or the land mass. The ship fired some kind of missile, but the screen of bodies slid apart just enough to allow it past, where it spiraled and fizzled and sank toward the sea far below.

The ship's engines flickered next. Again, Haral couldn't tell whether the General had ordered a landing or had lost control of the vessel. The whales joined the wall, adding to the threat to the ship, and Haral received another message, a message of welcome and embracing. Below, the lowest fliers swam across the open basin, then out the other side, meandering a bit as if losing their way, or their concerted direction…

This continued, and quickly Haral realized the basin was beginning to fill with gray fluid rolling down from the edges. The released hosts… Here, for whatever reason, the Unity could survive on its own, and it was gathering. The gray tide rose and rose as the dome dwindled. The ships in the dome landed, humani and Flexxe marching down ramps and falling at the edge of the growing sea. Rivers of gray converged. The fluid rose to hide the transport's landing gear, the lower edge of the hull.

The rear entrance was opened from one side, torn across the hinges by the unsteady landing. Rider's prison's brilliant light flickered chaotically within.

A blue sheen covered Haral's vision. A scene of two humani looking at one another, making expressions and noises at one another. The content of the discussion was lost in the wordless memory of the whale's rider, but the intent was clear enough.

Swimming down to the transport would take a lot of time and effort, so Haral snuggled close to the whale and transformed back into humani form, folding up his legs against the smooth, dark, skin and launching himself frog-like toward Rider and the General. The trip took long, strenuous, minutes where nothing he could do would kill off the seconds faster. He merely glided like a leaf falling from a tree.

Nearing, Haral could hear the General yelling at someone.

"…think you can force my hand? I've been guarding this planet for two hundred years, well before your first incursion, and I'll be here for hundreds more to fend off the next wave!"

"They can't understand you. They don't have language the way we do," Haral yelled across the dwindling void. "They never had a reason to come up with secondhand communication to get thoughts from one individual to another, because they're not individuals."

"What kind of malarkey are you talking now, Adjani?" the General growled, wheeling to face Haral, weapon drawn.

"No malarkey, unlike the line you were just spewing. 'Guarding this planet?' Hoarding it, maybe, strangling it, preventing expansion. The universe is so much vaster than you know. You've wrapped yourself up in the same kind of mind-trap that you've set on the people of Geode."

The General raised an eyebrow. "'Mind-trap?' Maybe you *are* unwell, after all. We thought you were adjusting to Rider, especially after you escaped and managed to survive for days… how *did* you do that, anyway?"

"I'm a little unsteady, but mostly because some maniac is pointing a weapon at me," Haral snarked.

"*I'm* the maniac? Who's nearly crashed two different trains, leapt out of a sky-restaurant, dived in a river—that ninety-nine percent of people don't make it out of—hijacked a military transport, and has more dolphin 'friends' than civilized race friends?"

"Having friends makes me a maniac? Saving a friend?" Haral asked. "I think you need to check your math there. Why are you doing this? You *know*, I'm certain you do, that the Unity doesn't pose a threat to anyone."

"Tell that to the dozens of people their pulse killed," the General growled.

"One, any injury or death was an accident. Two, they were desperately seeking their missing pieces."

"'Missing pieces?' They're goo. They don't have fingers or feet."

"And yet, their missing members are felt just as keenly as you would miss a limb."

"This is pointless. You're too far gone. But you've already lost. The riders… unity… whatever you called them—"

Haral cut in, "It doesn't matter what *I* call them. They don't have a name, because they don't have symbols. They have observation, memory, and emotion. Some of them have found a home here, despite you. They didn't harm a single human in a hundred years until the accident that set the fragment you call the rider into my body."

"And even now that it's out, it's controlling you. That's just one reason it's dangerous and needs to die. And it will, and so will you." The General looked off into space for a moment, no doubt using his Overlay.

Outside, a honk like a vehicle horn from the oldest of Gann's movies sounded. "U-ah U-ah!" After a few seconds, it came again. Haral turned to look out the destroyed back wall of the transport. Hundreds of ships crowded into just that small section of the airspace above the sky island that he could see. He took another step and craned his neck to spot many, many more.

"It looks like when the people hear their vote being disregarded, they'll vote with their feet," Haral observed. A flood of pings came through PullSys. He peeked while the General was unresponsive. Hundreds of invitations to sign petitions for new votes to stop the General from going after the Unity. Every HighPuller who had signed onto Merit's vote, and many others, had initiated their own votes. They were demanding their collective voice be heard despite the rejection of the earlier petition. As he read, more and more ships, mostly private HighPuller vessels, but also commandeered public vehicles, honked and hooted and blared alarms and flashed lights in support of the cause. Haral swept his mental finger down the requests, choosing every one that looked like the original petition, signing all of them at a click.

"General," Haral said quietly, but firmly, to draw his attention back to the real world. No response "General." Haral said again, more insistent.

"You are going to regret turning your back on your people," the man said, only half his attention on Haral. A light began to flash on the pilot's console.

"I haven't; I won't," Haral said as he moved across the space, splashing Unity before him as he trudged. The viewer read:

Self-Destruct Activated

"But you have. Have you looked outside lately?" Haral asked.

"What? More whales?" The General challenged. "I like animals as much as the next guy, but I'm not sacrificing the world, humanity and its friends, for them, or any aliens."

"More citizens of Geode, hundreds, *thousands* of HighPullers and their friends. If you detonate the ship it could kill them all. Is that really what you want? And if so, you have to ask yourself why. You love PullSys so much, but imagine the damage it will suffer without its main draws. People could… go back to reading books… or wondering about what's outside the Shell.

"*That's* what you're really worried about, isn't it?" Haral grasped. "This tired idea that this is the safest place to be, and no one should even *think* of other worlds? But that's not us. It's not who we've ever been, not in thousands and thousands of years. Before we settled into towns, we roamed. Even after we figured out how to survive in one place, we expanded, looking in new directions, crossing mountains, crossing seas, crossing the *sky* and then SPACE."

"You… don't know what you're talking about. Geode is a castle, a bastion against the horrors," the General shuddered, cutting himself off. The message on the console flashed red then returned to white.

"Horrors? Of course there are. Space is the new wilderness. Every new place we've been to some pioneers have eaten the wrong plant or annoyed the wrong animal. We celebrate them as heroes for trying. We are safer for their sacrifices. But if we don't learn our way in the wider world, if we just hide under the Shell, eventually something far less friendly than Unity will come visiting, and we won't know anything about it until it's too late. We won't have any allies, any means of fighting them off." Haral spotted the Unity stretching up from the surface along the pillar where the prison that held Rider stood. He looked away, trying not to draw attention to the effort.

"I've been out there, you know," the General said quietly.

"I didn't. The parts of our history where we reached outward have been erased from the searchable databases, the entertainment streams, the school channels. Tell me. What did you see?" Haral asked.

Chapter Twenty

"I was so excited during that first mission, making contact with aliens," the General said. While he spoke a small camera drone hovered into the cabin just along the ceiling and attached itself silently to the bulkhead. "It was a science fiction dream come true. Fifty of us landed on various points around the planet, teams of five. We approached what we took to be governmental centers. One team was beheaded by a single sweep of a weapon the recording drones never caught.

"Others were captured, experimented on, or fed to creatures in what we took to be either zoos or farms, others stuck in their own exhibits. Maybe we were interesting. Maybe we tasted good. I don't know. I just know that at every turn, they were faster, stronger, and possibly more advanced on every front. Any they didn't want anything to do with us."

"So treating other visitors the same way is right?" Haral asked quietly. He didn't want to disrespect what the General had gone through, but couldn't help but see the parallels.

The General ignored him. "Two of us made it home. We ended up just nuking the place from orbit and feeding the rubble into the furnaces to make the Shell… The survival rate of contact teams was less than half a percent."

Haral couldn't help but sympathize. "That must have been terrifying, but you can't blame all other life for opening one bad door."

"They're ALL bad doors!" The General screamed, hands shaking, spittle flying.

"What about the Xochat? The Flexxe, the Rulab? Each of them brought us improvements in our understanding of the world, our technology. Without each of them, Geode would be poorer, or not even exist. Our struggles would be greater—trying to make enough food and space for a growing population on a tiny rock ball."

"Three races out of hundreds," the General said.

"'*Hundreds?*'" Haral felt his eyes widen.

"That's the outside world they don't want you to know about. Sure, it sounds all wonderful—exploring, meeting new peoples, seeing all the myriad permutations of the known elements coming together in varied structures, art, music, culture… But most of them want to kill you and will do so on sight, or hearing, or whatever other more arcane senses they have."

"But we checked over every planet in our system, every moon, every rock," Haral said.

"Yes, and we-"

A gray filter slid over Haral's vision. He looked down and both his and the General's feet were invisible beneath the gathered Unity.

A new scene blotted out the ship interior. Tan, rippled walls, like melted wax with its own luminosity created an organically shaped room with nooks and cubbies and shelves and hallways off at angles. Some kind of woven tapestry led from a broad loft at the far end of the space, down the wall and across the floor out the nearby opening to the outside. A humani soldier stood before Haral's point of view, facing away.

"You won't play ball, huh? Maybe we'll just take what we need," the soldier said to a species Haral had never seen. It vaguely reminded him of an insect or crustacean, with hard-surfaced limbs and body, but narrow, flexible joints. The other clicked and warbled, then pointed with their right forelimbs to a point back beyond the viewer out the low, broad doorway. It seemed a clear sign for the visitors to vacate.

An urn was shoved into the point-of-view soldier's arms by another humani and he was pushed toward the door. Haral didn't need to see the murder to know the purpose of the energy blasts which followed—light reflected off the wavy walls of the chamber as he stumbled toward the opening into a plaza bounded by ridged cones with high, narrow windows.

A buzz rose up behind, and was echoed around the nearby buildings, growing more intense as more and more citizens joined in, appearing from doorways and holes in the tiled ground.

The memory swam for a moment, as though fast-forwarding through a weapons-heavy retreat to the landers, the memory holder still clinging to the urn and trying to keep it from spilling too much of whatever resource was worth thousands of alien lives. They got onto the lander, placed the urn into a crate where it spilled further, its pointed bottom preventing a stable position. The gray film receded.

"Because *you* were the monsters," Haral confirmed.

"What? No, we came in peace, hoping to learn…"

"Hoping to *gain*, to be *enriched*, but how many of those people held back their secrets, or didn't value what we had to give and *that's* what cost them their lives? The vestiges of imperialism and capitalism wend their ways through history like undead roots of true evil. Even when we'd cut down the trees bearing the poison fruit, leveling the playing field for the average person and allowing the basic necessities was only a smokescreen to hide your sins." The drone suddenly dropped into the pooled Unity, halfway to Haral's knees.

As if in reaction to this, the gray tendrils reached up, twining into the wires and components of Rider's prison. There came a crack and burst of light. Haral threw up an arm as a reflex. Something hot pierced the muscle at the back of his upper arm, while other objects sliced at the General and more struck the metal bulkheads with shattering sounds.

Rider splashed down into the surrounding Unity. Wavelets rippled and rolled across the surface of the gray lake while Haral's vision and hearing recovered.

A vision was shared with Haral, of a structure basically like a sine wave, but tapered at the ends, wider in the middle, and constructed of segmented panels he had seen before. This was their vessel, formed of themselves, and some connection to the universe that he could not perceive. There was certainly something to learn here, despite humani's need to cling to things they at least partly understood going in. No words. No math. Just experience, understanding, untranslated.

The words on the GDF ship's panel flashed more quickly. How long did they have until the vessel blew up, taking everyone with them? Taking their connection to the Unity away? Crashing the planet's economy, such as it was?

Haral focused on where the Overlay should be in his vision, but it was gone. Someone, somewhere, had cut off the feed. That's why the drone had dropped, he realized. No one would know what happened here. Like their ventures into space, recordings would be erased, experiences vanished. The explosion, if it was even reported on, would be called an anomalous accident, the results of scientific experiments, perhaps. All the missing and dead would be accounted for by said vague accident, or smoothed over entirely—bureaucracy swallowing any requests for information, any independent investigation. There would be no official investigation of an event that had officially never occurred.

"Check your Overlay. They're already sweeping this whole incident under the rug. You're no hero here, just something to be covered up, forgotten," Haral said,

"If that's the cost of Geode's survi—" the General began, but Haral cut him off.

"Cost of what? Centuries-old sins? Hiding away and hoping no one finds us? It's all terrible. You can do better. *We* can do better."

A barrage of crunching metal sounds came from outside. Haral looked and saw ship after ship bouncing off one another, careening into the sky island—drifting in the gravity-free space.

"Wha—" One of the General's crew woke up, strapped into their seat, disoriented. Then another and another awoke. They reached for their weapons, but found them missing.

Unity sent Haral a memory of gray tendrils reaching up and stealing them. He tried to send back a view of ships exploding from Gann's old movies, and memories of the insides of these panels, the wires and components, trying to get them to find the explosives and disarm them.

"But how?" the General asked, shoulders sagging, eyes pleading.

"First thing, we've got to shut down the self-destruct," Haral said.

"I—I was accessing it via the Overlay."

"Of course. And PullSys just shut it down. Maybe, in addition to keeping anyone from knowing what happened here, they cut us off so there was no way back," Haral observed.

The General's eyes widened a few degrees and then he nodded slowly. "Monsters…" he whispered.

Haral pushed his thoughts at Unity, trying to show them the ship they had shown him before. He placed all the people around them from the transport and the surrounding, out of control ships, on the alien ship and had it fly away from the sky island. The images kept slipping away from him, becoming crowds at the water park, or views from the underground river. The console began to beep, the message now flashing so fast it was a flicker.

"We've got to go!" Haral said aloud, falling back into verbal communication. He tried to step toward the door, but the Unity solidified around his feet. They didn't understand!

Safety harnesses snapped open. Humani and Flexxe bodies were crammed together in the middle of the space. A wall of Unity rose up around them. It wouldn't be enough, would it? Was the Unity's physical form stronger than the material of the ship? Stronger than explosives? Haral's mind whirled with questions while the bubble closed over their heads.

They all cried out as they were shunted in one direction, gaining speed as they moved, forced to hold onto one another to keep their balance. The General gripped Haral's arm with a massive, rough hand, a hand that had seen real, physical, labor and fighting. The pressure was intense, but Haral didn't try to squirm or knock the other away. They needed to stick together. The man needed to see them sticking together.

The Unity's motion shifted direction, though without the ability to see or gravity to orient them, Haral couldn't tell more. A few of the soldiers looked like they were going to be sick.

A cacophonous shock wave crashed through Haral, feeling like it rattled each bone independently. Immediately, he feared for Nez and Laeua, Chopper and Merit in turn—then more generally for the so many others who had been flying near the sky island.

A gray sheen fell over Haral's vision, showing him clusters of folk in gray bubbles, just like the one he and the General occupied. Many seemed frightened, covering their heads with their limbs, or curling up near the bottom of their capsule, or clinging to one another as they were doing here, but none seemed injured.

He saw Nez and Merit side by side, Laeua and Chopper close by in the same bubble. Haral breathed a sigh of relief at this. Then the view shifted, looking at the sky island, cracked around the edges, but largely between a string of gray bubbles like a pearl necklace below the island, such that the explosion had been absorbed and directed away. The dolphins and whales were clustered at the very peak of the inverted mountain, seemingly also well.

Slowly, the chain of bubbles rose past the island, showing many destroyed vehicles and a deeply cracked basin.

Haral showed the Unity a memory of Nez and himself together and felt the bubble move again, changing paths.

In minutes, Haral stood before his friends on a gray platform as more and more bubbles joined the edge wall, open sky above showing streamers of smoke sluggishly expanding in the weightless environ.

"Are we done here?" Haral asked the General. The man only stared for long seconds.

"They… saved us all… including me." His voice was shaky, filled with awe.

"They're not afraid of us, even you. Where words get in the way, understanding just is."

"What now?" The General asked, lost.

"Good question. I think first thing we need to do is get everyone back home. That means us back to the Central Band, and the Unity—all the pieces we might still hold—back together and above the Shell where they can exist without being inside anyone. For now, our technology is incompatible, but eventually, or maybe sooner with your team of scientists, we'll figure out how to work together." Haral looked up from the General to find a dozen or more people aiming their ID cards at him. PullSys might have cut them off from broadcasting for now, but the moment was captured. Things were going to change.

THE END

If you enjoyed Haral's adventure, please consider joining me for Abigail Beckett's battle to save her town and her family in **The Weight of Darkness:**

Silver Hill, Nevada - 1874

The 1870's offered a peaceful, simple, life after the strife of the Civil War. Its mine promised steady work. Abigail and Martin Beckett's parents owned and ran the mine, often away for days at a time, leaving the twins to... find their own fun. Tales of strange creatures, eerie cries, men and women gone missing in a blink... Folktales flow like whiskey amongst the miners.

When Abigail and her brother Martin go on an expedition, they find far more than they bargained for. With their parents and miners acting strangely and unseen influence beginning to take hold of her faculties, Abigail reaches out to her correspondence course professors for aid. Even when they arrive, though, these wise men can hardly believe what has become of the town and its people. Amid fires and armies of the undead and other monsters, how will they survive, let alone save their parents or the town?

Or, if you'd rather something more contemporary, **Down The Drain** follows Narayan Leon on a journey of discovery, about his family, about life and death, and about magic:

Narayan Leon's whole world is flipped upside down when his Gran falls suddenly and mysteriously ill. He learns secrets about her, magic, the afterworld, and his family, that he had never suspected, all while being chased by mysterious grim reapers called "Plumbers" and bouncing back and forth between the world of the living and the world of the dead.

Special Thanks

For years, I struggled to focus on my writing, sending only a handful of stories out, and having no luck publishing. When I learned I would be a father, it lit a fire under me. I resolved to write every day, or as close as I could get with kids. Within months, though, I had sent out my first story to be accepted, and over that year, I sold a dozen. Here you can see is the influence of my wife and motivation from my first son, Oliver.

As I went on, rejections piled up more than acceptances, and I failed to complete the many novels I started, yearly during a writing competition and sporadically otherwise.

That shifted as I again took on responsibility and someone to do the work for, this time in the form of Patreon. Ethan, Cindy, and Marilyn were my first supporters, and have encouraged me with friendship, kind words, and yes, their patronage. Others I have to thank on that same front include friends and family from across my life: Byron and Kristin, Grady and Christine, Andrea and Nancy.

Thank you all for your support across the years of my writing journey.

I would also like to thank Stephen and Seaneen from Black Thoughts Editorial Services for their help in fleshing out the ideas and words, sharpening the whole novel you have by now likely read. If you're starting at the back for some reason, no cheating! Go back to the start and read it properly!

For Sadie, my first reader for life, my kids, Oliver, Martin, and Abigail who all want to be social media stars, and everyone who has supported me on this journey.

Other Ascendent Media books
from John A. McColley:

Dark Motivators Series:
The Weight of Darkness

The Plumbers Series:
Down The Drain

Coming Soon:

Breaking The Word Series:
Breaking The Word

Ambervale Series:
Logicians of Ambervale

Stand Alones (so far…):
Where Smoke Walks, Fire Follows